THE BOY WHO COULD KEEP A SWAN IN HIS HEAD

THE BOY WHO COULD KEEP A SWAN IN HIS HEAD

John Hunt

UMUZI

Published in 2018 by Umuzi
an imprint of Penguin Random House South Africa (Pty) Ltd
Company Reg No 1953/000441/07
The Estuaries No 4, Oxbow Crescent, Century Avenue, Century City, 7441,
South Africa
PO Box 1144, Cape Town, 8000, South Africa
umuzi@penguinrandomhouse.co.za
www.penguinrandomhouse.co.za

First edition, first printing 2018
9 8 7 6 5 4 3 2 1

ISBN 978-1-4152-0966-0 (Print)
ISBN 978-1-4152-0983-7 (ePub)

Cover design and illustration by Sarita Immelman
Author photograph by Joanne Olivier
Text design by Fahiema Hallam
Set in Minion Pro
Printed and bound by Novus Print, a Novus Holdings company

For Kim, Michael, Luke and Jade
And, of course, Denise

1

Lickety-split

/liketi'split/ adverb, *informal*

Hillbrow, 1967. The New York of Africa. Apartheid kept the roads clean and the rubbish collected. There were buildings going up everywhere – "lickety-split", according to Mr Trentbridge. Large chunks of tin-roof houses were found in skips almost every day as the boy walked home from school. These homes were recently surrounded by honest gardens and the occasional peach tree. Someone wrote in *The Star* newspaper that soon Hillbrow would have more people per square kilometre than Tokyo. Everyone quoted that article to everyone. Some even cut it out and kept it folded in their wallets.

The boy, who went by the name of Phen, lived in Duchess Court. You'll find it at 20 O'Reilly Road, Berea. Technically it's in Berea, but for all intents and purposes it's Hillbrow. The heartland of Hillbrow, the parallel streets of Kotze and Pretorius, is barely a three-minute amble away. Duchess Court was built in the twenties, solid and grey with flirty bits of art deco. When first constructed it must have dominated the skyline. By the time Phen moved in, though, it had the look of an old, stout woman in a sombre overcoat that had been mended too often.

Not that the building was without its charm. At its core was the wood-panelled lift with its bevelled mirror, known to all simply as Mr Otis. He waited at the end of the foyer with three cast-iron ladies above his lintel. Joined together, they danced in a chorus line with their right legs held scandalously high. If you opened the heavy wooden door, then slid back the metal gate, the lift would take you a clanking six storeys high. The grill, when concertinaed closed, left big gaps you could peer through. As you faced forward the lift shaft was presented in vertical grey strips that drifted upwards in a slow-motion blur. This was punctuated by six square bursts of yellow if you went all the way to the top. The lift door at each floor had a small glass window allowing you to wave to people as you went past them.

Stopping was always a violent and inexact affair. Tenants would suggest to newcomers that they lean against the walls or, at the very least, hold on to the polished brass handle of the metal gate as the lift slammed to a halt anywhere between a foot and an inch away from the floor of your choice. The uninitiated would battle to see this as an arrival and presume something had gone wrong. It was only after the metal door had been brazenly slid open that they would sheepishly step up or down and then out.

Phen lived on the ground floor in number four. His trips with Mr Otis were therefore infrequent or for fun. And a fertile imagination grew more fecund when transport was on hand. There was a time when, based at military headquarters behind the washing line on the roof, he needed to find the v2 rocket base the Germans were using. London was taking a terrible pounding and it was all up to his commando unit. After days of relentless reconnaissance they found the cunning concrete shaft dug six storeys deep into the mountainside. Although they were vastly outnumbered, thanks to the element of surprise the mission was a total success.

If you sat on the bonnet of Mr Trentbridge's Ford Cortina and looked at Duchess Court, number four was situated on the extreme right-hand corner. A palm tree, planted years ago, blocked out ninety per cent of the view from the balcony and stretched up to the fourth floor. Doves cooed high up in the fronds as if the tiny strip of green between the building and the pavement was an oasis. Phen often Lawrence-of-Arabiaed around that tree, offering dates and nuts in the form of Wilson's toffees to the gathered Bedouin tribes. He would need their help if the Turks were to be driven out of the Middle East once and for all.

With a dishcloth on his head he blew up countless enemy trains as they moved through the desert and up O'Reilly Road. His plunger was a pencil he'd wedged into a hole he'd made in the top of an empty condensed-milk tin. As he rammed it down hard, the dynamite hurled the huge locomotives into the air. Volkswagens, Morris Minors, Fiats and the occasional Peugeot would launch helplessly off the ground and land on their sides and roofs.

"Tell your men not to waste ammunition, Sharif Nassir. There are still many battles to come for the Harith tribe."

It was an easy yet pitiless business finishing them off. Hidden behind the garden wall, his sawn-off broomstick picked them off one by one. It wasn't pretty but then war never was. He had to remind himself, "Mankind has had ten thousand years of experience at fighting and if we must fight, we have no excuse for not fighting well."

The flat itself was bigger on the inside than it looked from the outside. He lived in a flat while all the new buildings around him contained apartments. That was typical of words; they changed without rhyme or reason. And when you asked why, no one could give you an answer. His flat wasn't flatter. In fact, the older buildings had much higher ceilings. And those new apartments were built so tightly together they should be called closements. His father said flats came from Britain and apartments from America. He said those damn Yanks were getting in everywhere.

If you opened the front door to number four you could turn sharp left into the kitchen or proceed straight into the dining room. The kitchen floor was covered in one flat sheet of green linoleum that bubbled depending on where you stood. You could get the bubble to move but you could never get it to disappear. Much like trying to get the dent out of a ping-pong ball. Trapped air is happy to be transported, but, it will take its ballooned vacuum with it. Concerned visitors even suggested there may be a mouse problem in the kitchen. This, in turn, created such embarrassment for Phen's mother that his routine job became to force the bubble behind the fridge before anyone came to visit.

Not that walking in the dining room was without its challenges. Like the rest of the flat, it was all parquet flooring in what used to be a very close-fit herringbone design. Over the years, the perpetual pounding of feet in the high-traffic zones had begun to take their toll. Like a piano with a number of loose keys, the initial appearance of a smooth surface was deceptive. If you stood on the tail of the wrong wooden slat, its head would pop up like a snake ready to strike.

The most dangerous square lay, innocuously, directly on the path to the lounge. All three hardwood planks were loose and sat next to each other at slightly different heights. If you were carrying a tray you never stood a chance. And if you were a brisk or heavy walker one of the three would often flip out completely and smack you on the shin.

When Phen had caught his mother crying, even though she'd said everything was alright, he decided to fix the floor in an attempt to cheer her up. He was a bit of a hoarder and went straight to the top shelf of his cupboard. Under his two neatly folded school shirts he fished out the OK Bazaars plastic bag. Beside the egg from two Easters ago and the strips of liquorice, now a deep emerald green, he found his stash of chewing gum. He wasn't sure exactly how long to chew for. After the taste had left, was the stickiness gone too? He decided merely to make the gum moist then pull it out. Each piece was given a minute in his mouth. No more, no less.

He'd seen pictures of master craftsmen at work and tried to adopt their demeanour. He held the edge of the slats up to the light and frowned at their unseemly roughness. He traced his finger across the ancient lumps of bitumen, then took his mother's metal nail file and made them smooth. He'd put a newspaper on the dining-room table to catch their falling flakes, but most fell gently into the fruit bowl. Once finished, each six-inch plank was lined up vertically on the sideboard like a row of dominoes. He was uncertain about how to apply the chewing gum. One long stretch? Or a series of blobs?

After experimenting with both, he decided on the blobs. The measured distance between each mound of gum seemed aesthetically more pleasing and carried a greater sense of purpose. It reminded him of his Meccano set where a series of aligned holes solved everything. This choice demanded more material and depleted his entire reserve. By the time he was finished, a three-year collection of gum lay beneath the dining-room floor. Most were Chappies so he kept the wrappers to read the jokes and Did You Knows printed inside. However, there was also the faint whiff of peppermint and spearmint from other gums. Phen felt proud and exhilarated when he was finished. There is a kind of satisfaction that seeps in when a job requiring physical labour is well done. It's the sort of feeling that sustains you for quite a while even when no one else notices your handiwork.

On the south side of the dining-room wall was a door which opened into a cupboard that was so deep it was referred to as the storeroom. The three shelves at the back were packed with the finality of knowing no one was ever going to reach them. On the middle of the top shelf, bristling like a series of broken vertebrae, lay the deformed wire hoops of the record rack. Somehow on its journey in the delivery van from Shotley Residential Hotel, not even half a mile away, the leg of the sofa had been placed on its delicate spine. The wire channels were now splayed embarrassingly wide in the middle and impossibly tight on the opposite edges. *South Pacific*, *Brigadoon*, *My Fair Lady*, *Gigi* and all their contemporaries were therefore forced to lie on top of one other, flat and square. They, in turn, rested upon a hatbox from another age. Now empty, its circular velvet-covered lid captured the memory, if not the contents, of its beauty.

One shelf below, and slightly to the left, lay the likewise empty hamster cage that had once housed Philby. Phen had been allowed to buy the white hamster provided his father could name him. "That rodent should've been behind bars years ago." Only much later he learned that Philby was a British double agent who'd defected to the USSR. Teeth marks could still be seen where the hamster had gnawed through the pale blue powder coating of his steel feeding tray. Phen had placed the cage there himself, in a solemn ceremony shortly after Philby's demise. He hadn't been sure where you put the homes of the dead, let alone the dead themselves. He had wanted to ask, but couldn't find the courage. He sensed a plastic bag and the dustbin might have been the answer. When he'd returned from school, his mother had given him a hug, said she was sorry and now the subject was closed.

Which is why, two weeks later, when the hamster wheel began to run wildly deep in the darkness of the cupboard, Phen was at first confused and then elated. He'd read the stories and seen the pictures of the resurrection. He'd pored over those yellow rays that burst from behind dark clouds as white doves, caught in a whirlwind, spun up to heaven. He ran to the door and smote the darkness asunder. The huge black rat was clearly startled by the light suddenly flicking on. However, with size comes a certain confidence. He allowed himself a few extra whirls before darting out the cage door and through a pile of *London Illustrated News*.

There was no wall on the north side of the dining room. A sliding door with three frosted-glass panels on each side could be pulled across to meet in the middle, if necessary. Although this very rarely happened, its possibility seemed to make the room more sophisticated. It made you "pass through" on your way to the lounge, the way an important man makes you pass through his assistant's office before you can get to his. The lounge itself was dominated by the Grundig radio and record player that stared straight back at you. It knew it owned the room. Even the large ceramic bowl of potpourri, forced on its head, couldn't change that. The sofa and two armchairs tilted towards it, waiting for instructions even when it was switched off. And if its spindly legs made it look like a fat man with skinny calves, there was still no doubt it was the highest-ranking piece of furniture in the entire flat.

Behind the Grundig the lounge windows looked onto

the street. Because of the proximity of the pavement, barely two yards away, a thick lace curtain let most of the light in and kept the peering of most passers-by out. This allowed Phen to stand there and never be noticed. Although the windows stopped halfway, the lace curtain, mimicking the floral drapes, went to the floor. Some days when he didn't want to be seen from the inside either, he'd wrap himself in the folds and pretend it was an invisibility cloak. On a late Friday afternoon, when the two doctors discussed various options around the lounge table, he stayed enveloped for hours. Even when they called Phen's mother, he stayed where he was.

"Could you join us for a while?" the tall skinny one asked his mother.

Everyone loved his mother. Everyone wanted her to join them for a while. She was beautiful. She always denied it but could never be accused of false modesty. She had a deep acceptance of life as it had been dealt to her and emerald eyes incapable of disguise or guile. Almost everyone stared into her perfectly symmetrical face and full lips with a lust they immediately chastised themselves for having. By way of atonement they'd offer to help in any way they could. Her bedside drawer was full of business cards and scraps of paper from people she hardly knew, all waiting for her call.

"Of course. Shall I make a fresh pot of tea first?"

"Wonderful idea."

Confident he wasn't being watched, the fatter doctor rearranged his crotch and spread his legs wide. By the time the kettle whistled, his hands had grown impatient and rubbed the outside of his thighs. The other doctor pretended to make notes, scribbling then crossing out like a man battling with a crossword.

"No sugar for me."

Fatty took two.

"I'm afraid you have to sign all these papers. Rather daunting, but necessary."

Next they held up white envelopes full of pills and wrote long instructions on the outside, as if they were addresses she had to send them to.

"Correct dosage is critical. I suggest for the halves, you use a sharp blade."

"Bread knife won't do." His mother's attempt at humour went unacknowledged.

Momentarily distracted, the thin doctor referred back to his notes. "Now, this is likewise very important." He held up a tiny glass ampoule, tapped it, then snapped its neck. With cold precision he plunged the needle into the severed head of the vial.

"You'll get used to it. Straight into the hard muscle of the buttock. If we need blood samples, remember to pump the arm to raise the vein."

Through a thousand holes, Phen watched his mother practise.

"Good. Now push the plunger forward; we don't want any air left in the syringe."

The needle squirted in a wide arc, then collapsed in a damp line across the dining-room table.

"Sorry!" She dabbed at the moisture with a serviette.

"Don't worry, you'll get the hang of it."

The larger doctor smiled crookedly as if something rude had just happened.

Although the balcony led off from the left side of the lounge, it was not used much. It was open and therefore had no lace curtain, plus the single palm tree blocked the view like some massive peg leg. Two pots of bright red geraniums tried too hard to bring a little colour to the shadowed corner.

Like a pair of bloodshot eyes, they seemed to draw attention to themselves for all the wrong reasons. Their stems were soft and twisted from too much water, their leaves pale and pasty from not enough sun. The balcony did, however, serve one practical purpose. It supplied another way out. If the front door was being guarded, or if the question of home-work might be raised on your approach, there was always the balcony side exit. To avoid being betrayed by the bottom hinge, the trick was to move through sideways then leap the wall in a single bound.

Walking the full length of the dining room, past the kitchen and beyond the cupboard, Phen came to what was rather grandly referred to as the passageway: a dark, stingy channel with no windows. Its bend was so short and sharp, if you looked back after just one step the front room was no longer visible. Due to some architect's sleight of hand, big became small, wide squeezed to narrow and light disappeared to black. How could the world transform itself in a single step? Having lost the comfort of the dining room and not yet in the sanctuary of his bedroom, this was purgatory on wobbly parquet. It was rimmed by a ridiculously high dado rail painted a cruel midnight blue. This two-inch malicious streak tracked the length of the passageway before jamming itself in a macabre zigzag.

There were places of refuge in this no-man's land. The bath and shower behind the first door, the toilet behind the second. But when the night reinforced the interior blackness, sound could be malicious. A thirsty cistern acquired a viper's hiss. The drip of a tap was amplified by the certainty that it was not there before. A sheet of hanging plastic dotted with mermaids couldn't stop evil from brewing behind its curtain. While they frolicked in turquoise waves, metal hooks scraped against the rusting rod high above and waited their chance. The shower cap, split down the centre, hung from the taps. Phen wondered where the head was that had been wearing it when the cleft had occurred. Even in winter, he was no longer accused of lingering and using up all the hot water.

If he looked neither left nor right, it was six full paces into his bedroom. The far wall was bare. He had once considered buying a picture of a red E-type Jaguar. However, he'd then spent a disproportional amount of time on the next poster, which was of Ursula Andress in a bikini. The knowing smile of the store owner had made him blush and leave immediately. His single bed was covered in a used-to-be-blue candlewick bedspread. The tassels reaching to the floor were dog-chewed and uneven. Like roots no longer capable of searching for water, they fizzed and frayed on the edges. His grandmother had originally brought it from her hometown of Renfrew in Scotland when she'd emigrated with her husband in 1922. She couldn't believe this treasured heirloom had become a dog's plaything. "If I'd known, I'd have sewn bones on the bottom and been done with it."

The left-hand side of the cupboard opened all the way until it hit the wall, the right-hand side three quarters, until it hit the bed. Besides his school clothes, the shelves housed two pairs of shorts, one white, one black, both drawstring. Four shirts, three short-sleeved, one long. In the bottom compartment two jerseys lay on top of each other, though he could only wear one. His grandmother knitted clothes to grow into, claiming they lasted longer that way. Phen wanted to ask his mother for a pair of flared jeans, even if he was not too sure how wide he wanted the bell-bottoms to be. The single, empty wire hanger awaited their arrival.

There were two items of great value hidden in the cupboard. In the folds of his grandmother's jersey, secure in its woollen safe, were the papers that proved his cocker spaniel was a pedigree. The beautiful type with its embossed badge of the Kennel Club on the bottom corner indicated this was clearly an important document. It had a legal bearing about it. It declared emphatically that the sire was Six Shot Willy Wagtail out of the bitch Grand Empress Dowager Cixi. Phen saw no irony in such grand nobility producing an offspring he duly named "Pal". The tweezer-lipped breeder had fiddled with the leather elbow patches of her tweed jacket and pointed out there was still a lot more space left to fill in the name, but he stuck with the three letters.

"We don't normally sell to Hillbrow," she said, turning the suburb into the buyer. Phen held the puppy to his chest with both hands, unaware of the backhanded compliment. His mother asked if she accepted cheques.

The other important object was his grandfather's gold Zenith Elite watch. After thirty-five years as a fitter and turner at Rand Gold Mines, it had been presented to him on the day of his retirement. He had worn it proudly for four years before the cancer made him and his watch stop. It now lived in the heel of Phen's old cricket sock, underneath his underpants. Every morning, before brushing his teeth, he felt to make sure it was still there. He'd promised his mother he'd only wear the watch when he turned twenty-one. Phen had also been left his grandfather's First World War bayonet. His grandmother, however, had blocked the transfer of the long blade in its leather sheath. "It's enough that men still want to shoot and stab each other. We don't have to remind ourselves you can do both simultaneously."

The only picture in the room was of a clown juggling three balls while standing on one foot in the middle of a circus ring. Phen didn't like the picture, but had been told it was rude not to hang it up. When Phen was a four-year-old on holiday in Knysna, a part-time painter had taken a shine to him and offered it as a gift. His parents had said yes. The oil paint mixed heavily with the acrylic. The artist's palette knife scarred the canvas. The clown was in profile with an orange ball on his foot, a yellow one in his hand and a blue one hovering over his head. He had a pointed red hat like the ones stupid children are forced to wear in classroom corners with their backs turned.

The blunt edge of the knife ensured the clown had a slapped-on nose but no eye. It also meant the three balls could not be made perfectly round. Phen worried how a blind man could keep these irregular shapes in the air and wondered if the dunce hat meant he was being punished. Even worse, the tail of his jacket looked more like the tail of an animal. Was it just a clown suit? Had the tail fallen out by mistake? What beast lurked within? Who was being punished, the clown or the animal? And what would happen when those three balls finally dropped to the ground? The more he stared, the more they spun and floated. He knew it was inevitable they would fall. He knew the man watching just outside the ring would deliver his terrible punishment. Just like his grandfather's watch, time might've ceased, but nothing could stop the sense of dread about what would happen next.

The best way to calm the panic was to shift his gaze a little to the left and through the window. Between his bedroom wall and the parking garages lay the cricket pitch and Wanderers Stadium. He squeezed the famed arena into an area paved in concrete slabs precisely six wide and twenty-two long. Previously a wayward throw would've landed in the Bardeaux's garden, however, their four-foot wooden fence no longer played wicketkeeper. The jasmine didn't peep over any more and no pansies waited to be crushed as he searched for his ball. All six houses on that side of Duchess Court had been demolished and a twenty-storey building was under construction.

The huge wall, left unpainted and cement-grey, blocked out everything. It was already so high Mrs Kaplan on the fifth floor had been forced to draw her curtains. She'd been having lunch when a man in a tin hat on an iron beam had asked if she wanted to swap. He offered her one of his sandwiches as he slowly moved up past her window. She explained she was having her favourite Gedempte Fleisch, so clearly a trade was not going to happen. "Progress," she said, "should mind its manners."

Nothing could get in the way of a test match at the famed "Bullring", though. To ensure he had enough room for his run-up he'd had to use the full length of the boiler room. He'd burst from its door and let rip by the second slab to ensure a decent trajectory. The English were polite and acknowledged a good ball. The Australians were another matter. A thick edge a blind umpire would be able to hear and still they didn't walk. Caught behind, again, and still he stood his ground. Only when the tomato box was struck with such force it toppled over was justice done. The crowd understood, though, as they rose as one. The bowler acknowledged their applause with a gentle nod and a wipe of his brow. He was tired and racked with pain, yet good for one more over. He'd found his line and length and that hat trick was calling.

Back in his room with the roar of the crowd subsiding and his hand sore from all the autographs, Phen stared at the ceiling. He traced the crack in the plaster as it headed to the light fitting then turned left. His thoughts were good company; they filled a void, but he had to keep manufacturing them. Pal jumped onto the bed and lay next to his master. Phen ruffled his long spaniel ears and patted him on the head.

"Hello, Aslan," he said.

2

Enrapture

/in-rap'tyer/ verb

Number four Duchess Court had two storerooms. Besides the one in the dining room, the main bedroom was where they stored Phen's father. Or, on a good day, where he stored himself. This room was connected to the flat but also lived in a parallel universe. Although you always entered from the passageway, that didn't mean you always found the same room behind the door. Since the curtains were usually drawn, the darkness was thickest there. Yet, when they were open, this was where the light was at its brightest. How could the same gentle glow in the lounge hurt and dazzle his eyes in his father's bedroom? Once, the reflected light off the enamel bedpan had been so strong he'd had to cover it with a towel. The beam had streaked across the bed, burst against the wardrobe mirror and electrified the far wall. "A sign from the gods," his father had said. "A bowel blessing. I shall be regular from this day forth." Much later that night when he heard his mother emptying it in the toilet, his father loudly declared, "Thus spoketh the Lord."

The room consisted of two single beds separated by a slippery lookalike Persian rug which, according to the patient, was "cunningly designed to kill unsuspecting infidels". On the outside of each bed stood a matching side table. On top of these sat a lamp, each wearing a maroon velveteen shade. Similar to Phen's bedcover, they also had tassels. The tassels dangling on the right-hand side were scorched. The shade was worn like a beret, causing the strands of tightly bound string to lean directly onto the bulb. This made the room smell of burned toast. His father was aware of this, yet needed the direct light to read. Occasionally, when the stench became too bad, the shade was removed completely and placed over the glass ashtray like a tea cosy.

A stranger entering the room would initially notice none of this. He'd peer through the half-light and be taken aback by a massive wall unit bracketing the beds on either side and spreading across the wall where a headboard would normally be. To sit up and lean back meant a touch of Brylcreem or Vitalis on the spine of *Fahrenheit 451* or *Charlotte's Web*. The huge bookcase ate everything in the room. Thousands of vertical teeth, some narrow, some wide, waited to chomp. Any individual extraction made matters worse, leaving the insane mouth of a gap-toothed giant covering the entire wall.

Phen hated and loved reading to his father. The same way he hated and loved his father's bedroom. Although his mother slept there too, it was always his father's room. Over time they'd developed rules, some spoken, some not. As his father's glasses grew thicker and thicker and as the book moved closer and closer to his face, it became obvious he could no longer read. His magnified eyelashes stuck to the lenses like the bent legs of spiders waiting to scurry away. The size of his eyes was cartoon-like. The sticky tape wrapped earnestly around the bridge of his horn-rimmed frames only added to the caricature.

The game was predictable enough. Phen would return from school or from walking the dog and hear his father calling for him. Sometimes he'd pretend not to hear, although that always proved a useless exercise. Sick people develop a sixth sense about the presence of others. The only delaying tactic that worked was the offer to make tea and to then prolong the process as much as possible. Once the cup was placed on the doily, Phen had to move to the other side of the bed and sit in the cracked leather arm-chair. To get his shoulders flush with the backrest meant his legs would be parallel to the ground and the soles of his feet visible to his father.

"He was an old man who fished alone in a skiff in the Gulf Stream and had gone eighty-four days now without taking a fish."

"*The Old Man and the S-s-sea.*"

"Good. Let's start at the beginning and see how we go."

Having identified the book correctly, Phen now had to find it in the vast bookcase and read to his father until he fell asleep. This was easier said than done. He was not tall enough for the top shelves. Often the search involved the Formica kitchen chair and *Encyclopaedia Britannica*. If the book lay directly above his father's head, he'd have to take off his shoes and stand on the bed. The more he climbed the pillows the more they sagged under his weight. He also had to be careful his bare feet didn't snag the thin plastic tube bringing oxygen into the mask.

A reading took anything from ten minutes to two hours. It depended on the story itself, the recollections attached to it and the health of the listener. Phen supplied the words but where they went were not of his doing. Havana glows differently for each of us. Did Hemingway's fisherman see the mighty Yankee DiMaggio the same way as a sick man in Hillbrow? You read "The old man had taught the boy to fish and the boy loved him", but you don't know why that makes your father lift his head and stare far off into the distance. You are the voice to the words yet you have no control of their destination. You don't know why some merge into another story you're not reading. You stay true to the lines in front of you, although other thoughts are gathered along the way and memories you don't have are released.

Phen knows sometimes it's the rhythm of his reading and not the words that sends his father to another place. Like the steady drone of a transistor radio turned down low. He watches the calm face slowly fall asleep behind the oxygen mask and imagines his father is a Spitfire pilot. Echo. Foxtrot. Tango. Mission accomplished.

Sleep in that room needs to be tied down thoroughly. Creaking chairs, passing cars, yelling builders all wait to sabotage the slumber. The shrinking chest in the blue-and-white-striped pyjamas needs to rise higher and fall deeper before Phen can go. He sits patiently and continues reading. Although he keeps the same pace, he now turns the pages ten and twenty at a time. Soon the end of the book appears before his tired eyes. He leans forward and tips the page into the light. The edges of the letters turn crisp and focused.

"What's that?" she asked a waiter and pointed to the long backbone of the great fish that was now just garbage waiting to go out with the tide.

"Tiburon," the waiter said, "Eshark." He was meaning to explain what had happened.

"I didn't know sharks had such handsome, beautifully formed tails."

"I didn't either," her male companion said.

"Up the road, in his shack, the old man was sleeping again. He was still sleeping on his face and the boy was sitting by him watching him. The old man was dreaming about the lions."

It wasn't easy to silently get out of the armchair. Naked skin always squeaks against leather. Jumping off was not an option. The small frame had to slither off like a snake. That meant Phen ended up on his knees praying the gentle hiss of the oxygen cylinder had covered any unintentional sounds. It was obligatory to stay in this position for a while. His impatience had cost him dearly in the past. The body in the bed knew when the space around it had changed. Too much activity would cause its right hand to raise and wave him back into the chair.

Shutting the door meant much more than just sealing the room. Phen was now free of the four walls but not the guilt of the escape. Could he jump the perimeter walls as well and actually leave the flat? His mother would not be back from work for another two hours. If he waited until then it would be too dark to go to the park. His father could make it to the bathroom by himself, but preferred someone on standby. The thick plastic bottle, shaped like a weaver's nest complete with tunnelled entrance, and the bedpan were only for emergencies. "For dignity to be preserved, mobility must be maintained," his father often said. On good days his walking stick would rest against his shoulder like a rifle as he marched off.

The expectant eyes of a dog go deep. They watch even while Phen sings "If You're Going to San Francisco" and imagines wearing flowers in his hair. Safe in his solitude Phen allows his hips to roll and his fingers to click as he dances past the Grundig. He turns the volume of the radio up a little more in the vain hope it will deflect the stare. Pal sits motionless and unimpressed next to the hat stand that contains his dangling leash. Torn between the sleeping body in the bedroom and the waiting cocker spaniel, he makes a Solomon-like decision. He will walk the dog around the block and when his mother returns, they will go for a longer outing. Dogs, after all, also have to go to the bathroom.

The block is a building site full of pregnant women. Besides the huge construction next to Duchess Court, there is also a pre- and post-natal and baby clinic on the far side. It used to be a small synagogue, but now the congregation is either swollen or already divided in two. Everywhere you look, women in various degrees of wideness waddle or push prams between powerful black men who sing as they dig a trench to lay pipes in. The picks sway like a conductor's baton. Silence as they pause at the top, then pure harmony as they swoop down into the hard ground. It is, without doubt, the most beautiful thing Phen has ever heard. He is more than mesmerised; he is enraptured. The sound synchronises these humans into a perfect machine. Stripped to the waist, they are somehow holy. A church choir at work, sacred in their labour.

He thinks of his father hummed to sleep by his imperfect reading. Here words do the opposite. Here they wake you up and fill you with energy! These words don't stumble; they fly. They hold themselves perfectly in the air as they glide effortlessly. Like the birds at Zoo Lake they take off and land at the same time. He remembers his uncoordinated gyrations in front of the radiogram. He wishes he too had such a muscular body. Then he could also take his shirt off, tie it around his hips and let his chest sway in the late-afternoon sun.

The white foreman tells him to move back or he'll get hurt. He is wearing very tight black rugby shorts and thick khaki socks. The socks rise to under his knees, then fold back meticulously to create a two-inch ridge. The ridge accentuates his scrawny calves. Even when he bends down to help a young woman carry her pram over the broken pavement there is no sign of a bulge. She thanks him coyly, but it has the opposite effect. The foreman blushes, doffs his hat and rubs its leopard-skin band with his thumb. Three ballpoint pens in his left shirt pocket confirm his seniority. He checks if they are still there and fans himself with a clipboard.

Phen would like to stay, yet senses his presence is somehow annoying the boss man, who impatiently kicks the pipe that still has to be laid. Maybe it's the dog. As Phen walks off, the leader of the work party changes the song. The pace is much faster now. There is a whoop in the middle of the chorus and two pretend shoulder dips before the picks bite into the hard soil. They're all smiling now, even as the tempo increases. Between strikes into the ground, hips are thrust forward with a lurid intent. Phen doesn't understand the words but it's clear the new song is aimed at the boss man.

"S-s-s-spaz."

"D-d-d-dork." Phen can't stop himself from matching the staccato greeting.

Jimmy the Greek turns his roller skates sideways and screeches to a halt. His real name is Vakis Papadimitropoulos. He lives with his parents at the Chelsea Hotel, just off O'Reilly Road. Phen has it on good authority that the Greeks, like the Portuguese, only know how to run corner cafés. He, therefore, suspects Jimmy is lying when he says his dad is an engineer. In an attempt to emulate the Greek's confidence, Phen pulls his shorts down and tries to wear them like hipsters. Jimmy's jeans are brand new and tucked into his socks. His body is a year or two ahead of his age. According to Phen's gran this is typical of foreigners from the Mediterranean who eat the tentacles of octopus and wrap rice in vine leaves. Jimmy is athletic and has the self-assurance of one who's always picked first for every team. Unlike Phen, he has muscles you can actually see. His chest pushes against his T-shirt in a hard outline; his biceps fill his sleeves. He is as physical and powerful as his opposite companion is delicate and slight. Phen corrects his poor posture, jealous of Jimmy's sinewy frame and of the confidence it brings. He also gets words wrong, yet no one laughs at the Greek.

"Look super Spaz wearing school shirt. Especially button tied up to top neck and sleeves tied to bottom hands. Roll up! Why not? Want to match spaz dog? He got bump on head like extra bone, or what?"

Just to have Jimmy speak to him makes Phen feel important. Although they're virtually on the same street and are in the same class, they don't see much of each other. When he'd just come from Athens, they were almost close. There were cinemas to introduce him to. "What why you call this bioscope? And the Milky Lane, what why not call it Ice Cream Place? Milk nowhere. In shop, not lane. And why steak house? No home anywhere. No garden, nothing. And monkey gland sauce? You take pieces from apes and spread on T-bone? Africa, savage, savage country." He pounded his chest powerfully like an angry and disgusted Tarzan.

Most importantly, Phen could show him the best angles to take when sliding down Nugget Hill. The winter kikuyu, baked dry and flaky, offered the perfect slippery slope. All you needed was a flat piece of cardboard and a little courage. "Important you stay on, or grass toilet paper for you your arse."

It was not long before Jimmy's ability with a soccer ball put a distance between them. He was a brilliant centre forward and Phen was a last-pick goalkeeper. Everyone passed to Jimmy. Phen tried to hang around with him at break but whenever they played five-a-side, he never made the cut. Once he knocked on Jimmy's door at the Chelsea Hotel. His mother, dressed in black, opened the door and said he wasn't back from school yet. Phen saw Jimmy's satchel next to the rubber plant and understood. He thanked her anyway as she waved him away.

Since then he'd kept his distance. He missed sharing their tuck at second break. Exotically, the Greek's lunchbox often contained nuts, usually almonds, and biscuits covered in a thick, white dust. For this, he would gladly exchange a disproportionate amount of thick bread coated with apricot jam, or last night's chicken leaking tomato sauce.

Everyone was attracted to him even when he wasn't kicking a ball. All the teachers liked him. He could make a mistake and lighten everything with a shrug of his shoulders and a smile. Nothing stuck to him or flattened him. He could spray words everywhere and no one cared.

"Okay, Spaz, got to go."

"Me too."

"Maybe next time I take your dog. What why? He pull me on skates like Alaskan dogs. Call of the Wild. Mush, mush."

Phen watched the Greek jump the kerb and land right in front of an oncoming car. The angry hoot was met with a cheery wave and an over-officious salute. The driver of the Vauxhall shouted behind the windscreen to no purpose. The perpetrator was already a disappearing dot in his rear-view mirror.

Once Phen had walked past the prams all neatly parked on the diamond-shaped tiles of the old synagogue and turned left, the back end of the block was not that interesting. Everything had been smothered in tar or forced into submission by square paving stones. Huge metal rings protected the bases of trees from this new sea of solid. Here circles of soil clung to their trunks like black plug holes waiting to drain the summer rain. Nature had no place on the pavement. Wild plants and tufts of green had to be eliminated. There had even been talk of parking meters being installed. Poles of steel to guard over the freshly painted brackets that demarcated where cars were allowed to stand. His grandmother, who'd never learned to drive, found it unbelievable that you could be charged for keeping your car stationary.

By the time he had walked around the block, the sun was low and his hand was forced to his forehead like the peak of a cap. It was still in this position when Mr Trentbridge closed his car door. Phen couldn't see but heard the car keys whoosh through the air. He caught them waist high.

"Howzat?"

"Out!"

Though Phen wouldn't admit it, he'd sat down on the stairs outside Duchess Court to wait for the man's arrival. Mr Trentbridge was very punctual and always got home before anyone else. He said he liked to beat the madding crowd. He was also very proud of his car and needed to secure a parking space in the front where he could keep an eye on it. "Not just a Ford Cortina. A 1500 GT Mark I." Mr Trentbridge did most of the talking, which suited Phen fine. He was always friendly and enthusiastic, which is what his mother said salesmen were meant to be. "He could sell ice to Eskimos in winter," she'd said. "Look at the ridiculous price he gets people to pay for those imported shoes of his."

"So, Boyo, how's life?"

"Good."

"Good's good!"

Phen felt guilty to admit it, but he wished his father was more like Mr Trentbridge. Open-faced with lots of well-behaved hair, he looked fit and healthy and always smiled. His aftershave made him smell of the sea and success. He described himself as a man-on-the-move, a go-getter. He had two young daughters and Phen wondered secretly if he'd like a son. He was always throwing things at him and girls didn't catch very well. Once, during a test match Mr Trentbridge had peered down from the fire escape and offered to bowl. Phen had scored a scintillating half-century. "Magnificent!" Mr Trentbridge had said. "Maybe you should think of turning professional." His daughters didn't know how to cover-drive.

It worried him that the night after the match, he'd dreamed he was an orphan and Mr Trentbridge had arrived to adopt him. As always his jacket matched his tie perfectly and the three white mountaintops of his handkerchief ranged equally above his breast pocket. The flying duck that was his tiepin promised to lift him to a better life far away. The matron of the orphanage, dressed in a white uniform, also carried a cricket stump to confirm her authority. She asked if Mr Trentbridge intended doing a thorough job and he confirmed Boyo would find his new life top-notch and crossed his heart. "He'll get better shoes, too," he'd said. The Cortina had magically become a convertible. As they drove away, Pal barked happily and tried to chew the wind.

"Well, I suppose I should go up to my beloved and the two tykes."

"Yes."

"It's fish night and she-who-must-be-obeyed does not like to be kept waiting."

"Yes."

"Still practising your googly?"

"Medium-pacers."

"Well, Boyo, when they sign you up for the Springboks, remember you promised I could be your agent." He leaped the three outside steps, sped into the foyer then turned around. "And remember, a goal is a dream with a deadline – Napoleon Hill."

Phen opened the door to his flat as quietly as possible and took Pal off the lead. The metal links of the chain were carefully snaked around a sofa cushion to ensure they coiled silently. He tiptoed into the kitchen and filled the dog's water bowl. The linoleum bubble waited near the sink. There was no reason to chase it into the corner and place the dustbin on top of it, but he did anyway. This was a mistake. As he delicately trapped the bunched air, his foot caught the pedal. The lid opened wide as if eating what had just been placed underneath it. It hovered then slammed shut. The thud was faint, yet enough. Pal, resigned to the moment, clipped across the parquet and curled under the telephone table. Before the kettle could be switched on his father's voice called out. Phen pushed tentatively at the bedroom door. The blue-and-white-striped body was sitting upright, its head turned towards him with wide, expectant eyes.

"The village of Holcomb stands on the high wheat plains of western Kansas, a lonesome area that other Kansans call 'out there.'"

"*In Cold Blood.*"

"Some seventy miles east of the Colorado border."

"I said *In Cold Blood.*"

"Find it then."

3

Gullible

/gulebʼel/ adjective

Phen put great store by words and tried to treat them with respect. He knew that if they were understood, arranged and delivered correctly, they earned considerable power and meaning. He fully appreciated how some words, better chosen and aligned than others, created a much more forceful trajectory. Yet words continued to play practical jokes on him. They were always testing him, waiting with a bucket of water balancing on top for him to walk through the door. The gigantic *Chambers Twentieth Century Dictionary* he'd inherited from his father was a constant source of reference, although often of little help. Finding the actual meaning of the word was one thing. How people chose to twist it out of shape was another.

It didn't help that Phen stuttered badly. Nearly always on the ses, often on the ps and occasionally on the bs. The words themselves were there, waiting patiently; they just couldn't be delivered. Like a parachutist who'd received the green light but couldn't get himself out the door. Although the word had clicked through from the brain, the first letter of that word would catch on some r-r-r-rotating piece of machinery on the way down. He could feel his lips repeating the word soundlessly as people stared, trying to use their eyes to evoke a dialogue.

Phen wasn't sure which was worse: this guessing game, usually well-meaning, sometimes cruel, or the silent blocks that often involuntarily descended before he could speak. Silence in this case meant stupid. The inability to reply to a question. Even if the answer was a simple yes or no. On a bad day, every letter would run away. It was a game of hide-and-seek. Sometimes he would count to ten, sometimes a hundred, and still he couldn't find them. It was pointless smiling to buy time; this just confirmed he was the village idiot.

The worst was when the lazy circles of Mrs Smit's ruler would suddenly stop and point at him. Who didn't know the first Governor of the Cape of Good Hope was Simon van der Stel? It was even there, in black and white, in his history book lying open in front of him on his school desk. Yet the fear of the opening and closing s stretched the block of silence to such an extent he was eventually asked to sit down. He knew the answer. He could see the words. He just couldn't get them through the dense forest in his head. And in some moments, on some days, the pathways were more overgrown than on others. A sniggering Hettie Hattingh supplied the answer and did a little curtsy on receiving the teacher's compliment.

Confirmation of his stupidity was not needed by his classmates; however, it was nonetheless supplied by what he would only later know as dyslexia. "Thick" was the adjective most often used to describe him. And anyone who turned a dog into a bog while up at the blackboard certainly deserved it. No wonder the chalk was irritably snatched from his hands, its white dust spreading wide as it fell and covered his shoes while he stood waiting to be dismissed. His internal reading of the word was fine. There was no back-to-front switch, no silent block or stammer to ambush him here, it was just that, by the time it reached his hand, it came out incorrectly. Usually he saw this mistake, sometimes he didn't. Either way, if it was in public, it was too late. Spaz is as spaz does.

The teacher's comments, written in red ink in the margins of his books, were always the same. He was an untidy worker who should pay more attention in class. Rows of exclamation marks, like angry pinpricks, highlighted her mounting frustration. If he worked in pencil, he'd often rub a hole in the paper to correct his spelling. If it was ink, the page would look like a war zone, railroads of crossing out and ink blobs leaving craters on almost every line. The more he panicked, the smaller he wrote. The corrections to his words and sentences became indecipherable. This was often interpreted as a peculiar kind of cunning, a craftiness the teacher would not fall for.

He longed for the silver and gold stars of Hettie Hattingh and Vernon MacArthur. From a distance he envied the perfect slope of their writing and the whiteness of their unblemished pages. Their sense of control, both verbal and in written form, created a gulf he couldn't cross. When Vernon MacArthur wrote a love letter to Margaret Wallace and signed it with Phen's name, she immediately knew it didn't come from him. "It's too neat," she said. "Nothing's crossed out or going the wrong way." To confirm her forensics, she showed it to him. His nodding head agreed that he could not write like that. Though the ink arrow through the ink heart joining their names together seemed to pierce his chest clearly enough.

If words hijacked him when he tried to talk or write, they were much better behaved when he read them in his own mind. Here they flowed without bashing into anything. In fact, sometimes they took on a speed and a life of their own. Like flying down Nugget Hill on a flattened cardboard box, they accelerated to a point where he was barely in control. Words zoomed past, blurred but recognisable, just managing to stay connected to sentences and barely holding on to paragraphs. Pages flowed into chapters and the end suddenly appeared like Mr Otis slamming to a halt.

Often the words would leave the page and softly bounce as if on an elastic thread. Phen would lean back and give them a chance to settle. They took their time as they drifted on those magic thermals somehow created between author and reader. He loved these moments. It was proof of the other life that existed between words written and words read. As each letter floated down, he'd start again, this time a little slower, not wanting to tire the story unnecessarily.

So he read continuously, understanding he had a place to lose himself in. It was comforting to know there was somewhere else to go. When he overheard Philip Denton, who always tried to talk like his older brother, calling him "the dumbest fuck since the dodo" and suggesting the polony in his school sandwiches had more brains, he could always call on Holden Caulfield. He knew he could go home to *The Catcher in the Rye* and find someone else who was "concealing the fact that he was a wounded sonuvabitch".

Yet even in his head, words continued to play games with him. The more he read, the more he understood they often carried meaning well beyond their formal and published explanations. His father had called him gullible. He'd looked it up and had to agree. Phrases deliberately camouflaged themselves. Metaphors twisted whole chapters out of shape and anything to do with adults was never what it seemed. They could never say what they meant. There were always secrets. Their words had hidden compartments. If they said it with a smile, they usually meant the exact opposite. "Of course," she said with a smile, "my balcony door will be locked tonight. Besides, you would never be able to climb the tree to reach it."

This was never more evident than with Miss Zelda Hillock in number forty-three. When he first moved in to Duchess Court, Phen watched her intently. He was barely eight years old and in addition to being gullible tended to be very literal. As she walked back from the shops he waited for her to fall apart. He wasn't sure how this would happen. Maybe a leg would become unhinged or possibly an arm would suddenly drop off. At the very least he expected a foot would be left behind and she'd have to hobble back to fetch it. The more this didn't happen, the more intrigued he became. The walking of the dog, carefully planned to coincide with her return from the supermarket, showed from close up that she seemed sturdy enough. Not only that, she smiled, waved and, over time, even engaged in conversation. She understood his stammering shyness and didn't rush to fill his silences. Best of all, she laughed a lot and usually at herself. Burning the toast three times in a row was hilarious; so was finding her cat in the wash basket. And the time she ordered her steak tartare medium rare, well, she was in stitches.

Although Zelda worked in a bank she called herself "free-spirited" and "a child of the sixties". Phen didn't know what that meant but he liked what he saw. Most of the women in Duchess Court called her other names. Zelda said this was a "happening time" and asked him why she had to be barefoot, pregnant and in the kitchen. A somewhat startled Phen could find no good reason. "Fab!" she'd said, and straightened his hair.

Still, the more her condition didn't manifest itself, the more Phen was convinced she was being brave and hiding it. The way his grandfather had told him his cancer was indigestion, sometimes severe. He looked for signs of her ailment from every angle, yet could find none. As his puzzlement grew, so did his fear that something terrible would happen to her, just as it had to his grandfather. It began to affect his sleep. He imagined her strewn across her flat. Her hand still mixing the pot on the stove while her feet tapped in the lounge to the music everyone said she played too loud. After months of anxiety he decided he'd have to ask her. He tried to cover his apprehension by casually lying across the bonnet of the Cortina as she walked past. Zelda asked if he'd hurt his back. He immediately sat up straight and enquired if she was alright.

"Why?"

"Just asking."

"But why?"

There was a long silence as he groped for the words. He'd rehearsed it many times in his head, yet the sentence had scattered. There were also a number of ses waiting with a smirk. He breathed in deeply. Zelda seemed to have all the time in the world.

"S-s-some women s-s-say …" Having got over the first hurdle he perversely decided to reconstruct the sentence. "I was wondering if there was any way I could help hold you together."

"I beg your pardon?"

"They s-s-say you s-s-suffer from being a loose woman. They s-s-say s-s-sometimes you're very loose."

Zelda smiled and kissed him on the forehead. "Pancakes upstairs if you're interested."

When Phen told the story to his father, the upward curve of his mouth widened past the tight plastic edge of the oxygen mask and stayed there for some time.

"I'm happy to hear she's well bolted and bound," he said.

"Now … Mr Jones, of the Manor Farm, had locked the hen-houses for the night, but was too drunk to remember to shut the pop-holes."

Phen knew the book; however, he didn't want to go there yet. He still had the perfect blend of cinnamon and a rich sweetness in his mouth. Zelda had been true to her word. She'd opened the door to number forty-three and a plate of fresh pancakes immediately greeted them on the kitchen table. They smelled delicious. Next to them lay a green-and-gold tin of Lyle's syrup.

He knew the label well. He'd read it like a book many times. The lion lay on its side, bees buzzing around its stomach.

"Is this going to take long?" Zelda asked with an exaggerated opening of her green eyes.

The knife was initially a little tentative until she took his hand and made him plunge it deeper into the thick, sticky gold. They then spiralled it up and expertly flicked the blade onto its side. Together they made intricate designs on the flat circles of dough. He loved the way she urged him to have more, to spoil himself. He'd been taught the opposite. Good manners required a guest never to take advantage of the host. In the face of temptation, restraint was the highest honour. He overcame his guilt and had a second pancake while stoically refusing a third.

"With the ring of light from his lantern dancing from side to side, he lurched across the yard, kicking off his boots at the back door, drew himself a last glass of beer from the barrel in the—"

"*Animal Farm*."

"To the left, third shelf if I'm not mistaken."

Although his father owned thousands of books, Phen noticed his choices were dwindling. Before, there seemed to be hundreds he had to remember, now they were down to twenty or so. Not that it had ever been a real problem for Phen. For all the incorrect wiring in his head, he could remember them, he just couldn't say or spell them very well. "Stammer away," his father would say, "I'm not going anywhere and practice makes perfect." He'd stare at the ceiling in deep concentration while words sputtered and wobbled around the room. When a particularly difficult word finally made it out, he'd breathe deeply and close his eyes for a moment. "Thanks be to the god of vocabulary. Never mind the staggering, you got it over the finishing line."

Perhaps Phen's speech impediment reminded his father of his own life. He'd left England so his sickly mother could find good health in warmer climes. Within days, though, he'd lurched into a burial at sea as the tuberculosis and Atlantic took her. He landed with her hatbox in Cape Town and a determination to get to Johannesburg, the City of Gold. Bright and determined. he talked himself into a job at a stockbroking firm just as duty and the British Empire called. He was initially defeated by and then finally victorious against Rommel. It would take five years for the airman from North Africa to return to his posh leather seat at the Stock Exchange.

Yet his soul had begun to hem and haw. So much had been seen and experienced it was difficult to squeeze it back into a tiny office even if you had two phones and a secretary. The immigrant stockbroker airman decided he should be a farmer. Opportunity called. The colonial office offered large tracts of farming land for "a bob and sixpence" in Northern Rhodesia. This was the stuff of Kipling: "Take up the White Man's burden –/ Send forth the best ye breed – / Go, bind your sons to exile / To serve your captives' need." But what he'd said about Asia was also true for Africa: "Asia is not going to be civilised after the methods of the West. There is too much Asia and she is too old."

The Wind of Change blew his father back to Johannesburg. All Phen could remember was that the first Pal, a large black ridgeback, had to stay. Although chained to a wheelbarrow, he chased after their truck, it seemed for miles. Sitting on his mother's lap Phen twisted around and watched the dog keep coming through the red dust. The wheelbarrow bounced behind him, occasionally flipping in the air before being dragged again on its side. Eventually his mother, using two hands, gently turned his head towards the windscreen.

Maybe a life that's always stuttering begins to make you sick. All the stopping and starting, the breaking of rhythm, has to take its toll. How many times can you change direction until you have none? What is the opposite of the verb "to flow"? And whatever it is, did it turn the minuscule pinprick in his father's heart, hidden since childhood, into a hole? By the time he was trying to be a stockbroker for the third time, he was literally running out of air. Although it was his pump that had sprung a leak, it somehow affected his lungs, which produced their own heady mix when accompanied by a migraine.

In a cunning attempt to smoothen his reading, Phen introduced a new rule. If he saw a word further down the sentence that he knew he would battle with, he could change it, provided his father didn't notice. If this verbal detour was, however, spotted, a hand would immediately lift from the bedspread. Like an errant motorist halted by a traffic cop, Phen would have to reverse and park the correct word into the sentence. In *Cry, the Beloved Country*, he was caught out claiming the road that meanders through the hills, which are lovely beyond any s-s-singing of it, climbed for eight miles. "Not on my odometer." The s-s-seven miles twisted and turned in his mouth like the road to Carisbrooke, but he finally got there. Revenge was sweet, though, when barely five lines later, he entirely skipped the "Umzimkulu Valley" and moved on unimpeded. The body of his father lay blinking at the ceiling yet Phen knew the mind was far, far away. Although he was reading a story, what he was really offering was transport. Even his stumbling words made wheels good enough to be driven somewhere else.

There was another rule that was his and his alone. It was only enacted when sleep was at its deepest. And that was when the morphine had seeped in and made his father's chin crumple into his chest. This caused the transparent oxygen mask to pull his nose up as the mask came to rest between his eyes. Phen would quietly get off his chair and check the heavy breathing from the drooped head. He'd then stare at the now Porky Pig nose and whisper "Th-th-th-th-th-that's all folks!" This benediction allowed him two options. He could slowly move to the door and close it behind him. Or he could resume his seat and once more pick up the book he was reading. Only this time the story and the words were his.

The book on his lap was a guide, a general reference. He was not bound by its lines nor intimidated by its narrative. He read more loudly now and often melodramatically. His father's heavy snoring and occasional farts only added to the theatre of it all. Phen's arms swept and his fists clenched. They'd watched *The History of Shakespeare* in the assembly hall in preparation for the school play. Everyone else had laughed at the acting. Phen, though, had loved the extra-wide eyes, the wrist on the forehead and the pretend sword fights. This was an adult cartoon with grown-ups acting like children while throwing thees and thous at each other.

Whatever he was reading, he now performed with similar gusto. If he battled with words or didn't like the characters, he changed them. If the story was slow or boring, or in any way not to his liking, he changed that too. He would decide who won. His heroes were exalted with passionate praise and animated adoration. The mean, the greedy, the evil suffered terrible consequences. Anything he wanted, any time he wanted.

His mother caught him in full flight. He turned around to find her standing at the open door. He had no idea how long she'd been there for. She patted and straightened her apron as if some of the words might've splashed there too.

"Dinner's ready."

He wanted to explain over the cottage pie. As his fork dipped through the mashed potato and into the mince, he wanted to say how that curtained bedroom was a prison and an escape. How he never felt closer and further away from his father than when reading to him. How, sometimes, when the words and the stories caused chuckles and smiles, the body in the bed was almost Dad. And how sometimes, no matter how or what he read, the body stayed motionless.

But, as usual, he couldn't find the words.

4

Sputnik

/*sput-nik*/ noun

"Your mother," Uncle Ed said, "was some looker," and then correcting himself, added, "she still is." Uncle Ed wasn't Phen's real uncle but that's what he called him. His full name was Edward, which seemed to suit his double-breasted jackets and cufflinks better. It also matched his head, which sported the world's most marginal side parting. To all intents and purposes Uncle Ed was bald except for two narrow strips which started at each temple then petered out as they moved towards the back of his skull. In addition, no more than a few dozen hairs looped over a polished landscape from one side to the other. These survivors were the cause for a side parting to be maintained with incredible precision. Equally spaced, they half-orbited Ed's head like the trajectories of the Sputnik Phen had seen in a *Life* magazine.

He had heard from his grandmother that Uncle Ed had been "sweet" on his mother although he'd gallantly stepped aside when Dennis, his father, had won her hand. There was much debate on whether this had been a wise course of events. "When life turns as black as the Earl of Hell's waistcoat, you don't want a man who's all bum and parsley," his grandmother had said to Aunt Aida. "Anyway, he's doon if not oot so now's not the time to sew his life with a hot needle and a burnin' thread." Dennis and Uncle Ed had met on an Egyptian runway during the Second World

War and stayed best friends ever since. Proof of this lay on the sideboard in the dining room. The silver frame held the black-and-white picture stiffly to attention. Dennis smiled widely next to his beautiful bride, while the best man, already losing much of his hair, tried to do the same.

When he overheard that Uncle Ed "would always fly solo" he nearly, stupidly, asked if he owned his own plane. He had, after all, been a pilot in the war. Phen stayed hunched over his homework, leaned a little to the left and waited for clarification. It appeared an affair of the heart was not to be trifled with. It was also confirmed by his gran that love was not a mathematical equation. Just because A loved B it didn't necessarily mean B loved A. If B loved C there wasn't much A could do about it. Even if, truth be known, A would've been a better match for B. Aunt Aida agreed and pushed a thin slither of fruit cake between her red lips like an envelope sliding into a postbox.

Phen looked at A in the wedding photo. His hands, with nothing useful to do, were joined together behind his back. This pulled his arms straight and pushed his double-breasted chest out. B and C had their arms wrapped around each other's waist, eyes wide and expectant as they waited for the camera to click. Although all three letters were lined up equidistant from the photographer, there was a telling gap between A and B. It wasn't very big, but Phen understood it was large enough for his uncle's entire life to fall through.

Mairead was a large, imposing lady. She was neither apologetic about her height nor bashful about her width. Only her oldest friends were allowed to call her May, so this abbreviation didn't extend to her grandson. Phen was left to work out his grandmother on his own. All he really knew for sure is that she'd left Glasgow by boat shortly after "The Great, Stupid War". She'd travelled third class with her husband and discovered on her arrival that her sea sickness was also morning sickness. For years he heard her described as a door Scot. He presumed she came from a clan in the Highlands that made, or in her case, possibly blocked, entrances. It was only when Reverend Clayburn surprisingly popped in, that he realised this was another misunderstanding. His father had said his visit was a little premature unless he wanted to administer the last-ish rites. The minister had replied he was not Catholic. This had led his father to say, once he'd left, that he found him a little door. Phen asked if he also came from Scotland. "No, he originally came from the Cotswolds. His pale and bony knees, always bent in the service of the Lord, have never felt the rough tartan of a kilt."

Mairead might have been dour, yet there was no doubt she was sweet on Uncle Ed. She said he was "good with money", implying that Dennis was not. She used her baking prowess as an offensive weapon in declaring her feelings for him. Her affection was made real with butter and flour, yeast and caster sugar. She tried to ensure her visits coincided with his. When this didn't happen, sealed tins of scones and shortbread were left behind with his name neatly written on the sticky tape. After playing a particularly tough cricket test series against the Australians, Phen had helped himself to one of these biscuits.

He'd returned home from school on a Tuesday afternoon to find her sitting at the dining-room table. Tuesday was not a normal visiting day, and as Mairead found bus fares exorbitant, he knew she'd walked all the way from Ivanhoe Mansions in Joubert Park. Even taking the lesser gradient of Hospital Hill, instead of Nugget Street, it would've been a strenuous hour in the sun. The opened shortbread tin was on the table, the lid lying helplessly on its back. This caused a sharp reflection to bounce off its silvery surface, which underlit her not insubstantial chin. His glowing grandmother said nothing as he put his school bag down and fetched a glass of water. By the time Phen returned, she hadn't moved an inch. He wondered how long she'd been sitting there.

"I better check if …"

"He's fine."

She said nothing more but he knew the chair opposite her was the only place to sit. Having his father blocked as a potential distraction, he turned to his dog. Pal stayed under the telephone table, opened one eye, then feigned sleep. Deserted on all fronts, he sat on the chair and tried to smile.

"Is something funny?"

"No."

"There has been a theft."

Phen said nothing. He knew the tension would surely make him stutter. Plus he couldn't think of anything that wouldn't be immediately incriminating. He thought he'd resealed the tin perfectly. His mistake was to underestimate his grandmother's sixth sense and her deeply Calvinistic accounting. Confession or denial seemed equally damning. Instead, he took the last sip of his water and, frowning, pretended to be genuinely confused.

"How do you square a circle?"

He shrugged.

"I bake my shortbread in a square tray. I then cut them into fingers one inch wide and three inches long. How do I fit them into a circular tin?"

Silence. He tried to drink the water that was no longer in the glass.

"I place them horizontally in a crisscross pattern in the centre of the tin. This allows for six levels until the tin is full. However, given the nature of a square and a circle, this causes a gap on each side. Into these two gaps I place three vertical fingers of shortbread. Two times three when I went to school equalled six. Has there been any change in the times table that you would like to make me aware of?"

Phen pondered for a moment then shook his head. His grandmother slowly slid the tin across to his side of the table. He stared into the buttery circle. Some edges were baked a deeper brown. Did these represent the parts of his soul burned by greed?

"Three plus two equals?"

"F-f-f-ive."

"Indeed."

The silence that followed brought the picture above his grandmother's head into focus. Although only a print of a Pierneef-type landscape, Phen ran into its geometric canopy of trees and tried to hide in its flat planes and smooth lines. While he was there, her hand, made curiously more powerful by all its wrinkles, slowly turned the lid over. Deprived of her glow, she now matched the dark, swollen cloud as it enveloped the acacias behind her.

"Is there a name on the lid?"

"Edward."

"E-D-W-A-R-D. Do you think there is any possible confusion relating to whom the contents of the tin are intended for?"

"No."

"Do you think theft comes in sizes? Like shoes? And do you think a little theft is not as serious as a big one?"

Phen was back in the trees.

"And does a tiny theft deserve just a tiny punishment? Or none at all? Do the Ten Commandments say 'Thou shalt not steal' or 'Thou shalt not steal too much'?"

It was an umbrella acacia. The foliage was thickest at the top. Phen climbed as high as he could and wedged himself into a narrow fork.

"It always starts small, but it never stays that way. If you don't nip it in the bud, one becomes two. Two becomes four. It starts off as a biscuit and before you know it, it's your mother's change, the greengrocer's apple, then it's that transistor radio you want and suddenly it's a car. You promise yourself it's only going to be *one* car, just like it's only going to be *one* biscuit. And all the time you're forgetting when someone steals, they take something away from themselves. They take away their self-worth, their ability to look their fellow humans in the eye. It is impossible to steal without taking something from yourself at the same time. Therefore, the more you steal, the less value you have."

Broken and contrite, Phen unsuccessfully tried to hold back his tears.

"So," his grandmother said, suddenly allowing her accent to stream through, "it's clear we have a moose in the hoose." When she talked like this his father said it was English as spoken through a bagpipe. "I'm happy to put this theft down to that raving rodent you found on your hamster wheel. But you're the man o' the hoose now. Make sure it never returns. Stay calm. Keep the heid. Am I clear, laddie?" She put the lid back on and, with both hands, placed the tin on her lap. Phen had stopped crying although his eyes were still red and puffy. He nodded and waited for permission to leave. "Dare to be honest," she said, "and fear no labour – Robbie Burns … I believe there is homework still waiting to be done?"

Since his father's illness, everyone kept telling Phen he had to be the man of the house. He was desperate to oblige, but had no idea how he was meant to behave. Read the stock market pages? Smoke a pipe? Shave? He was also perpetually told he had to "be there" for his mother. But where was "there"? As Phen opened his geography book and sharpened his pencil, Pal finally felt safe enough to leave his shelter and join him under the dining-room table.

If his feelings for his grandmother left him confused, he had no such problem with his mother. He adored her. He loved her the way sons do. It was impossible to find fault. He worshipped her, sometimes in the literal sense. In his darkest moments he prayed for her, through her and occasionally to her. This perfection created a distance, though. Phen felt unworthy. Like his father, he was damaged goods. He was incapable of simple speech, and painfully thin. "A set of pretzel sticks with a belt around the middle." When he looked in the mirror he couldn't find anything that resembled his mother. Although there was much evidence to the contrary, he often went to sleep believing he was adopted. They said the grainy black-and-white pictures taken at the hospital were of him. Yet the tiny body was so wrapped up you couldn't really see anything.

His mother, on the other hand, was impeccable in all things except her choice of husband and son. Her attractiveness radiated all the more because she never acknowledged it. Any compliment was met with surprise or embarrassment. The more demurely she dressed, the more her physical beauty was shown in contrast. The skirt of appropriate length, the blouse always buttoned, and the tiny scarf worn the French way with a knot on the side were bewitching. Her total lack of awareness of the infatuation she caused lent her an air of serenity. While others scrambled and breathed heavily, she sailed blissfully through, offering another cup of tea or a slice of Madeira cake.

This calmness, this inner beauty, was as mesmerising as her outer appearance. The brokenness of her husband and son only added to her Madonna-like qualities. Here was a woman who could have had anyone, yet she'd ended up with those two. Could there be any greater self-sacrifice? They'd all seen the pictures of her baking bread in an anthill somewhere in the wilds of Northern Rhodesia. The next picture in the album showed her still smiling, in shorts, outside an old army tent. How long had they lived like that while Dennis tried to make bricks from the river sand and build them a house? And that python the workers were all nervously holding? Eighteen feet long! Measured thirty-six times by the six-inch ruler she kept to make lines for her diary. You couldn't see the hole in the python's head, but everyone knew Dennis had to reload his service revolver before actually hitting the target.

There were no shortages of stories to prove her saintly qualities and eternal patience. The one most told involved Phen's entry into the world. Not surprisingly, he'd contrived with his father to make it a stop-start affair. He was almost two weeks overdue. Perhaps intuitively aware of what awaited him, he'd chosen to delay his arrival as long as possible. The hospital was two hundred miles away by dirt road, so daily visits were not an option. Nor could she simply "wait it out". There was work to be done back at the farm. She was in charge of the chicken battery and the daily distribution of its eggs. It was also the only part of the farm that brought in any meaningful income. The doctor agreed on a compromise of weekly check-ins. There was the obvious caveat that "should she feel anything happening" she would immediately head for the hospital.

How "immediate" could relevantly relate to two hundred miles of dirt road and an ancient Ford truck was not discussed.

Phen had heard the story so many times, he'd begun to remember it first-hand. He clearly recalled his mother telling Jam, the kitchen helper, to fetch Boss Dennis. A panting man from Mars arrived and asked if Lil was okay. Lily said she couldn't hear him and suggested he take his beekeeper mask off. He was reluctant to do so as there were still a few bees on the neckpiece. Jam obliged by flattening them with a fly swatter. This allowed Lil to tell Dennis to his face that "something was happening". Dennis said maybe he should leave the last two hives until later; Lily felt this was a good idea. When his father looked at his watch, his mother knew something important was flashing through his mind. Time and its measurement were never very high on his list of priorities.

"It's nearly dusk," he said.

"Yes."

"The truck's lights aren't working and I'm not sure about the fan belt. The motorbike's fine, though."

Even the Blessed Virgin Mary has her limits. "The air turned purple," his father would always cheerfully recall, clearly proud that he finally got his wife to voice her exasperation. Jam stopped sweeping the dead bees with his broom, placed both palms over his ears and looked out the window. Once Lil had run out of breath, Dennis suggested a glass of orange cordial. Through clenched teeth, she explained thirst was not her paramount concern.

If it was not going to be side-saddle on the Triumph Tiger, it would have to be the front bench seat of the Ford. Fresh off the assembly line, it must have been a thing of great beauty. British racing green with matching runner boards, the grill seemed to smile above the heavy black bumper. Time, however, had taken its toll. The baked enamel was eczema-ed with rust from bonnet to tailgate. On the passenger door, the small brown craters had joined together to create a hole the size of a fist. You could now stick your hand through and open the door from the inside while standing on the outside. In a clear manifestation of colonial optimism, when the truck had been sold to them, this had been mentioned as a positive feature.

"She's no Bentley," the salesman at Victoria Falls had said. "Still, I doubt you'll be driving her to Buckingham Palace."

Driving her to Livingstone was the challenge. Jam fetched a pillow to allow Lil to rest the small of her back against the peeling upholstery of the seat. He was about to leave, when he found two torches thrust into his hands. He knew not to ask any questions at this stage, as he was sure he wouldn't understand the answer. Instead, he went to the back to check if the boiled-egg sandwiches had been packed into the picnic basket. He found them next to the brown-and-white-striped thermos flask. He lifted it to make sure it felt full, carefully placed it in the cubbyhole and wedged a spanner against its neck to ensure it stayed upright.

Unfortunately, Lily, having regained her composure, seemed to give Dennis the licence to lose his. "I want all the stockings and *Siddhartha*! Now! Quick!"

Jam had been chosen for both his patience and his ability to get the job done. He ran the household with an easy smile that belied his methodical tenacity. He enjoyed solving problems, even if many of them were created by the man now standing in front of him. He'd taught this man how to plant maize and soya beans, how to kill and pluck a chicken. Where to place the rain tank and why welding near thatch is not a good idea. He'd even helped him with the birth of the calf that had been facing the wrong way. But now he was genuinely mystified. He stood there, again clutching the two torches, waiting to find a link to logic which might make him move.

"Stockings! Silk or nylon, doesn't matter! *Siddhartha*! Finding individual meaning! Hermann Hesse!"

The man had clearly lost his mind. The condition of his wife had made his brain bulge and explode. She was about to give birth and he wanted to wear her stockings. Plus, that was the one drawer he never went into. It was the ladies' drawer full of things he couldn't touch or even think about. When these things were washed, they were put on another line and the women hid them from view by hanging blankets on each side. And who was Siddhartha? He knew no such name. And now there was this Hermann man? He switched the torches on; at least they worked.

The mad boss opened the bonnet and leaped in as if being eaten by the engine. The pregnant woman called Jam across and gently laid a hand on his shoulder. She explained Siddhartha was a book the crazy one was reading. It was on the bedside table. She also asked him to get Abigail to bring all her stockings in a paper bag. They would have to use them as a makeshift fan belt on the journey to Livingstone. Massively relieved, Jam put down the torches and did as he was requested. He was happy to see on his return that the truck had started and was answering to the deep plunging of its accelerator. There was black smoke everywhere. This led to some joyous ululating from the staff who had spontaneously gathered to form a farewell party. His relief was short-lived, though. Lily shifted sideways to make room for him and handed the torches back. "You," she said, "are our headlights."

As the truck spluttered and jerked through the farm gate

that had no fence on either side, Lily leaned over Jam and waved through the window. In the rear-view mirror, she watched the women dancing as they cradled imaginary babies in their arms. Dennis spotted his book on top of the dashboard and thanked Jam. "It's made up of two Sanskrit words," he said. "'Siddha', which means 'achieved', and 'artha', which means 'what was searched for', hence *Siddhartha*." Stuck between the door and the lady who took up the space of two, all Jam could do was remove the window winder from his ribs and stare through the windscreen.

The first fifty miles devoured a single stocking and an unfortunate jackal that inexplicably ran in the same direction as the swerving truck. The driver apologised profusely, although no one in the front seat quite knew to whom these sorrys were directed. Dennis was talking into the rear-view mirror as if it were a microphone. Perhaps he thought the jackal, which was embedded in both the front and rear wheels, had left a family behind. At the very time he was trying to add to his own bloodline, he was guilty of subtracting from another. To calm him down, Lily suggested a tea break.

She thought it wouldn't be wise for her to move, so while she sipped from the metal cup, Jam attempted to dislodge the jackal with a stick. He showed Dennis how it looked as though the rear wheel had grown a tail. Maybe it was the liquid, still hot in the stainless-steel flask, that caused the first contractions. Either way, the yelp from the cab caused both men to leave the tail where it was and run to the front of the truck. For fear of it not starting, the engine had been left running. Within seconds, they were on the road once more. Jam took the cup from Lily and screwed it onto the top of the flask. Lily, in turn, grabbed his thigh and dug her nails deep.

Nightfall on the southern tip of Northern Rhodesia was not an even process. The light lingered and teased. Sometimes the fading glow even increased in intensity as it bounced off clouds or set the horizon on fire. And then it was gone. Like the flick of a switch, the dark was so deep you couldn't see your hand in front of you. Dennis leaned forward as if getting closer to the windscreen would help. What road there was disappeared. They were boxed in black. He wound his window down, hoping the fresh air would somehow increase his visibility. Jam lifted Lily's hand from his leg and switched a torch on.

"Slow down."

"I'm only doing thirty."

"Slow down or you'll crash."

While the husband-and-wife team argued in the cab, Jam stood on the runner board with a torch in his free hand. It served absolutely no practical purpose except, perhaps, to offer some erratic illumination to a vehicle coming in the opposite direction. On two occasions, cars veered out the way at the last moment as they realised the single bulb belonged to something larger than a bicycle. As the light bounced and swayed in every direction, Dennis prayed for the moon to finally break the tree line. Just over halfway, the contractions increased both in frequency and in intensity. As Jam's thigh was out of reach, the ancient and seeping foam of the dashboard became the grip of choice. With fifty miles to go, stuffing lay all over the seat. The battery on the second torch was almost gone, yet Jam felt it was safer outside the vehicle. There was no room for him, anyway. Lily was now sprawled across the front seat with her head on the driver's lap.

They were saved by a full moon, a clear sky and a surprisingly large number of stockings for a farmer's wife. By the time the tyres felt tar under their treads, the buildings on the outskirts of Livingstone cast clearly defined lunar shadows. Their arrival also heralded a huge gush of fluid onto the seat, then floor. Jam's torches were long extinct, yet he still symbolically pointed one into the night and kept his eyes focused forward. Dennis defied all the neatly arrowed signs and the frantic waving of the night watchman as he parked in the rose garden at the entrance of the hospital. The high roof and wide turning circle of the truck would not allow a more sedate arrival under the neat canvas canopy. The good news was all this turmoil also produced the doctor on night duty. Dennis ran around to the passenger side and whipped open the door like some frantic presenter revealing the climax of his main act.

"I see," said the doctor, "most of my work is already done."

The next morning Dennis cleaned out the cab. Yellow tufts of sponge lay everywhere. He flattened a piece and made a bookmark out of it. And although he had since read *Siddhartha* many times, the pressed yellow strip always stayed on page thirty-three where the last paragraph was underlined in pen.

At that moment, when the world around him melted away, when he stood alone like a star in the heavens, he was overwhelmed by a feeling of icy despair, but he was more firmly himself than ever. That was the last shudder of his awakening, the last pains of birth. Immediately he moved on again and began to walk quickly and impatiently, no longer homewards, no longer to his father, no longer looking backwards.

5

Avant-garde

/av'an-gärd/ adjective, *French*

It was the weekend, so Uncle Ed had left his cufflinks at home. He had, however, kept the double-breasted jacket and tucked a burgundy cravat where his tie would normally be. His unexpected arrival turned everything upside down. Already Phen's mother had apologised twice for being caught in her apron. Further embarrassment had ensued by her not having anything to offer with the tea. The flat was a mess, the kitchen barely clean, and the passageway rug still hung over the balcony wall waiting for a beating.

It was eleven thirty on Saturday morning and Edward was basking in the moment. He didn't often cast himself in the role of unexpected guest. There were many words to describe him, but spontaneous was not one of them. You wouldn't call him mischievous either, yet here he was, being positively coquettish. He crossed and uncrossed his legs like an impatient schoolboy, his coy, crooked smile creating a single dimple on the right side of his face. Unable to contain his excitement, he'd carelessly rubbed his head, leaving the normally smooth arc of his individual hairs crisscrossed and tangled.

"You have to tell us, Edward."

"Not until Dennis wakes up."

"You're such a devil."

It was strange to see a man who was an elder in the local Methodist church and lead baritone in their choir burst with such pride on being called Satan, thought Phen. Uncle Ed ran his finger around the back of his cravat as the temperature in the room suddenly rose. From beneath the table, Phen watched his uncle squeeze his own knee in an attempt to contain his enthusiasm. He'd chosen this vantage point because his Meccano set was on the floor anyway and, besides, it allowed him to feign disinterest. He also didn't like the jovial and almost intimate chatter between the two of them. He preferred his uncle more subservient. He was a supporting actor, not the star of the show. He smashed the crane against the table leg and watched the wheel of the headgear roll under the sideboard.

"Accident below?" asked Uncle Ed as if he was suddenly in charge. "Shall we send for the ambulance?"

The epicentre of all the intrigue lay on top of the table in a large square cardboard box. That in turn was surrounded by wrapping paper that designated neither a birthday nor Christmas. Phen decided it was happy-nothing paper. Tiny stars streaked out of a toy trumpet and burst against a blue sky like some feeble Tinkerbell Guy Fawkes. Silly yellow birds with large, wide eyes gawked in amazement. One of them was so stunned it covered its beak and face with its wing. What annoyed Phen even more was the weight didn't match the frivolous paper. He'd seen its heaviness had lopsided his uncle's shoulders and he'd needed two hands to place it gently on the table.

Whatever was in the box, its importance grew as they waited for his father to stir. This led to a second cup of tea and a "poor rescue act" of four dry Marie biscuits served on a side plate. Phen reached for one, but was stopped by his mother's glare and arched eyebrow. "Visitors first." The stupidity of the moment was compounded by Uncle Ed declining. To punish his mother he was forced to refuse her second-round offer. The box was causing problems and it hadn't even been opened yet.

"I'm sorry," his mother said. "It was a bad night, had to give him morphine."

"Migraine?"

"Yes, and battling to breathe."

From under the tablecloth Phen watched his mother surreptitiously point at him, then place her finger on her lips. Uncle Ed nodded.

"Well, I'm sure he'll be much better when he wakes."

As if on cue they heard the clink of the water jug, and the bedside lamp being switched on.

"His Lordship arises."

The routine was always the same after morphine or pethidine. His mother would go in first to "make the room safe". She was never sure what she'd find behind the closed door. Often she'd discover his body as she'd left it, lying on its back with both sleeves still forced above his bony elbows, her amateur needlework on full display. The black and purple bruises spreading like continents across his forearms. "Africa," he'd once said, staring at his veined atlas. "You've even got the Blue Nile in the right place." If he was drowsy or being teased with nausea, she knew he had to be coaxed back, gently persuaded to fully return. There were whispers of hot tea, warm baths and did he know "Test the Team" would be on the radio tonight? Could she open the curtain just half an inch? It was a beautiful day, could she let it in?

On other days the opioid worked a fuller magic. The body would be sitting upright, the pillows already stacked, throne-like, and the pyjamas neatly buttoned from collar to cuff. As the door opened, there would often be a request for a dance. On hearing that her card was full, he'd mischievously stroke his imaginary pencil moustache. He was taking the yacht down to Antibes tomorrow – would she care to join him? Only if she could bring her mother along too, was the usual reply. Perhaps the Moulin Rouge later in the week, then? Perhaps.

It was a full fifteen minutes before Phen and Edward were ushered in. Until then, he had refused to move out from under the table, even though his uncle's upside-down head had popped beneath the cloth a number of times in an attempt at conversation. The curtains in the bedroom were open enough to see the dust travel through its single shaft. It danced and spun before disappearing into the dark corner where the oxygen cylinder stood erect, awaiting orders. His father had been given a shave and had had his hair neatly combed back. His Old Spice clashed with the disinfectant and metal smell that seeped from the scrubbed and covered bedpan.

It was obvious his father hadn't dressed himself and this embarrassment made his body sit ill at ease. Like a child forced into a new uniform, he tried hard not to show his grumpiness. He'd been changed into a newly laundered pyjama top that was way too big for him. The sleeves stretched over his knuckles and the freshly ironed shoulders sat like tents on either side of his head. Each button, dutifully fastened all the way up to the neck, mocked the torso it was bringing order to. The heavy square box at the bottom of the bed bullied his father into concertinaing his legs. This created a mountain Phen couldn't see over.

"Hello, Ed. What brings you to these parts? And on a Saturday morning to boot. We haven't fully recovered from our champagne-and-caviar shindig last night."

"Sorry to interrupt your hangover, but I've bought you a present. Saw it in the shops this morning and thought, 'Why not?'"

"He won't tell me what it is. Said I had to wait until you woke up!"

His mother rubbed his father's knees at the top of the mountain. After a pause this prompted him to feel for his glasses, which lay on the cover of *The Spy Who Came in from the Cold*. He stalled again while he rubbed the large indents on each side of his nose. The weight of his glasses had left deep crevices that could no longer be massaged out. Finally, he slid the heavy frames on. Instantly his eyes doubled in size. Like a dramatic magician's trick it confirmed he was now fully engaged. Slowly he rolled his head from one side of the room to the other.

"We are missing one."

"I'm behind your knees."

"Well, get yourself in front of them."

Ed pushed the box further up the bed then bowed to Phen to indicate he should do the unwrapping. His mother asked him to be careful and he cheekily said you can't unwrap something without tearing the paper. He was suspicious of this sudden eagerness and anticipation. He didn't like the way all the adults were joking with each other as if everything was instantly, miraculously perfect and normal. His father's cartoon eyes looked at him reproachfully. It was all meaningless anyway. Once the wrapping paper had been ripped off they were left none the wiser. Strips of corrugated cardboard now surrounded the square. Phen picked tentatively at the thick sticky tape that held everything together. In addition, a thick twine secured the package in tight vertical and horizontal lines.

"Perhaps I should take it from here?" Ed brought his middle and forefingers together to indicate scissors.

"Back in a jiffy; they're in the kitchen."

With his mother gone the three men suddenly felt awkward around each other. The pause was too pregnant. Ed began to pat the box.

"Not another dog, Ed? We've already got one of those."

With the string and cardboard armour lying on the floor, the present looked flatter and more streamlined. The box had its individual flaps fastened together by thick copper staples. The only new clue was the type that ran in capitals across the top. STÉRÉO CONTINENTAL "401". One of the staples was punched through both the O and the C, metallically defying everyone to separate them. Phen had no idea what a STÉRÉO CONTINENTAL "401" was and felt relieved to see that nor did his parents. His mother let out an excited gasp, but didn't know where to send it. His father looked over his glasses like a bored professor waiting for his student to come up with the answer.

"Nearly there."

While Ed attacked the thick staples with his pair of scissors, Phen continued to read the box. He knew the word stereo, but had never come across stéréo before. It seemed so much more exotic, even alluring. He felt a guilty pleasure as he rolled the word around his mouth and made different attempts at pronouncing it. This pleasant feeling was accentuated by the continental that was bound to it in shiny metal.

Hillbrow was full of continentals. There was even a Café Continental. They drank coffee that wasn't from a Frisco tin and bread not sliced, but shaped like plump torpedoes. They dressed differently too. His grandmother had said everyone's pants were too tight and everyone's skirts were too short, but the continentals had something else. They had style. The men didn't just wear shorts with long socks, or safari suits. The women, well, the women weren't trapped in Crimplene. He had no idea what that meant, but when his mother had said it, it sounded like a good thing.

The final endorsement of continentals had come from Zelda. She'd said she liked all these Europeans pouring into Hillbrow, especially the French and the Italians. She said she knew the National Party was just letting them in because they wanted more whites to counterbalance the blacks. Still, they were a breath of fresh air. Not so conservative and uptight. She enjoyed talking to them and loved their different accents. Even the Germans, believe it or not, had a sense of humour. She said the continental thinking was much more avant-garde. Again, Phen had no idea what that meant, yet it sounded positive. Later on this was more than confirmed by his *Chambers*. Who wouldn't want to be part of a noun that gave its meaning to those who support the newest ideas?

The scissors were a little small and the staples particularly tenacious. They were not giving up their prize without a fight. Uncle Ed was becoming a bit flustered as he now dug holes around the metal clasps rather than attempted to pry them loose. His mother tried to maintain her excitement with pitched eyebrows. His father, meanwhile, opened Le Carré's spy novel to check which page he was on. All this allowed Phen to contemplate "401". It was such a strange number. He felt it was meant to have been "400", but someone, at the last moment, had added an extra something and now it had to be "401". That's avant-garde for you. Those continentals were a different bunch.

The STÉRÉO CONTINENTAL "401" suddenly seemed

to promise only good things. His sense of dread and ill humour began to recede. To see better, his mother opened the curtains another inch and the expanded sunlight reinforced his positive shift. Ed tilted the box sideways and pulled the now-exposed plastic handle. The box clung on like a second skin. He shook it violently but to no avail. Phen's father continued to look over his glasses while his finger kept his place in the book. Uncle Edward was beginning to perspire. He took a moment to dab at his forehead before carefully refolding the handkerchief and sliding it back into his pocket.

"Perhaps if you lift it up and I pull the box down?"

Inexplicably Phen felt a surge of jealousy. It was as if his mother was helping his uncle undress something. His dread returned. They laughed together as the box squirmed and turned in their hands. He saw their fingers overlap as she gave one final heave and the box fell like a dropped skirt. Ed was left holding it high as if waiting for applause or maybe a photograph.

"Shall we put it down?"

"Of course."

Still clutching the white handle, he laid it gently on the bed and smoothed the blanket surrounding it. There were more words for Phen to read. In small metal relief on a raised portion in the middle was the word "Philips". Two white dials on the left said "Volume" and "Tone". Moving right and housed in the same raised section that proclaimed "Philips" were seven square cubes. The first one was bright red and labelled "Rec". Pause, Play, Multiplay, Stop and the two cubes marked with double arrows pointing in opposite directions were all white. On the far right were two more dials marked "Micro" and "Phono".

Phen's father stared blankly then moved his legs further

away as if the contraption might bite. Uncle Ed was crest-fallen by this reaction. He slowly let the handle go and began to seek comfort by stroking his cravat. He then suddenly pointed at the machine as if it had given him an idea.

"Of course! It needs these!"

From a large envelope no one had noticed behind the scatter cushion, he produced two reels. One was empty, the other full of a thin brown tape. He placed them both on their awaiting metal spikes, threaded the tape through an adjoining slot and then secured the full reel to the empty one. Confidence restored, he demanded a double adapter so the machine could be plugged in. From a secret compartment on the side of the device, he pulled out what looked like a torch. Except there was no light at the end. Instead, a metal bulb of polished steel punched full of tiny holes stared at them.

"A microphone," said Uncle Ed.

"Terrific," said his father.

"Say something."

"Why?"

"I am trying to record your voice."

"Why?"

"It's a tape recorder, the latest."

"You're the one with the voice. I don't sing in the choir."

"You don't have to sing. Just say something."

"I am saying something."

"Say something more profound."

"Fuzzy Wuzzy was a bear. Fuzzy Wuzzy had no hair. Fuzzy Wuzzy wasn't fuzzy. Was he?"

"Deep."

"Your turn. 'Amazing Grace'."

"No."

The red record button was released from its pressed-down position and popped up obediently. The white cube with arrows pointing backwards then took over. Once that too had snapped back into position, Ed paused for effect then pressed Play. It was the funniest thing Phen had ever heard. Delivered second-hand, the two quarrelling voices sounded like a pair of comedians. How could the two of them be so hilarious without even trying? Why was listening back so much more amusing than listening to? He'd never realised his father's voice was so low, a tractor trying to talk. And his uncle – so posh! 'Sa-a-ah-a-y something. I ham trahying to record yarrh voice.'

It was their voices, but it was not them. Phen marvelled at the mystery of it all. Everyone seemed delirious! His mother giggled incessantly while trying to wipe the tears from her eyes. His father's body shook as his pyjamas ballooned with his chuckling. Phen wondered if his father, bloated with laughter, might lift off the bed and float towards the ceiling. Each time his heaving chest tried to catch his breath, he'd let out a loud snort and trigger the whole room again. Uncle Ed paced the room, eventually seeking refuge behind the oxygen cylinder, where he cackled and guffawed into the corner. The room had never ever been so happy. The magic box had turned a dark cell smelling of hospital into an enchanted place by merely playing their own voices back to them.

This was wizardry Phen could not fully understand. He laughed and laughed yet felt the distant anxiety return. He was made nervous by the speed of it all. The change had been so quick, so violent. Didn't magic spells carry a price? Abracadabra wasn't for free. There had to be a cost. Had they unwittingly practised the dark arts and would they now be held to account? He didn't trust the machine; there would be a ransom. He just didn't know what form it would take.

He didn't have to wait long for the answer.

Slowly the room returned to normal. Ed apologised profusely, cleared his throat and straightened his cravat. His father's laughter turned to a cough and the oxygen mask resumed its normal place. His mother stopped giggling but continued to cry. She smiled through her tears and left the room to make everyone some fresh tea. The light dimmed and the dust refused to dance. Pale and anaemic, its gleam barely reached the bed before extinguishing itself on the brown bedspread. By the time his mother came back with the tray and the smart cups, he knew it was a cheap conjuring trick.

"I've let the leaves settle."

"Excellent."

Ed accepted the tea strainer and nodded dumbly. "Suppose I should've phoned in advance."

"Not at all."

The oxygen had been turned up in an attempt to stifle the cough. The high pitch of escaping air made conversation difficult. To accommodate his father they had to talk much louder. Phen hated this. It was as if an idiot had suddenly entered the room. People often did it to him when he didn't answer immediately. He turned to leave; Pal was waiting at the door. He was stopped by Ed, who turned the strainer into a sword and pointed it at his chest.

"Look," he said, "besides all this silliness, there is another purpose behind this purchase."

Uncle Ed was feeling guilty. He spoke as if in his own defence. He knew he should never have been spontaneous. He knew, in his world, this led to calamity. What was he thinking arriving on a Saturday morning unannounced?

He'd tried to mix it up a little, play it off the cuff, and now he'd paid the price. He wasn't quite sure what had gone wrong, but that's precisely what happens when you don't carefully plan things in advance. Everything was in a state of turmoil and it was all his fault.

"You know Mavis?"

Everyone shook their heads. No one knew Mavis.

"Well, anyway, toiled away for years in our accounts department. Good worker, failing sight, though. Something to do with diabetes I think. Had to let her go. Here's the point, we passed the hat around and bought her one of these things."

He pointed to the tape recorder.

"Not quite such a spiffing model, but pretty damn good. Not so that she could play silly buggers on it, rather so that she could listen to books."

Phen knew at that exact moment everything was about to change. Some key had turned, some moment had passed and there was no going back. He was being left behind as the world moved on. He was being unhitched. Sidelined. Made to watch. He looked at the metal box; the still reels stared back. The plastic strap curled from one side to the other in a smirk. He didn't understand it fully, but he knew there were new rules and these would dislodge everything. What had been built before wasn't very strong, yet it had managed to stay standing. Now things would start tumbling. Although no one had asked for his opinion or permission he knew he was ceding control. He dragged his eyes off the tape recorder and returned to his uncle's conversation.

"They're a wonderful organisation called Tape Aids for the Blind. You don't have to be blind, just battling to read. They've got all the books. Huge library. And best of all, they're read by South Africa's finest voices. All these men and women you hear on the radio, the professionals, they're the ones who do the reading. If you miss something or fall asleep, just click a button and rewind. Volume? Well, as loud or soft as you wish."

Phen's clawing apprehension was perfectly counter-balanced by Ed's growing enthusiasm. As his uncle fought to win the room back, his mother turned the oxygen valve down to ensure his father could hear. Ed continued to shout. Although imparting information, he was really seeking converts. As he gained confidence he began to evangelise. His arms left his sides as he welcomed all to this new tech-nology. His hands coaxed Lily and Phen to come closer and examine the future. An automated Shangri-La waited, nest-ling on the bedspread. All they had to do was embrace it.

"Want a break? Make a cup of tea or a trip to the bath-room? Just press Pause. Tone allows you to add treble or bass. It's press down or up. The turn of a dial, the flick of a switch, you call the shots. You are master of your own listening pleasure, Dennis."

Dennis put up a hand to show that he understood.

"Threading is easy once you get the hang of it ..."

Dennis now raised both hands in a sign of surrender and in an attempt to lower the volume or, better yet, induce silence. Ed's sermonising slammed to a halt. The oxygen mask was pulled from the mouth and onto the chin. Half the air escaped down his father's neck, making his chest bulge and billow again.

"Thank you, Edward. Wonderful idea." *The Spy Who Came in from the Cold* was plopped behind the bedside lamp. "How do we get hold of this Tape Aids place? Rather like the idea of my literature being read to me in perfect enunciation."

Phen felt the first block of what used to be begin to topple. He'd never known what his father thought of him; he'd suspected he was loved although this didn't make being made redundant any easier to take. It felt like he was losing not only a hesitant love, but also a sense of purpose. He wondered if it would have made any difference if he didn't stutter. He had gone for pages, sometimes even chapters without a problem. He'd made up paragraphs to get around ses, changed heroes' names and altered stories. Day after day, he'd remembered those changes so he wouldn't be caught out. Now he could see it was all for nothing.

He'd been replaced by a machine. A machine that would have no problems with any words. One reel would feed the other and the story would flow. They would spin together in perfect time as if the voice itself were lubricating their lazy circles. There would be no silent blocks, unless the finger pressed Pause to make it so. The Philips didn't have to go to school, walk the dog or want to listen to the Top Ten on the radio. It was the *deluxe* STÉRÉO CONTINENTAL "401". Phen knew he hadn't just been replaced; he'd been surpassed.

6

Rendezvous

/ron'di-voo/ noun

It hurt that a better version of him could arrive delivered in a box. He disliked the indent it caused in the leather armchair that used to be his. He didn't approve of the way the room had to be rearranged to ensure the cord could reach the plug. But most of all, he hated the way it commanded *all* within the room to do its bidding. The Grundig in the lounge was passive and benign by comparison. While the Continental spoke, everyone else had to be silent – even if his father was asleep. The moment you pressed Stop the white cube would answer back with such a loud click his father would wake. So the Philips just kept on talking, holding court even if no one was listening.

The bedroom was now literally always full of stories. Phen would stop and listen from the door. Although standing in the passageway made him feel uneasy and antsy, he was not prepared to give the machine the satisfaction of seeing him in any way interested. By deliberate design, the first book ordered had been the same Le Carré spy novel still wedged behind the bedside lamp. Phen leaned against the wall and teased Pal with an ancient tennis ball.

"You bastard," hissed Leamas, "you lousy bastard! You knew I wouldn't trust myself to your rotten Service; that was the reason, wasn't it? That was why you used a Russian."

"We used the Soviet Embassy at The Hague. What else

could we do? Up till then it was our operation. That's perfectly reasonable. Neither we, nor anyone else could have known that your own people in England would get on to you so quickly." …

"Goodbye," he said to Leamas. "Good luck."

"Come," Phen said as he pulled the ball out of his dog's mouth. He'd heard that part a few times already. His father was always dozing off and then rewinding too far back. "It's time for a walk. We have to get to West Berlin. The Ruskies aren't playing nice and I don't want to have to drink vodka with my dinner again."

He decided Checkpoint Charlie would be Villa de Eston Mansions. The building stood midway between Duchess Court and Nugget Hill Park. As he did a careful reconnaissance from behind the jacaranda tree, he noticed the East German border guard sitting on the steps of the entrance. The Zulu night watchman with his knobkerrie and khaki uniform leaned back on his elbows and yawned. Phen would not be fooled by this seemingly casual behaviour. He pulled Pal diagonally across the road and half into the privet hedge. He'd need to assess the situation from another angle.

The guard leaned further backwards, causing both the badge on his cap and the zcc star on his chest to face upwards to the sky. So, that's how he wants to play it, thought Phen. He imitated his nonchalance by allowing his dog to sniff a passing poodle. But something about that encounter stirred the Stasi's interest. He suddenly sat upright, tapped his weapon and stared straight at him. Phen wondered if he should just make a run for it. Would he make it to the other side? He could see the park beckoning to him; vast stretches of green and rows of white daisies planted next to the slide waved him on. He had a safe house there. No one knew about the willow tree. Freedom was calling. He hated this Cold War. This damn wall that made you choose! This scar of brick built straight through the heart of a nation.

Now you could trust no one. Even as he looked towards the entry gates of the park, he wondered if they'd infiltrated that too. Was he really secure there? Or were they waiting for him disguised with open arms and false smiles? He'd have to decide soon. The guard had stood up and was looking restless. It seemed he wanted to cross the road. And what? Check his papers? Luck favours the brave. Phen pulled his dog towards the menacing sight of the man now rubbing his thigh with his knobkerrie. This was the moment! No turning back. He had to get past or live the rest of his days as a guest of East Germany's State Security.

"Wait!"

Phen froze in terror. Even Pal lifted his head and cocked his ears.

"Wait!"

He studied the ground and expected the worst. His cover was blown. The guard approached him, walking briskly. There was nothing he could do but accept his fate. Whom had he trusted too much? Who was the turncoat? Someone had ratted him out and he'd probably never know the name of that faceless swine. And then the miracle. The guard kept on walking. Past him, across the road and to the car parked on the corner. Not wishing to be obvious, Phen slowly turned his body once he'd reached the sanctuary of the chrysanthemums. The Chinese man who controlled the local Fa-fi syndicate had almost left without collecting the guard's bet for the week. Coincidence or planned diversion? Either way, Phen and his dog hurried to the park happy and relieved.

Once there, though, he couldn't let his guard down. He allowed Pal off his leash, but immediately found the lady at the baby swimming pool suspicious. Firstly, the pool was empty so why would she choose to sit next to it? Perhaps it was a prearranged rendezvous? Shortly, a man of average height wearing a forgettable raincoat and a bland hat might sit down next to her and place a parcel between them. He would say nothing, then leave a few minutes later with the brown paper bag still on the bench. Plus, her hair was beehived and her face fully made up, yet she was by herself. Why get so dressed up for a date with no one? What did thick lipstick and enormous stuck-on eyelashes mean at five in the afternoon? Too much for the office, yet too early for any nightlife. He'd read about female spies in a photo-story magazine while buying bread at the corner café. It was titled "The Honey Trap". She looked like the lady on the cover, although her skirt had no long slit up the side.

"Agent provocateur," he said aloud.

"I don't think so."

Phen nearly jumped out of his skin. He spun around to find a man standing not six inches behind him.

"Look at the smudge of mascara, especially under the right eye. She's been crying."

Phen stepped back to create some distance between them. The man's face and forearms were baked a deep nut brown. Nothing else matched. He wore white tennis shoes with a pair of smart suit pants and a blue, yellow and purple paisley shirt. The collar was clean, although frayed. The loose threads sprayed everywhere, some trying to climb up the side of his neck. He had no socks, yet cradled a brand-new felt fedora in his hands. Phen knew the make and material of the hat; they'd been on display at Harry's

Hattery, a shop he passed every day on his way to school. For all this clash of colour and style, the man appeared strangely confident, even a little suave. This self-assurance was confirmed by the way he spun his hat around his forefinger without even looking at it.

"She's been crying. At the moment, more inside than out. Her heart is heaving. And all we have as a clue is a path one teardrop wide through her mascara."

Phen looked at the woman again and was suddenly overwhelmed by her sorrow. The empty pool made sense now. Where better to sit when your life had run dry? She stared at the leaping dolphin made of small white and blue tiles, its bemused, smiling face confirming they'd both been duped. Phen wondered how he'd not noticed this sadness before. It was now so obvious he could feel it seeping into him.

"Love makes the world go round," the man said, "and sometimes stops it, too."

He placed the hat back on his head and did what Phen presumed was a romantic dance with an invisible partner. He thought it might be a tango. The man's body shot right, suddenly turned and burst left. He did this a number of times before ending dramatically with his back curled forward as his eyes smouldered at the emptiness he gently cradled in his arms.

"Don't worry," the man said as he straightened up and released his partner. "This is not your story to join. Someone was meant to come and didn't arrive. That's the problem with ultimatums – you have to choose. Binary. Yes or no. No si, so adios. Nothing in between. You cannot dither deeply. No indecision to marinate in. She did love him and, in time, she will also realise that he loved her."

Phen looked at him blankly, still trying to arrange his

words and dress sense into some kind of order. It was impossible to guess his age. Forty-five, perhaps even sixty? The extraordinary blue of his eyes belonged to a baby, yet his face was heavily lined. Tiny holes pitted the skin that stretched across his cheekbones. His nose almost beaked then turned friendly again at the tip. His hat didn't sit on his head; it rode a massive wave of hair. It sloped forward then back in a huge sweep like a lion's golden mane. If he hadn't had so much hair going sideways, he would've looked like Elvis Presley without the grease.

Equally eye-catching was the black-and-grey square of facial hair that spread beneath his lower lip and covered most of his chin.

"My placemat," he said, watching Phen's eyes.

"It's square."

"Holds my face together. Like a room that needs a rug."

Phen nodded.

"The boyfriend," he continued, "comes from Spinalonga. Small island off Crete. Beautiful in a rugged way. His family want him back. There's a local girl waiting there. It's, sort of, been arranged. Complicated. Second cousin's sister. If they get married the bakery then becomes his, so his parents' future is secured."

"H-h-how do you know …?"

"They came here often and discussed it. I'm usually stretched out on the bench opposite, sometimes with a newspaper over my face. No one notices me. When people don't see you they don't put up any barriers. Not that you have to hear everything. Your body tells a lot, too. You can listen with your eyes if you have the time or patience."

Phen continued to stare vacantly at the jumble sale in front of him.

"By way of example, right now your face is saying you

don't know what I'm talking about, even if your mouth isn't."

Phen's mouth opened, said nothing, then closed. This he repeated twice.

"You also keep staring at my hat. It's brand new and you think I must've stolen it because I can't afford it. Well, a man came out of Tattersalls, the horse-betting place, and insisted on sharing some of his winnings. People can be kind."

Phen was saved by a stifled moan. The woman placed her elbows on her knees and cupped her face in both hands.

"She needs to meet her emotions … been delaying for a while."

"You live here? In the park?"

"Most days, when the weather is good."

"For how long?"

"A while."

"And at night, when they close the gate?"

"Sometimes I stay. Sometimes I go."

"Where do you go?"

"I have a number of addresses."

"Flats are becoming apartments now." Phen didn't know why he said that and immediately felt the need to continue and explain. "Words change all the time. I battle with them."

"Wouldn't have guessed."

"I s-s-s-stutter too." The instant admission took him by surprise. Why would he suddenly put a spotlight on his speech? And why choose to do this with someone he'd never met before? His mother and grandmother kept telling him not to talk to strangers.

"Really? When?"

"All the time."

"All the time? But hardly when you talk to me."

"I …"

"It's probably because you don't have to worry about the likes of me. Nothing to get nervous about. No need to impress."

"I … I … I …"

"Is that stuttering or just repeating yourself?"

"S-s-s-s-ses are the real problem. My father s-s-says it's a letter curved like barbed wire to catch my tongue." Phen wondered at his words; this was becoming a confession.

They both turned as the girl's body began to convulse and shudder. She kept her face tightly held behind her hands. This made the shaking of her shoulders seem more violent, more out of control. Her head was still but the rest of her body became unmanageable. Phen felt in the pocket of his shorts and pulled out his handkerchief, still neatly folded.

"My mother says you're not a true gentleman if you don't always carry a clean hanky." He couldn't stop himself from talking to this man, even if it was drivel.

The man nodded as Phen slowly walked up to the girl. The sound of her sobs was stifled by her palms, but the tears were leaking through her fingers. He stood there patiently with his arm outstretched, not sure how to get his offering noticed. He cleared his throat a few times to no avail. In desperation he touched her on the shoulder. This was a mistake. Her eyes opened in joy, narrowed in confusion and closed in the deepest despair. Clearly she had thought he was her errant boyfriend. At first she didn't even see the handkerchief. It was only when she opened her eyes a second time that she accepted the white cloth with the briefest of smiles. As she dabbed her eyes his kindness suddenly made her cry even more. Her face disappeared behind his hanky.

Phen stood for a while knotted with guilt and totally bewildered. Kindness had somehow added to sorrow. He was now complicit in her deeper suffering. How could good intentions turn bad so quickly? He apologised then turned and slowly walked away.

Intuitively, Phen headed straight for the willow. A temporary board explained the tree had recently been planted as part of the "Hillbrow Beautification" project. Its thin trunk sprayed even skinnier branches like a green fountain. Although it was barely two metres high, its flopping limbs provided a perfect curtain. Phen was about to slide through it and escape behind its narrow leaves when he saw the hat.

"Don't let me stop you from vanishing into your cave of leaves."

"How did you get here first?" Phen paused, suddenly feeling like a coward for wanting to disappear.

"I saw your encounter was going to take a little time. That's a lot of emotion to fit into one hanky." He turned his hand into a hanky and the hanky into a parachute which he let drift through the air before landing it on the grass. "When they've finished building the waterfall I think this will be the prime spot in the park. Your special tree. Shady. Water gushing. Beautiful view of Jo'burg. Voila! I notice you often use it as a hidey hole. Good choice. Once you're in, no one can see you."

"I thought Pal was the only other one who knew."

"How do you think the weeping woman is doing?"

Phen felt uncomfortable. Not only had his secret hideaway been discovered, he also didn't like the way the man casually lay stretched out on his back talking to the clouds, taking over his space. He wasn't sure if he should sit next to him or remain standing. It felt as if sinking down to his height was giving in. Instead, he leaned against the pole of the heavy metal sign that said "Whites Only. Slegs Blankes", and, mimicking the man, addressed his answer to the gathering cumulus.

"I made it worse."

"How so?"

"She's crying more."

"So you think the volume of tears equals the degree of sadness?"

"Yes."

"What about tears of joy?"

"What?"

"The more you cry them, the happier you are?"

"Don't know."

"Do you think you can have both of them at the same time?"

"Don't know."

"Maybe some are tears of sadness for Thanos – that's his name, the almost-husband. And some are tears of gratitude for a boy who offered his handkerchief?"

Pal found Phen and brought some much-needed relief. He threw the tennis ball a few times before the spaniel drifted off to a pair of wiry Airedale terriers. The man had gone silent, yet was still staring at the sky. He wondered if he was in some kind of trance. For all his talk before, it intrigued Phen that the long silences between their conversations didn't worry him. This was confirmed by him pushing his hat over his eyes and seemingly going to sleep. A cue to leave, or was he meant to stay?

"Please," the man said without opening his eyes, "do whatever you feel."

Phen looked at him stretched out with his sockless feet casually crossed and his tennis shoes vertical. He spotted a thin pinstripe in the man's trousers that had previously gone unnoticed. He also now saw the shoes were at least two sizes too big and their laces were made from industrial-strength twine. The last time he'd seen such thick string, it had been wrapped around the cardboard box that held the Philips tape recorder. He leaned forward for a closer inspection and decided it was exactly the same.

"Pulled them out of a dustbin behind Duchess Court."

"That's where I live."

"There's a coincidence."

Phen turned to go, feeling perhaps he had been dismissed.

"And before you ask, the shirt was also a gift. From a gentleman with a beaded bandana and a rather large rolled item in his mouth. I told you people can be kind."

Phen stopped and leaned against the sign again.

"He said it was the Age of Aquarius and that all we need is love. And at that exact moment that Beatles song began to play on his transistor radio. You know, 'All You Need Is Love'?"

Perhaps Phen frowned for a moment, or didn't reply quite quick enough. Either way, by way of clarification, the man began to sing, loudly. Phen was so embarrassed he had no idea what to do. Here was living proof that there was nothing you can sing that can't be sung. The man stayed horizontal and had a lousy voice, yet was happy to warble at full volume to the sky. What was even worse, he chose to do the instrumental parts too. He tromboned to the horizon and trumpeted to the cosmos. People all around the park were turning to see where the noise was coming from. In desperation Phen slowly lowered himself until he was crouching next to the pole. To further distance himself from the noise he stared at the huge Catholic church down below. It was built not far from the Casablanca Roadhouse, where waitresses in short white skirts raced and did tight pirouettes as they brought toasted sandwiches and pink milkshakes to car windows on their roller skates.

Thoughtfully, Pal trotted back to see who was in so much pain. He licked the man's face and knocked his hat off. The rough tongue served as an off button and silence resumed.

"Because of the coincidence, Felix – that was his name – took off his shirt and handed it to me. He said it was a sign. The stars had aligned with the radio waves to send a message. He had to share a little love. So he gave me his shirt. He said he had more clothes than me and liked my vibrations. He dug me."

"Are you a hobo?"

"I certainly could be."

"Don't you sometimes start …" Phen pinched his nose.

"Well, don't tell anyone, but the kiddies' pool early in the morning is pretty handy. Of course, it helps if there's water in it. Then there are a couple of taps. I keep some soap and a bucket in my sack."

"Maybe when the waterfall is working?"

"Good point … How am I doing now?"

"Not great."

"I do have some aftershave I found outside Gainsborough Mansions. Lots of bachelors there."

"It's not that bad."

"Good … Do you have a name?"

"Yes."

"Is it a secret?"

"No."

"May I know it?"

"Phen. Phen Baxter. My proper name is S-S-Stephen but everyone calls me Phen. I can say the F sound through my nose better than I can say s in my mouth.

The man stood up as if he was about to go and brushed the grass off the seat of his pants. Suddenly Phen didn't want him to leave. He seemed taller and broader across the shoulders now that he was facing him straight-on. The man pointed just in time for him to see the beehived woman nearly fall into a bed of orange flowering aloes. Her stilettos were drilling into the lawn with every step she took, leaving deep tunnels in her wake. Every yard gained was a stop-start extraction of the heel she left behind.

"Better go and help her before she breaks an ankle. She just wants to give you your hanky back."

Phen ran to her and accepted the damp cloth. It was presented with two hands like some holy shroud.

"You are a very kind young man," she said, smiling. "I'm sorry it's all covered in mascara. I hope your mother will understand."

Phen nodded and smiled back. He turned immediately, yet knew in advance the man would no longer be there.

7

Stoicism

/sto'i-sizm/ noun

Sarah looked at him and loved him, loved the lines of his face, the darkish blue of his eyes, the straight brows. She saw laughter and need in those eyes, felt strength from his hands flowing into her, saw the background of crimson curtaining at the window.

Her breath caught and she said foolishly, "I'll be able to finish Ruth's book with her. She'll be delighted."

"It'll have to wait till we have a honeymoon. I'm not one of those chaps who can wait around for heaven. I want mine red hot!"

"Oh, darling," she said with that delicious feeling of help-lessness, "you say the craziest things. Who ever heard of a red hot heaven? I love you!"

And that, naturally, was more than enough encourage-ment for Brent. He proceeded to convince her, with a passion both savage and tender, that she was the most adored creature in the universe.

And just for a second, she thought thankfully that of all the women in the world, only she could be Sarah, wife of Brent.

Phen watched the final inch of tape on the right slither off and wrap itself around the bulging reel on the left. His humiliation was complete. Tape Aids for the Blind had mistakenly sent his father *Denise* Baxter's literary choice. In this case a Mills & Boon book titled *The Tulip Tree* by

Kathryn Blair. And still he'd preferred to listen to it rather than have his son read to him. It didn't matter that his father said he'd listened to it for a laugh. That it was full of square jaws and trembling lips and thrusts that went upwardly and inwardly while hearts soared outwardly.

There was little solace, too, in the fact that his father slept most of the time. So he really didn't know about the tulip tree in Dr Ruth Master's garden that refused to flower. And how Sarah Knight wondered if it was a symbol of her love for Brent Milward. When Phen heard they'd delivered the wrong tape, he'd gone and stood at the bottom of the bed. He'd even held *Grapes of Wrath* in his hands because it was the book his father most often chose. "Always lyrical," he'd say. "Indignant yet lyrical." Instead he'd been asked to help thread the tape.

The machine's control of the room was now absolute. It sat deep and centred in the leather chair that used to be Phen's. A white hand towel even caressed and supported its far-right-hand corner, to keep it perfectly level. Its two smug revolving eyes saw everything and demanded respect. "Easy," his father had said when he'd tried to force the tape through the narrow slot. "It's not a toy, boy." If he couldn't damage the recorder at least he could crinkle the tape occasionally. He enjoyed hearing words suddenly stretch or fold in on themselves. If the crease made with his nail was really deep, the word disappeared entirely. He wanted his father to know that the STÉRÉO CONTINENTAL "401" wasn't perfect either, but he never seemed to notice.

Phen watched the full reel continue to spin while the empty one slowed to a halt. He knew the machine was still telling him everything was changing. He sensed his life shifting; he was losing his mooring. The ropes and chains that held him secure were being thrown overboard. Although he desperately wanted to steady himself, he wasn't sure what to hold on to. Nothing seemed firm. His father lay upright with the top pillow hugging his head like a helmet. The oxygen mask completed the look of an astronaut. Maybe a part of his father was already in outer space?

His mother was different now, too. She shrugged her shoulders even when no one asked her anything. When he did ask her a question, all she'd do was run her hands through his hair. He asked her why his father chose to listen to a love story instead of him reading *Grapes of Wrath* or even *Animal Farm*. Phen explained how his father loved his Old Major voice and how in the past they'd even sung "Beasts of England" together. She just smiled and walked away. He followed her and, as she turned the kettle on, he imagined himself climbing onto the vinyl seat of the kitchen chair and singing loudly.

> *Bright will shine the fields of England,*
> *Purer shall its waters be,*
> *Sweeter yet shall blow its breezes*
> *On the day that sets us free.*
> *For that day we all must labour,*
> *Though we die before it break;*
> *Cows and horses, geese and turkeys,*
> *All must toil for freedom's sake.*
> *Beasts of England, beasts of Ireland,*
> *Beasts of every land and clime,*
> *Hearken well, and spread my tidings*
> *Of the Golden future time.*

"Have your tea," his mother said, "or it'll get cold."

Uncle Edward wasn't the same either. He came more

often yet for shorter periods. As if he was seeing a patient rather than a friend. Somehow, in his mind, there were now visiting hours he had to adhere to. "Don't want to wear the fellow out!" He always arrived too cheerful and hated himself for not leaving in the same vein. He felt he was letting the team down and apologised to Phen's mother continually. "I'm absolutely hopeless at this sort of thing."

"What sort of thing?" Phen had asked and once again there had been no answer.

Ed also knew the arrival of his tape recorder had altered everything. The transference of so much power to the box had repositioned him too. More and more he was forced to stay silent as they both listened to the third voice. The story would fill the room as paragraph after paragraph took them further and further away to another place. Ed would sit straight-backed with a pained look of concentration on his face. Occasionally he'd lean forward as if trying to hear some announcement that might clarify their destination.

"Become the story," his father had said.

"Righto," said Uncle Ed.

Mairead pretended she was exactly the same. And the more she did so, the more it became obvious even she was affected by the whirling that was picking up speed all around her. She refused to spin but could not stop herself from occasionally being turned. She carried stoicism like a club. All the better to beat those who might be feeling sorry for themselves.

"Who exactly is the sick one here?" she asked Phen. "I'm beginning to think you're confusing yourself with your father."

Phen had been caught angrily ripping the brown paper

off the exercise book he'd been trying to cover, and hurling the scrunched-up mess at the wall. The crumpled ball had ricocheted onto Pal's head and into the passageway. Mairead had bent down slowly to pick it up, examining it on the floor and then in her hand. She held the crushed paper to the light like a prospector confirming his find.

"You've wasted a perfectly good sheet of paper, the book remains uncovered and you have a cocker spaniel slinking under the bed thinking it's his fault."

"Mom normally does this."

"I'm aware of that. However, in the greater scheme of things, this is a problem unlikely to cause the universe to implode. There are more pressing issues right now. Ones that require you strap on a man's pair of shoulders. In addition, the curve of the blade on a pair of scissors used to cut your nails is not appropriate for the cutting of a straight line across a sheet of paper. If you fetch the correct tools from my sewing bag, I am prepared to help."

It wasn't just the crooked cutting and the mass of twisted sticky tape that made him angry. It was the thought of school beginning again. The term break was over. One weekend stood between him and his ridiculously wide grey shorts. "It's not the shorts, it's his legs," he'd overheard his mother reply defensively to his gran. "They're so skinny, I have to put elastic garters in his socks to keep them up. I've known thicker toothpicks." Kobus Visser, who had legs like swollen pork sausages, pretended he was being original by calling them Wednesday Legs. Wens day going to break. The joke had stuck.

In an attempt to dampen his anxiety, Phen decided to visit Zelda. Number forty-three was the only door in Duchess Court he had the courage to knock on. He tapped gently then respectfully stepped away. It didn't feel right to stand all over a mat that had "Welcome" written on it. Zelda's blurred head appeared through the frosted glass. She comically squashed her face against it then held up a length of ribbon by way of explanation. He watched her head fly backwards and forwards a number of times as she tried to get her hair to fan out equally. At last the knot was done and the door opened with a grand sweep.

"Your majesty, how kind of you to grace me with your presence." She bowed low and bade him enter. "You timing is excellent, I have just finished."

"What?"

"Finishing."

She checked her vast ponytail, opened a packet of Peter Stuyvesant, and slowly drew a cigarette out. "My passport to international smoking pleasure. Do you have a light?"

"No."

"Good. Keep it that way. If you ever start, I shall be forced to tell your mom or even worse, your gran. And she'll make you eat haggis and black pudding."

"Term begins on Monday."

"You don't sound happy."

Phen shrugged.

"How's Jimmy the Greek?" The question was asked behind a plume of smoke she tried to drive away with an impatient hand.

"Okay. Doesn't play with me much any more. S-S-Sometimes I'm reserve goalie."

"New term, new beginning. Maybe you'll find a new friend. Maybe someone who's just moved into the area? You know what Hillbrow's like. A gigantic train station. I've just met a man from Yugoslavia. He said his president was called Tito. Great name for a dog, don't you think?

'Come here, Tito! Sit, Tito!' Evidently he's one tough guy, so I better watch myself."

"We're doing a play this t-t-term. Everyone has to be in it. Everyone has to go to auditions."

"I see." Zelda plucked a flake of tobacco from the tip of her lip and placed it in the ashtray. The thin crimson gown, tied tightly at her waist, was full of embroidered tumbling hearts that fell all the way down from her shoulders. Phen guessed there was nothing on underneath. Her body seemed more liquid than usual. It flowed and bobbled, sometimes in two directions at the same time.

"My gran s-s-says I have to put on a man's pair of s-s-shoulders."

"She does, does she? Well, I think the pair you've got are pretty broad already."

"Putting on a man's pair of s-s-shoulders really means my father's very ill, doesn't it?"

Zelda nodded and let the faintest "yes" escape from her lips.

"I wish people would just say what they mean."

"Maybe they're trying to protect you."

Zelda waved away another cloud of smoke and offered Phen a chair. He chose the corduroy couch. Usually he would go for the orange beanbag. This time, however, it had a used look about it. The leatherette was spreadeagled across the floor and looked exhausted. Its hollows seemed violent and deep. Besides, he was too shy to beat it like a punchbag to get it back in shape. Zelda sat on a bar stool, although there was no bar, and began to brush her ponytail.

"Remember Ziggy?"

"The s-s-saxophonist from s-s-sixty-one?"

"Yes. He had wonderful hair." Zelda examined her split ends. "Wish we could've swapped. What a ponytail! When he let it loose, it almost reached his waist. He was very good, not just with that saxophone."

"I heard he's playing for a top band in America now. Even has his own record coming out."

"I hope so."

The doorbell rang. Zelda frowned and pulled her gown around her neck.

"Busy day."

Phen turned to watch as she padded to the door in her bare feet. This time it only opened an inch or two. There was a pause followed by a whisper, followed by another pause. The sweet, salty smell of aftershave spoke loudly, though. It was Mr Trentbridge.

"Hey, Boyo!" he called from the door. "Just borrowing a cup of baking powder for the missus's dessert!"

Zelda came straight back to him and smiled. She'd obviously run out of baking powder.

He had wanted to tell her about the dancing man he'd met in the park and the lady who'd been crying next to the empty swimming pool. How the man could spin his hat like a top without even looking at it and sing at the top of his voice while lying down. How his face was square and round at the same time. And how his hair exploded as if someone had put a hand grenade in there and pulled the pin. How you shouldn't issue ultimatums if the potential ownership of a bakery on an island off Crete is involved. And how stilettos leave holes even deeper than hadeda beaks. But now, something had changed in the room. Although Zelda continued to blow smoke, she no longer tried to wave it away.

Once again, Phen felt he was the cause of a detour. Life was going on around him. Another story was sidestepping him. Words were winking. He felt angry and left out. Like the empty reel on the tape recorder, he was turning mindlessly with nothing to say. He stood up and, copying the man from the park, dusted the back of his pants.

"Better go."

"So soon?"

Phen shrugged.

"Well, come back, maybe Sunday. I'm planning a marathon baking session. All-you-can-eat pancakes and chocolate brownies to go. Add a little luxury to your school lunchbox."

He didn't want to admit it, yet he knew it was true. Every walk with Pal was now a hunt to see if he could find the man with the felt fedora. He thought he'd seen him high up on the construction site next to Duchess Court. He'd pulled Pal to the other side of the road for a better look, but the hollow concrete block he'd been standing in was suddenly empty. Phen also thought he'd spotted him at the bottom of the almost completed waterfall. He'd run down the rough slope of Nugget Hill, filling his socks with blackjacks, almost falling twice, and found nothing. Three cardboard boxes had been joined together to make a tunnel bed. When he peered inside, all he could find was an old blue blanket, half a candle stuck to a tin plate and a key ring in the shape of a crescent moon with no keys attached to it.

He wondered if his laces from the tape-recorder box still held and why, if the man had said he lived in the park, he couldn't find him there. He ended each search by burrowing under the flopping willow tree. He'd wait for his eyes to adjust to the dark and hope he'd find another silhouette calmly leaning against the trunk. On the fourth day of his search, he assumed the role of Sergeant Bill Dawson, the mainstay of Lieutenant Pitt's platoon, formed from the rifle regiments of the Oxfordshire and Bucking-hamshire Light Infantry. It was Sunday and Phen was scared he'd not find him before the start of school. He knew Sergeant Bill Dawson died on page nineteen of *Pegasus Bridge*, the Battle Picture comic he was reading. Still there was no better man for the job. He'd rallied his men in Calais during the dark days of 1940. Thanks to him, a number of survivors had been evacuated across the channel to fight another day. A tougher and more resource-ful Tommy you would not find.

"We're not leaving," he said to Pal, "until we get our man."

They combed every inch of Nugget Hill Park from west to east. The long, narrow stretch of green was crisscrossed again and again. A man asleep on his stomach, with the *Sunday Times* protecting the back of his sunburned neck, initially had them excited. On closer inspection, they found the shoes were too new and the hat was missing. They crawled under a purple flowering bush, *Brunfelsia pauciflora* 'Floribunda', according to the metal plaque embedded at its base. It was time to calmly take stock. Phen turned his hands into binoculars and slowly scanned from left to right.

"Reconnaissance," he explained to Pal. "When they can't see you, they sometimes show themselves."

He saw an exhausted-looking man lean against the white painted wall. He became his own dark shadow as he battled to gain his breath. Phen guessed he'd been trying to sell mielies all day. It seemed impossible that such a huge sack could be balanced on a single bicycle saddle. He wiped the silver dots of sweat from his forehead and slid down onto his haunches. His long pants were held high around his waist by an old piece of rope knotted in the front. This ensured his bare feet had uncluttered access to the pedals. Phen watched the park attendant in his dark, gold-buttoned uniform tell him to move on, waving his baton like a Keystone Cop. "M-i-e-l-i-e-s!" the man shouted as he battled to push his bike uphill, "M-i-e-l-i-e-s!" And once more Phen understood "mielies" was the word but, by the way he screamed, it was not the meaning.

He refocused his binoculars to the left. A toddler in a sailor suit tried to kick an orange plastic soccer ball. His right foot missed entirely, forcing him onto his padded rear. A cloth nappy is a thing of substance, yet it cannot soothe a howl of indignation. The earnest mother arrived in her kaftan and sandals, determined to right all wrongs. She placed a hand on her hip, question-marking her body and demanding an answer from her child. Sailor Boy immediately pointed an accusing finger at the ball. Her eyes grew wide as she bent down and picked it up. "Naughty ball! Naughty! Smack! Smack!"

Phen trained his glasses still further left. The green door of the tool shed came into focus. "We haven't looked there." Pal was losing interest; they'd have to move soon. The thatch hut, Phen knew, was home to lawnmowers, gardening tools and compost bags. "Stay low. Move slowly." He took the leash off the collar and gently broke through the *Brunfelsia* bush. You had to admire an opponent so devious and cunning. Phen held a stick he'd found like a machine gun. "Spread out." Pal over-obeyed and ran to a bunch of children with ice creams. With two yards to go, Phen shoulder-charged the wooden door.

It swung open violently, smacking a terracotta pot and dislodging a rake that fell sideways, blocking his entrance. A startled cockroach left via the back window. Phen wasn't sure what to do next. He peered into the dark room and kept his stick in the ready position against his shoulder.

There was a gas burner, pot, mug and some Boxer pipe tobacco. He decided to duck under the rake and investigate further. He found a footprint in the spilled fertiliser; even in the half-light, though, he could see it was from a workman's boot. The only other item of interest was a brown tortoiseshell comb. It leaned against the wall, delicately balancing upside down on the metal handle of a shovel.

"Too late." Sergeant Dawson lowered his gun dejectedly.

"Not necessarily," came a voice from the sunlight.

Phen was still trapped inside by the rake. He squinted directly into the sun.

"I'm glad you didn't touch any of the park attendant's things. He's a very strict and ordered man. Especially when it comes to his old copies of *Scope* magazine, which you didn't find because they're wedged behind the chicken wire in the ceiling. He's told me many times that this is his office and he doesn't like trespassers."

Phen slipped under the rake and closed the door behind him. Pal returned with flakes of ice-cream cone around his mouth. Now that Phen had found the man he was looking for, he had no idea what to say to him. The three of them walked, for no reason, to the bench next to the kiddies' pool. Phen rather exaggeratedly turned his machine gun into a walking stick. He'd seen how old people strolled. He sauntered to the bench, giving each step a poke in the ground and a twirl of his wrist. They sat down with a large space between them confirming they were essentially strangers. Phen resisted the temptation to start talking immediately. He waited for what he thought was a mature, grown-up length of time before opening his mouth.

"I go back to school tomorrow."

"I know. All the dustbins are full of empty school-shoe boxes."

"How're your laces?"

"Fine."

They looked down at each other's shoes.

"I didn't get a new pair this term."

"Me neither."

"New shirt, though. Very stripy."

"Yes. The label says 'Perma-Prest shaped for the fashion crowd'. I found it flapping like a flag on a car aerial. Last night's wind must have dislodged it from some washing line … Are you looking forward to school?"

"I have to audition. For the s-s-school play."

"Don't worry about it."

"It's tomorrow. First day back."

"Don't worry about it. You'll be fine."

"How do you know?"

"How do you know you won't be?"

"Last time all I had to say was 'S-s-stand and deliver!' I was a s-s-sentry. I took s-so long, the king and his cavalry just rode over me and into the castle."

"That was then, this is now."

"S-so?"

"So last time we were here the pool was empty and now it's full."

"So?"

"Things change."

Phen looked at the man looking at him. His fedora was at an angle, his left eyebrow raised as if that was the cause of the tipped hat. Who was this man? He'd taken the cup-shaped cap off an acorn and stuck it in the middle of his placemat. It looked as if the square of hair under his chin was held in place by it. A bolt perfectly placed in the centre.

"One ruined hanky doesn't mean a life of misery. The woman you helped might be wiser and stronger now. You might have done your bit to prepare her for an even better life. One bad term of stand and deliver doesn't mean the next will be the same."

Phen felt slightly annoyed. He didn't like the way the man turned to face him, twirled his thumbs and waited for a reply. His walking stick became a rifle again. He shot an Alsatian and the hysterical dachshund barking at it. He then took aim at the mother in the kaftan who was now smacking the swing for hitting her screaming child on the head. Sergeant Dawson had found his man, yet clearly he wasn't like those Jerry prisoners who always refused to talk.

"Nobody knows if things aren't going to get worse to-morrow."

The man stopped twirling and prodded at the exploding hair behind his head. It could not be contained by his hat and sought freedom in every direction. From this tangled mess, he produced a tube of Life Savers. Phen declined his kind offer as the green sweet disappeared into the mouth opposite him.

"And nobody knows if things aren't going to get better." He sucked loudly and put his tongue through the hole in the middle of the sweet.

"My gran says it's all fun and games until you lose an eye."

The man pushed his hat further back and decided to suntan. Phen studied the narrow, deep lines that erupted from the edges of his closed eyes. Blown sideways, they fanned out towards his ears, but never quite made it. And in those distant whorls, more tufts of hair grew wild and rampant.

"And how many one-eyed people do you know?"

"None. If you exclude pirates."

"Tomorrow, tomorrow, tomorrow," he said, apparently tired just at the thought of it. "Everybody worries about tomorrow."

"Shouldn't we worry about the future?"

The man sat upright again. He plucked the acorn cap from his chin, licked it and stuck it in the middle of his forehead. He stared at Phen through his new, middle eye.

"Ooooommmmm," he chanted three times. "Tomorrow is just today in one day's time."

8

Serendipitous

/ser-en-dip'i-tes/ adjective

Pal was delighted his master had decided not to go straight home after the park. Instead, although it was turning to dusk, they had veered right down O'Reilly Road and headed in the general direction of Yeoville. The further they moved away from Hillbrow, the more bunches of houses began to reappear. They huddled next to each other in a sincere attempt at respectability. Tiny mowed lawns reached freshly painted front gates, some left half-open in a cautious welcome. This was the road less travelled, full of new sights and smells. Pal was allowed to take the lead. His master seemed distracted as he let himself be pulled in any direction. Even the quick devouring of half a chicken-mayonnaise sandwich found in the gutter went unnoticed.

By the time Phen reached Harrow Road his mind was no clearer. He decided to cross over and give it a few more blocks. He was feeling confused about Sergeant Dawson's discovery. He wasn't even sure why he'd gone looking for the man in the first place. He'd stalked and found his prey, yet somehow felt he was the one who'd been caught. The more they talked, the more he became entangled. Often he'd seemed to give the answer just before Phen would ask the question. But that answer just led him to thinking about another question. He had looked asleep half the time although his head would slowly turn half an inch left and right as if his fedora housed some secret radar.

He'd said our job wasn't to fight time, just to piggyback on it. He'd then done that hat-twirl thing and stated, with both eyes open for a change, that so many claimed they suffered from not-enoughness, when the real problem was too-muchness. Phen had tried to look intelligent because the man spoke as if he'd known this all along. Phen nodded perpetually, meanwhile his brain was tying itself in a bigger and bigger knot. It wasn't helped by the irregular way the man spoke.

Phen began to imagine him powered by the ancient circuit board behind the only metal door in Duchess Court. The stencilled DANGER sign and the broken lock beneath it offered the perfect ingredients for an enquiring mind. It was full of switches, exposed copper wire and spiders' webs spun from one fading label to the other. s1 Ground Flr and s2 First Flr were beautifully written in dark-blue fountain-pen ink. An electrician full of serifs and exaggerated curls had, long ago, written a love letter to the current he was installing. Faded white rectangular pieces of paper lined up square and proud were neatly trapped on all four corners by triangular pouches. He'd seen these same pouches before in his parents' photo album. As he shined a torch over the rubber insulators, silver lines of gossamer spun out, dressing everything in fine silk. More an alchemist's concoction than hard science.

That something so beautiful and untidy could power all of Duchess Court mesmerised Phen. When the lift stopped or the lights went out, he imagined a rain spider trying to tiptoe off a live wire. He saw the hairs on its legs go static and blue as the charge lit it up like a Christmas decoration. Phen felt that some similar magical, yet interrupted, source powered the man who enlightened and confused him at the same time. His silences seemed to surge suddenly into voice, only to return to silence again. Sleep, or half-sleep, descended at the same speed as it lifted. A tilt up or drop of the chin and the switch was flicked.

Although the sentences had been irregular and his startling blue eyes anything from tightly shut to wide in wonder, he had clearly said that good could be as unexpected as bad. That we should be careful not to play the victim in advance and by doing so attract the wrong luck. "Tonight," he'd said, "could prove serendipitous." Phen didn't know what that meant and had waited for another clue. None had been forthcoming. He'd tried to sniff surreptitiously to see if he could catch a whiff of alcohol on the man's breath and felt ashamed to come away with a strong smell of Pepsodent toothpaste mingled with the sweetness of apple-flavoured Life Saver.

"You'll wonder where the yellow went …" was all the man said, allowing Phen to finish the radio jingle in his head.

He'd also told Phen to stop worrying about his role in the school play. By then, they had moved to the willow tree. They sat next to it and stared at the horizon for a long time. Instead of singing, this time he'd recited some poetry: "Oh Willow gray, I may not stay / Till Spring renew thy leaf; / But I will hide myself away, / And nurse a lonely grief." Again Phen had looked at him waiting for an explanation and again none was forthcoming. Instead he had lowered himself slowly onto his back, as if testing the elasticity of his spine, and stared at the sky. Phen had waited a few moments and then done likewise.

"You'll be fine," he'd said into the clouds. "Look at this tree. It grows up to grow down. No one understands gravity better."

You would've thought the snoring of the man next to

him would ensure the exact opposite, yet Phen had also drifted off. By the time Pal woke him, the sun was much higher. The willow had created a triangle of shade that saved his face, but not his knees. Bony hills of angry red stared back at him. Miraculously, the man was still there, body straight, arms at his sides, sleeping at attention. His forest of chest hairs, some turned gold by the sun, rose and fell in deep and regular intervals. A scar the shape of a horseshoe u-turned just beneath his chin.

"Bottle," he'd said without opening his eyes or breaking his breathing.

"Better go," Phen had said, getting up and clipping Pal's lead on.

Initially the man had stayed horizontal and just nodded.

"Do you have a name?" Phen had asked. "I gave you mine."

The question forced the man onto his elbow and then his feet. He patted himself down again. Dry grass shot off his pants and showered down on an unimpressed Pal. His master picked the dry flakes off his ears.

"Hmmm. Do you think names are important?"

"Well, everyone needs one."

"If I said I was Algernon or Ebenezer, would you look at me differently to a Peter or John?"

Phen shrugged.

"What about Xavier? I've always wanted to be a Xavier."

The man began to stretch in a number of positions as if preparing for a major sporting activity. He started by elongating various parts of his body in slow motion. He swivelled his neck while rotating his hips to the point of a pirouette. Then he raised both hands before bringing them down sideways and holding them parallel to the ground. He hung there for some time, suspended east to west, then sank down, folded his arms and, Cossack-like, tried to shoot each leg out alternately. He wasn't very good. Twice he nearly toppled over as his knee joints battled to carry his weight. His body appeared to be hinged differently. If the exercise was designed to remind his frame how it was supposed to work, it wasn't particularly successful. He became stuck on his haunches. Unable to move, he eventually toppled onto his back, lay there for a while and eventually stood up.

"What if I said I was Lord Marmaduke the third? Heir to a massive fortune. Castles everywhere and my own private golf course?" His voice was believably posh as he gave a twitch of his superior nose. "Or Mad-eye Malone? Still on the run. Ha, ha, ha, haaa!" He laughed insanely. "Them coppers will never get me! They'll never find the money!" He pointed to his squint eye while his other hand shot randomly through his forefinger. "What about, say, Thomas, loving husband and father of two? Family tragically killed in a car accident – and he's never been the same since. I like Jack: simple, strong name. Ex-army, special forces. Seen a lot, maybe too much. In time, that has to affect you."

Phen held Pal close as he tried to construct one man from the many that stood in front of him.

"So which one is it?"

"Heb."

"Herb?"

"No, Heb. If you want to call me something, let's make it Heb."

"Okay."

"Heb Thirteen Two."

Heb Thirteen Two took his fedora off and cleaned the brim between his thumb and forefinger. He then replaced the hat on his vast expanse of hair with the firm clamp of a Lego piece finding its exact position.

"You'll work it out. You have a bright, dancing mind."

Heb Thirteen Two had cha-cha-cha-ed a few steps forwards, then had done a few backwards.

"Gotta go."

The fedora had begun to rise and fall as he'd changed to the twist, his unlubricated hips corkscrewing painfully.

By the time Phen reached home he'd travelled in a large square up Harrow, left into Abel, left into Quartz and back into O'Reilly Road. Aside from the owner of a pink-eyed pit bull on a studded lead, he'd spoken to no one. If he did have a dancing mind, it was now sitting on the pavement outside his flat, exhausted. The more he tried to clear his head, the more it blocked up. In the end he had let Pal zigzag him from one island of grass to the other. Even the rich smell of roasted coffee beans from the Gobble & Go hadn't slowed him down. Normally he'd pause and allow the colossal triangles of chocolate cake to tempt him from the glass shelf that lined the window.

Finally he forced himself to stand up and imitated Heb Thirteen Two with a few exercises of his own. As he turned, he saw a watchful Mrs Kaplan stick her arm out of her fifth-floor window and shoo him inside. Phen opened the door to number four as quietly as possible. Pal headed straight for his water bowl while Phen tried to slip unnoticed to his bedroom. Somewhere in the dog's rush, he stood on a loose plank of parquet. It plinked as it leaped out and plonked as it returned.

"A little late tonight, aren't we?"

Although Phen recognised the voice, he was confused by its location. The panels between the lounge and dining room had been drawn slightly, so he was forced to peer around the frosted glass. His father, sitting relaxed yet upright, with a *London Illustrated News* on his lap, gazed back at him. His hair was neatly combed, his face perfectly shaved and, most surprisingly, he was fully dressed. You could say he was almost overdressed. The very slightly checked sports jacket and white shirt spoke of a sophisticated cocktail party. The grey slacks with the perfect crease were underpinned by a pair of stylish black brogues. They hadn't been dusted; they'd been polished. The dotted design on the toecap circled itself twice before shooting up the side of the shoe. Phen had never seen his father shine from the feet up before.

"We thought we'd all listen to the radio tonight. As a family," his mother tried to explain. She spoke as if the lines had been rehearsed. "Family time," she reiterated, as though hoping the label would stick.

Phen was astonished. He'd been prepared for anything except an attempt at normality.

"Fine."

He looked for the oxygen cylinder. It wasn't behind the curtain or the last defiant leaf of what was their only indoor plant. His father inhaled and then exhaled in an exaggerated fashion to supply the answer. This was followed by a totally unnecessary thumbs up, until Phen realised it signified not just that he could breathe, but that he'd also been told to be on his best behaviour. He couldn't remember the last time all three of them had been in the lounge together. Perhaps his last birthday? His father's migraine had allowed for the singing of "Happy Birthday" but had stifled the three cheers that were meant to follow.

"Why don't you get a book and join us?" his mother continued. She was attempting to make it sound as if this happened every Sunday evening. "What with tomorrow being your first day back at school, I thought it might be nice to have a sort of family send-off?" As hard as she tried, his mother couldn't help ending the sentence with a question.

"I'll just wash my hands first."

He wasn't sure why he had to wash his hands, but the thought crossed his mind that in normal families this might be what sons did. He combed his hair too and tried to hide the dirt on his shirt by tucking it into his shorts. He was about to pick up a war comic. The cover showed an Australian with one side of his hat flipped up, defending himself against a banzai-crazed Japanese soldier. The soldier, much smaller than the Australian, was attacking him with a bayonet the length of a Samurai sword. The occasion, however, seemed to call for something less graphic. Instead, he traded it for C.S. Lewis's *The Last Battle*. It was a book he'd almost read a number of times. He found fantasy in novels unnecessary. Real life provided enough of it.

"We're listening to the A Programme." His mother continued to add clarity and sense to the evening. She was keen to provide the necessary decorum in the hope that her husband would follow suit. He gave a protocol-correct smile. "It's a lovely music hour. Why don't you sit here?" She pointed to a cushion already placed on the carpet. It lay between his parents, close to the radiogram. "Later on, I'll get you some Milo." He hadn't been offered Milo in two years. The last inch of it was now rock-solid in the bottom of the glass jar behind the packet of rusks. She would need a drill to dislodge it.

He sat down on the cushion as requested, although he'd have preferred a chair. Herr Grundig, on his bandy legs, seemed offended that his personal space had been interfered with. Phen opened his book and pretended to read. Everyone was pretending. No one could intelligently scan a page while Louis Jourdan was noticing that Gigi had breathlessly turned into a woman overnight. While he questioned whether he was a fool without a mind, or had merely been too blind to realise, Phen's father feigned interest in a picture of Queen Elizabeth walking her corgis. By the time Louis questioned whether he'd been standing too close or back too far and wondered when Gigi's sparkle had turned to fire and her warmth become desire, his mother gave up entirely. She closed her book and eyes at the same time, leaned back into her chair and tried to rest deeper in the song. Her husband watched her over the top of his glasses and allowed himself to smile. It was only after the compère had finished praising the lyrics of Alan Jay Lerner and music of Frederick Loewe that her eyes opened.

"We had a portable record player on the farm," she said to Phen. "On the last Saturday of every month we'd hang paraffin lamps on the tree next to the kitchen and have a dance evening. I know you've heard this a hundred times before. Your father was quite the Fred Astaire."

Phen felt guilty for nodding. He wanted her to go on but she'd run out of words anyway. Instead, she closed her eyes again. Now there was a bright golden haze on the meadow and the corn was as high as an elephant's eye. All the cattle were standing like statues and the ol' weeping willow was laughing. His father smacked his knee like a cowboy at a barn dance and tapped his brogues in time.

Oh, what a beautiful morning
Oh, what a beautiful day
I've got a beautiful feeling
Everything's going my way.

The next musical pieces were all instrumentals. This period was therefore interpreted as intermission. His mother disappeared into the kitchen and returned with a swing of her hips he'd usually only seen on the roadhouse waitresses. She'd baked scones, famously known for not being as good as Mairead's, and placed them on the coffee table with a sassy twirl. Although he was a little embarrassed by his mother's playfulness, it also made him deeply happy in a way he could not describe.

"And for you, my handsome one."

Although there was very little Milo in his milk, he thanked her all the same and placed it on the last chronicle of Narnia. When he lifted it again, a damp circle had formed around the horn of the unicorn on the cover. His mother was now pouring another cup of tea for the cowboy who eyed her somewhat mischievously.

"Why, thank you, ma'am."

"You can call me Lil. I've seen you round these parts before."

"They call me Dennis."

"That's a mighty fine name." She hovered above his knees, pretending to want to sit on his lap. Phen turned a bright red. Dennis chewed on the edge of the sugar spoon as if it were a stalk of corn.

"Well, little lady Lil, you make a fine brew."

"Thank you kindly, sir. You'll let me know how else I can meet your needs."

By the time his mother had returned to her seat, Phen's ears were burning and his face was on fire. He had no idea why his father's wink, although aimed at his mother, had hit him so squarely. He spilled some Milo down his chin, but wouldn't let his mother near him to dab it with her serviette. The very proper voice on the radio apologetically stated that they would now play a piece of jazz. By way of seeking forgiveness, the voice explained it was written in E-flat minor and made use of the unusual quintuple time. Dave Brubeck's "Take Five" did little to change the awkward atmosphere surrounding Phen. The repetitive two-chord piano and scaling saxophone seemed to be looking for trouble rather than trying to avoid it.

My Fair Lady came to the rescue, although it was only in the second half of "I Could Have Danced All Night" that things started to return to normal. As Eliza explained that she could have spread her wings and done a thousand things, his father went back to the Queen's corgis and his mother began wistfully to try to find the page she'd forgotten to bookmark. Phen no longer even pretended to read. He let the music go through him while watching the cloth in front of the speakers vibrate. He imagined his skin doing the same thing as the sound entered his chest then pounded out his back.

Somewhere in *West Side Story*, he drifted off. Neither awake nor asleep, he'd heard the compère's request that they hold on tight, this was a modern *American* musical. It was a rumbustious affair yet entirely infectious.

By the time the animated Puerto Rican woman had explained that skyscrapers bloom and Cadillacs zoom in America, the room had returned to its old self. His father tried to remain dapper although was powerless to stop his padded shoulders from rising to meet his ears as he slid down the chair. The foot still tapped but with less rigour. It couldn't keep up, anyway. His shoe twitched to its own beat while the hand on the knee, bruised a deep purple all the way to its fingers, was now motionless.

"Are they that bad?"

"What?"

"My scones. You haven't tried one. If they're tasteless, the jam will help."

"No. Of course! Just f-f-forgot." He reached for one and stuffed it in his mouth.

The voice on the radio said "cheerio" and "toodleloo". It hoped to have our company at the same time next week and wished us all we wished ourselves until we met again. "And, as always, we sign off with 'In the Blue of the Evening'. Take it away, Mr Sinatra."

Heb Thirteen Two had been correct. The night had surprised with unexpected happiness. Phen knew it couldn't last, though. Nor did he expect it to. Such lightness couldn't be maintained; the heaviness had to return. Maybe he too was beginning to understand gravity. His father started to cough while battling to get out of his chair. His mother grabbed one elbow and Phen took the other. Slowly they lifted him up. He stood still for a moment, trying to get his balance and breath back. They could not move. His father had no waist and, although the belt was tightened to the maximum, his pants had now fallen to his thighs. He was standing on his turn-ups.

9

Apoplexy

/apo-pleks-i/ noun

The first day back at school was not as terrible as he had initially imagined it might be. To start with, he met a stray dog as he strolled out of Duchess Court. It sat on the pavement with one ear up and one ear down, as if waiting for him. After Phen had patted him a few times, the mutt decided to walk with him. Almost instantly, the empty feeling in his stomach was filled. He liked the fact that it didn't just follow him the way most homeless dogs did. Instead it trotted next to him, peering up occasionally to ensure he was keeping pace. Phen smiled at the way the elongated body hovered over its short legs. The faster they walked, the more it bounced.

He remembered Mr Trentbridge talking about his SPCA special, before it had been run over, as a high-quality mixture, a pedigree mongrel. This seemed a good description for his hybrid. It was clearly made from spare parts yet displayed a street-smartness, an intelligence, Phen enjoyed talking to. The conversation became particularly animated at red traffic lights. The dog would patiently sit on his hind legs, cock his head and try hard to get both ears up. He was longer than he was high. This made him torpedo forward when the light changed to green.

They chatted and walked together pretty much the entire length of Kotze Street before turning right into Edith Cavell. Normally Phen would have worried about how the dog would get back home, or even if it had a home, but the thought never entered his mind. In a strange way it felt as if the dog was making sure *he* reached his destination. There was a purpose in the way his padded feet always stayed just in front of Phen, the way he'd look back after rounding each corner. By the time they arrived at the gates of Roseneath Primary, the over-sleek body and tail, broken and bent in the middle, was still with him. They sat down on the pavement and stared at each other.

"You can't come inside."

The dog appeared to understand. Nonchalantly it began to scratch under its jaw. Phen swung his haversack off his shoulder and reached for his lunchbox. He offered half a ham-and-tomato sandwich.

"I know the tomato makes the bread soggy. You should see what they're like by second break."

Two brown eyes, first incredulous and then deeply sympathetic, peered back at Phen.

"Suit yourself."

Phen repackaged the damp bread into the greaseproof paper and stood up. He patted the dog in farewell, yet found it difficult to move. His palms were beginning to sweat; he could feel the panic coursing through his body. His temporary source of refuge returned to scratching himself. The distant nightmare that had been school was now barely a yard away. The cold, deep fear he thought had disappeared had merely been biding its time. He wanted to run away. No one would notice him gone. Not on the first day. No one was waiting for him. No one wanted to know what he'd done on holiday. His parents didn't have a place at the Vaal like Philip Denton or a holiday home in Margate like Hettie Hattingh, even if it really belonged to her grandmother. The dog stopped scratching and started staring. Clearly he was waiting for Phen to turn and disappear through the gate.

"I have to go," he said as he put his cap back on in an act of mock courage.

The dog agreed by moving away, then stopping as Phen remained rooted to the spot.

"Hey, Spaz!" said Jimmy the Greek, rushing past. "You like late or you coming with me now?"

By the time they reached the assembly hall, Jimmy was still dragging him by the shoulder of his blazer. Phen twisted sideways and saw the dog imperiously moving in the direction of Hillbrow. The chin was held high and if a chest that low could be puffed out, then that's what it was. He wanted to see it safely across the road, but the headmaster called them to order and demanded the doors be closed. The prefects obliged, slamming them shut as loudly as possible to underline their authority. Clutching his Dracula cloak in both hands, the head of the school commanded that they all sit and be silent.

The lawnmower and the white paint used to mark the soccer field seemed to be Mr Kock's main concern. Both had been tampered with during the holiday break. The culprits *will* be found, he promised. He then asked the assembled masses how much a diesel lawnmower capable of mowing a sports field cost. No one had the courage to suggest a price. When he explained "over fifty rand" there was a chorus of amazement from the hall. Someone let out a long, low whistle, which was immediately choked by a firm sideways tug of the cloak. The headmaster theatrically held the black material wide to scoop up all the unnecessary noise.

The need for their rapt attention soon became clear. "Now, the matter of the theft and or use of the white paint."

On matters of extreme importance, Mr Kock tended to a more legalistic formation of words. He'd studied law for two years before changing to a teaching degree. Everyone knew of the sacrifices he'd made in order to contribute to the South African educational system. The older boys called him Counsellor Kock and drew pictures of him wearing a powdered wig. "The perpetrator or perpetrators of such action *will* be brought to book." The less the audience understood the words and sentences, the more they realised the severity of the crime. "Theft and the wilful, illegal use of school property is one thing. However, to combine this act with profanity is quite another issue. It goes beyond the pale."

"Say what, who?" said Jimmy the Greek, battling to follow. In frustration he slapped Phen on the back of the head.

"The lawnmower's been messed with and the paint."

"That," the headmaster continued, "your expletives, your obscenities, can no longer be found on the embankment next to the change room is not the point. The purpose, the intention of this act, is clear. That this ... this vulgarity de facto was meant to greet everyone on their first day back at school makes the crime all the more heinous. I thank our groundsman, Mr Swindon, for his timely action in this regard."

At the mention of Mr Swindon's name, the audience's attention was temporarily returned. He'd never been referred to before from the lofty heights of the hall's stage. He was a rural member of staff. Someone who lived in the country under his massive straw hat with its chewed brim. He worked on the outskirts of the fields and in the furthest corner under the bluegums where he made compost. He'd never actually been seen in the school corridors or classrooms. Irrespective of the weather, he wore a khaki shirt, pale blue shorts that shaded his knees, and brown boots that ended mid-shin.

He did, however, have one unique feature. He spoke with a posh accent. Vernon MacArthur knew for a fact that he'd been a soldier in the Korean War. There he hadn't just stopped communism; he'd halted the Chinese kind. This was even worse than the type of communism you got in Russia. The Chinese did terrible things with sharpened bamboo while the Russians just packed you in snow and left you to die. For all these heroics, Mr Swindon had apparently caught a little shrapnel in the head. "It's still there," Vernon MacArthur promised. "The brain is a complex thing," he explained. "You can't just go in there with a pair of pliers. You hear how he speaks," he concluded. "Could've been a millionaire, owned a bank."

What added still more to Mr Swindon's mystique was that he rarely spoke. And on the occasion he said something, he'd use long words wrapped in an accent normally reserved for English royalty. Three people heard what he said to Miss Ravensbrook, who took tennis on Tuesday afternoons. She'd arrived, and for some reason, the nets weren't up yet. When he ambled from the storeroom, carrying them on his shoulders, she began to express her displeasure. In the middle of her sentence, Mr Swindon had put his hand up and cautioned her against apoplexy. The word had stunned Miss Ravensbrook into silence. For a full term thereafter it had become a playground favourite. It was used with particular effect by bowlers during the more competitive cricket games when opposing batsmen were in violent disagreement about their LBW decisions. Even Jimmy the Greek began to use it, although he turned the Ps into Bs and found the word more useful as a threat. "Fetch my ball or I aboblexy you."

Besides Mr Swindon's occasional effect on the school's vocabulary, it was clear he enjoyed being invisible. His camouflage was made complete by the six black staff members he worked with. He was part of a group of shadows with no status that existed solely to carry, cut, paint and repair. The fact that he often spoke in Zulu or Xhosa wasn't seen to highlight his linguistic skill, but merely confirmed his choice to be unimportant and inconspicuous. That a man of this nature was now being mentioned in complimentary terms from behind the lectern was big news. All the pupils had assumed his muddy boots and sweat-stained armpits would ensure he was never referenced.

There was not much other riveting news at assembly so Mr Kock's legalese began to trail off. What did surprise the school was that Miss Tulip, who taught grade two, would not be returning. She had decided, for personal reasons, to move to Rustenburg. She would be replaced by Mrs Kramp, which was close enough to crap to make the hall titter. The headmaster once more spread his cloak wide to absorb the sound. A Tulip versus a Kramp is no contest, anyway. The fact that Miss Tulip had been young, blonde and beautiful made it even more of an unfair fight. Although Philip Denton claimed he'd had a long look up Miss Tulip's skirt at sports day and seen nothing special. Philip had been held back a year and, as the oldest in the class, was therefore qualified as an expert in these matters.

The news of Miss Tulip's departure was followed by the telling of "the dramatic story of Wolraad Woltemade". The story might have been dramatic but the telling of it was not. Mr Kock rattled it off as if reading out a new timetable. Maybe he'd told the tale too often.

"Wolraad was a Cape Dutch dairy farmer. He died rescuing imperilled soldiers on the ship *De Jonge Thomas*. The ship was in Table Bay. The year was 1775. It was mid-winter. Many were lost to the storm; however, a number of survivors clung to the hull. Wolraad Woltemade drove his horse 'Vonk', which in English means 'Spark', into the waves and asked two sailors at a time to jump into the sea and join him. He then ferried them to shore. He did this seven times, bringing back fourteen men."

Headmaster Kock paused briefly to straighten and stretch, as if the weight of those men had somehow also affected his back.

"Exhausted, he tried this one more time. The waves were big. The wind howled. The ship began to list – which means topple over. The men on the ship panicked. They thought this was the last chance for them to be saved. The desperation amongst those remaining was tremendous. Six men plunged into the sea, grabbing at the horse. The weight was too much for the tired steed."

The highly strung Hettie Hattingh bit down on what little remained of her thumbnail while Carlos de Sousa began picking his nose. His foraging expedition was brought to an abrupt halt when the supremely beautiful Margaret Wallace, who was sitting next to him, looked his way. Encouraged, he angled his knee an inch closer to hers and waited in vain for her to do the same.

"All were dragged down below. Wolraad Woltemade's body was found the next day, but not that of his stallion."

The matter-of-fact reading of the story left his audience bereft and uncomfortable, as if they'd just witnessed a priest hurry through a funeral service. The headmaster himself seemed a little startled by the silence he'd created. He checked his moustache was still there and slowly rocked from one leg to the other. Eventually, somewhere near the front of the stage where the grade ones sat, a young girl whimpered. Mr Kock held out his cloak, but with less determination this time. Jimmy the Greek was battling with the whole concept. "What? So the man does cavalry into the sea and drowns his own horse?"

To break the bleak mood and keep things flowing, Mr Kock shouted at everyone to stand up so they could close with the Lord's Prayer. He had hoped a heroic drowning would've been a little more inspirational; instead, all he could demand now was strict piety, loud and clear. Discipline is always a more tangible deliverable. He watched a sea of heads bow as one and waited for the shuffling to stop. The headmaster then clasped his hands and cleared his throat. Keeping his head high and eyes open he barked out to Our Father which art in heaven.

Once Phen reached his class he noticed that Zelda had been right. There was a new arrival. The boy wasn't very big, yet carried himself as if he was. He was quietly powerful. Phen noticed how he said nothing yet everyone took notice of him. His skin was "certifiably Mediterranean", as his gran would say, and his thick black hair clung to his skull. It wove a mat over his head, keeping low and rooted to his scalp. The class knew immediately Miss Smit didn't like him. What made him unique was they could also tell he didn't care. She smiled at him with too many teeth involved. He looked her straight in the eye and over-grinned back.

"No. Sit here." She moved him away from the fragile whiteness of Margaret Wallace. Like a thin, delicate bone-china cup being lifted off a rough enamel saucer, she made Margaret stand so the darker boy could push past. "You can sit next to Kobus."

Kobus Visser was not impressed. He had presumed the celebrity of a freshly broken leg would guarantee him the extra space. "It stuck out both ways." Visser had sent his top lip and bottom lip in opposite directions to make his point. "I could see the bone sticking out my sock. Snapped like a piece of biltong." Although each bench and desk was made to accommodate two, he'd thought his large bulk and one limb in a cast had filled the space adequately. He belatedly heaved his damaged leg out of the way and placed his crutches on the floor. The new boy likewise registered his displeasure by sitting with only one cheek on the bench.

"Sit properly."

The new boy made it a cheek and a quarter.

"Now stand and tell us your name."

"Adan Karim. But everyone calls me Adam. That's okay, you can do that too."

His self-confidence was incredible. It bordered on insolence. Here was the newest member of the school telling the teacher what his name was, and then that she could call him something else.

"Thank you, *Adan*. You can sit now."

Adan sank in the slowest slow motion and smiled, again ensuring his grin was as wide and as false as his mouth would allow.

The next piece of his puzzle fell into place at the beginning of first break while everyone stood in a line to sign "Fat Visser's" leg. In addition to elaborate signatures, there were a few Tweety birds and flowers from the girls. If he'd expected hearts with arrows through them, he hid his disappointment well. The boys provided some barely recognisable Batmen and Popeyes. Visser's mother had made it clear nothing rude was allowed, and this had clearly cramped their imaginations. Phen dangled loosely at the back of the line, not sure if his name was worthy of the plaster of Paris. He held his pen absent-mindedly as if it was really for another purpose.

Carlos de Sousa stood waiting in front of him with a Marmite sandwich in his hand. He was the only boy in the class with a mole on his face. It sat midway between the bottom of his nose and the top of his upper lip. When he spoke it was impossible not to watch it undulate like a buoy in rough seas. He turned casually to Phen and offered him a bite. This unexpected act of kindness took Phen by surprise. Although he was more of a Bovril man, he obliged and ended up with half the crust in his mouth. Carlos meanwhile brushed a few wayward crumbs off his tie. Those that were a little more stubborn, he patted against his tongue.

"Porras use fists and feet." As Mr de Sousa was originally from Lisbon this statement seemed credible enough. He made two fists and assumed a boxing position. "Portuguese kiss." Carlos spun then rammed his elbow within an inch of Phen's nose.

Phen tried to stay calm and not back away. He just nodded and stared at the mole, waiting for the next wave. Carlos had missed a blob of Marmite in the corner of his mouth, but now was not the time.

"Lebs, on the other hand, use knives and broken bottles." He transformed his right hand into a flick knife and his left into the neck of a broken bottle. His stance dared Phen to take him on. Phen stepped forward for a moment, feeling he had a part to play in this ballet, then stepped back and held his ground.

"And that is the difference between us." Carlos returned the ends of his arms to hands. "So, watch out for that new boy."

Up until this point the Lebs were purely a gang from

Mayfair, a suburb of corrugated-iron houses that hugged the railway line as it left Johannesburg. They were the same as the Braamie Boys or Hell's Angels. Or the Jets and Sharks from *West Side Story*. Phen had no idea they also represented a nationality and had a country. He'd seen restaurants advertising Lebanese food, but had never put the two together. It only dawned on him now that Mr Karim was fresh from another land and automatically part of a notorious gang. Porras had Portugal, Lebs had Lebanon *and* instant membership to the toughest, meanest gang in South Africa. No wonder he was so confident.

"White kaffir," was Visser's contribution to the conversation, although Phen noticed he'd checked the classroom first to make sure Adan wasn't still in it. "De Sousa," he continued, "are you signing or not?"

De Sousa's pen didn't work on the rough plaster, so Phen lent him his. It was a fair exchange for the sandwich. It also made his signing more natural. It didn't feel as if he had to ask Visser if he wanted his name on the cast or not. He looked for some inspiration. Besides Jimmy the Greek's horse head with snorkel and goggles, there wasn't much originality. In the end he settled on a white patch just below the knee. He decided he'd just write his name, his proper name. The capital S in Stephen was large and proud. The top curl even crept a little onto the kneecap.

The three of them then walked down to the embankment next to the change rooms. A certain popularity is transferred when you walk with a boy who has a broken leg. You get stopped as a group and asked a lot of questions. Even if you don't say much, you are part of a team that causes circles to form around you. And, the larger the circle, the more brutal the break. He was playing with his older brother's friends. It was meant to be touch rugby but "those guys klap you into next week". He was about to score when the garden hose "wrapped around his foot like a snake". At the same time, Gerrit, who played first team for Helpmekaar, tackled him full-weight. The ensuing crash caused Visser's leg to embed itself on the edge of his father's braai. The forty-four-gallon drum, cut in half, sent his knee left while the trapped ankle turned in the opposite direction. "It was amazing," Visser admitted, "that I didn't cry."

No one believed the last part of the story. Yet some first-day-back code existed which allowed the telling of tales to go untested. Later on there would be those who claimed all he did was slip on a hosepipe and cry like a baby. There was little evidence of Visser's sporting skills. It would also be pointed out that, in the previous term, he'd howled when a tennis ball hit him in the nuts during a game of stingers. And it hadn't even been a hard throw. But today he was a hero and it was contagious. Phen noticed when he finally reached the sports fields that he, too, was limping slightly and favouring his left leg.

The embankment was something of a letdown. Most people had already drifted off. Only the truly hardened detectives remained. Mr Swindon had indeed done a good job. He'd obviously repaired whatever damage had been done to the mower. He'd then cleverly mowed the words vertically and horizontally, so the direction of the cut grass gave no clue as to what lay beneath. This didn't stop Vernon MacArthur, who lay with his head on the ground squinting through the grass. He kept changing position then staring at the ground like a snooker player lining up his shot. He tapped the side of his head as if it was all slowly coming to him. He always came top of the class, and this gave him the right to wait for an audience before he spoke. Those who lingered obediently gathered around him while he pretended to be deep in thought.

"There were three words originally," he said definitively. "But I can only make out one." It was a rare act of humility designed to entrench his credibility. "This one here," he said.

Everyone looked at the slope of the grassy mound and saw nothing. The heat had already turned the freshly mown grass a silvery brown. It lay over the slanting surface of green, hiding all its secrets. A small boy from grade two blew at it, hoping to lift its veil. Vernon MacArthur gave a heartless chuckle at the stupidity of the gesture. He bent down on his knees and lined up his shot again. He nodded to himself and confirmed his genius.

"It's cock or penis," he said.

The girls were genuinely shocked. They blushed and put their hands to their mouths. They were so embarrassed they could no longer look at the embankment. The boys smiled ruefully as if they'd known all along. Phen couldn't believe what he was hearing. Without thinking, he opened his mouth and tried to get his tongue to respond. His anger did not act as a lubricant for his speech. He was surprised that even the Bs refused to behave. They queued up behind each other, refusing to advance.

"B-b-b-but which one is it?"

"B-b-b-both."

"B-b-but there's not even a s-s-s-s … a sing … one letter the s-s-same in either word."

When you're a straight-A student and the winner of the academic prize *and* your father drives the latest Valiant Barracuda Fastback, you don't have to answer spazzes. As the school bell rang, everyone turned to run back to their classes. Vernon paused just long enough to do his monkey impersonation. He stuck out his jaw, scratched his armpits and picked lice off his chest. "S-s-s-s-stupid," he hissed with chimpanzee-pursed lips before running off with his knuckles dragging on the ground.

Visser might have been a crowd-puller on his way to the sports fields, but on the way back he was pretty much a loner. He swung between his crutches as fast as he could but his weight and general lack of aerodynamics made for slow progress. Uphills were particularly tedious. His broken leg had to loop out sideways. This sometimes caused his foot to hit the rubber stopper at the base of the crutch. Twice Phen caught him as he tilted sideways. He thought of the *De Jonge Thomas* listing, "which means topple over". Either way, there was no Wolraad Woltemade welcome when they finally made it back to class. Mrs Smit shouted at them for being late and Visser didn't keep his word and say that Phen had been helping him.

"If this is how you choose to behave on the first day of school, you will regret it until the very last."

This direct threat produced more current than Phen's head could handle. A deep anxiety grabbed him and began its cruel dance as new history textbooks were handed out. On the cover, Jan van Riebeeck stood at the base of Table Mountain with a feather in his hat and his hand resting on a gold-capped walking stick. In the top right-hand corner two Bushmen, naked except for their loincloths, stared back. One had his bow and arrow raised, not sure if the men from the Dutch East India Company, with buckled boots, constituted prey. Clouds gathered at the Cape of Storms in swirls of white and smudgy grey. Phen wondered, if the wind was blowing across the top of the cover, why were the sails of the *Dromedaris* still droopy and lank? They hung from their masts like exhausted sheets still recovering from their long trip from the Netherlands.

He wanted to go down to the bay and help those dots, which were sailors' heads. He'd climb the highest rigging if needs be to fold and roll up those sails. And when that was done, he'd be happy to join the brown, barefooted men. They must have a cave somewhere he could hide in. They could teach him how to survive off the land and chew cactus roots when he was thirsty. Maybe they could even climb Table Mountain and use the approaching tablecloth to become invisible. Once you were in its billowing thickness, no one would find you. Not even Mrs Smit.

She had returned from first break determined to stamp her authority on the class. Clearly Adan Karim had shaken her. Phen and Visser's late arrival was exactly what she didn't need. Any transgression of the rules was now interpreted as a direct challenge to her sovereignty. Even Hettie Hattingh, who was teacher's pet, had been told to sneeze like a lady. Bewildered, she'd dabbed her nose with her hanky and sent the embroidered pink lamb up each nostril just to make sure. Jimmy the Greek, who sat in front of her, had wiped the back of his neck as if caught in her spray. Everyone had laughed. Mrs Smit had slapped Van Riebeeck's face five times with her eighteen-inch ruler. She would have none of this insolence. The pile of books had still trembled on her desk as she waited for absolute silence. Head down, Hettie had examined the recently returned lamb. It was a little damp, but otherwise no worse for wear.

Phen's fear was that his late arrival would somehow affect the last class of the day. This class lived under the broad term of "art". Monday-afternoon art encompassed anything from tearing up old *Huisgenoot* magazines to make collages of the Voortrekker Monument, to having a member of the Johannesburg Philharmonic explain how a tuba, "the largest and lowest-pitched instrument in the brass family", worked. Phen knew, though, that today was all about auditions for the school play. Mr Kock had announced that Mrs Smit would assist Miss Delmont to produce this term's "extravaganza". This amounted to a demotion for their class teacher. Her previous staging of Charles Dickens's *A Christmas Carol* had not been a success. It had been forced upon her, even though it wasn't a setwork, in an attempt to create a little year-end festive spirit. Her Scrooge was mean enough, yet seemed to lack the will to repent.

Daphne Delmont, on the other hand, had graduated from the Arts and Drama College and had been on stage "more times than I've had cups of tea. And I don't drink coffee." Her long red hair fell both in front of and behind her shoulders. Philip Denton swore she never wore a bra. He said when the weather was cold they stuck out like those circular roofs you get on top of rondavels. She had changed out of her smart teachers' clothes and now wore jeans, sneakers and a poncho with Red Indian motifs down the side. The soft leather hung like a large bib, so no one could deny or confirm Denton's observations. "Come, dahlings," she said as she waved the class into the hall. Mrs Smit, in her black skirt, high heels and puffed white blouse, stood beneath the portraits of past headmasters. The thick wooden frames and gold lettering offered little refuge. As it became increasingly clear that this would be no co-production, she edged closer and closer to the exit before disappearing entirely.

Phen's sense of panic now lifted to a new level. The ease of Miss Delmont's chatter, the way she threw words into the wind knowing where they'd land, terrified him. She would surely assume everyone had this ability. She sang her words, laughed in the middle of them and then continued as if nothing had happened. She deliberately put obstacles in her way so she could jump over them. Phen watched her paint the hall with her voice, then use her hands like a conductor as she made her audience stand in a semicircle around her. He was finding it difficult to breathe and was about to pee in his pants. He rubbed his sweating palms on his shorts in case she extended her hand. He did mouth exercises and practised "how now brown cow" a dozen times in his head.

"So," she asked, scanning the curved gathering left to right. "Where do my Ingrid Bergmans, my Judy Garlands and Audrey Hepburns hide? And where are my Laurence Oliviers, my Cary Grants and Humphrey Bogarts?"

Phen looked up at the bare wooden cross on the fascia board above the stage. Metal strips shot out of it optimistically, but the Son of God had already left.

With Jesus being absent or perhaps too high in his ascension, Phen decided to join his two hunter-gatherers again. The weather had cleared on top of Table Mountain and the view was spectacular. They shared berries and nuts and watched the two mighty oceans collide into one another. Far out to sea, whales dipped their massive heads and sent fountains of white upwards against the perfect blue. Closer in, waves curled a deep green before flattening themselves against the shore.

"The problem with the world is that it's always one drink behind." Daphne Delmont took a deep draw on her imaginary cigarette and stared at Phen. He apologised by straightening his tie and refocused his eyes on her. Her voice was suddenly deep and morose. She continued to look at him over hooded, melancholy eyes. Eyes full of old pain and scarred memories. "Of all the gin joints, in all the towns, in all the world, he walks into mine." She toasted Phen over a tumbler of whisky and gave just a hint of a wistful smile. He returned the smile but didn't quite have the courage to toast her back. Someone started clapping and soon the whole class was applauding. Jimmy the Greek slapped him on the back, although he'd really done nothing.

Miss Delmont bowed and her poncho billowed out before her.

"Right!" She clapped her hands like castanets above her right ear. "To work! We're going to do *A Midsummer Night's Dream*. However, it shall be our version. Lots of fun. It's about a daughter who doesn't want to listen to her father. There's kings and queens and fairies. There's even a man with the head of a donkey. And snicker, snicker, his surname is Bottom. There are also herbs involved, which as you all know is another name for hallucinogenic drugs." She said "hallucinogenic drugs" soundlessly, her mouth clearly forming each syllable to ensure all those paying attention would understand. Her eyes went so wide they nearly popped out of her head.

Mrs Smit, just returned, visibly stiffened as she forced her back against the wall. Her bell-shaped hair, stiff with hairspray, scratched against the paint.

Miss Delmont had, in the meantime, commandeered a chair, spun it around and sat on it the wrong way round. She looked like a cowboy with her legs straddling either side and spoke to her audience briskly. "Let's keep it simple. Come up to me one at a time. We'll talk and then I'll decide which part you get. I'm the casting director … impress me!" No one moved. "I said casting director, nothing about juvenile cannibalism." Still no one moved. Daphne Delmont placed the back of her wrist onto her forehead. She began to weep.

"Crazy," said Jimmy the Greek as he walked towards her. "Even more crazy than cavalry sailor man." Daphne stopped crying immediately and burst into a huge smile. Soon everyone was queuing to see her.

Phen was last in the line. He noticed most people left the chair cheerful enough, although a number of boys wanted to play Puck because it sounded like a really bad word. He tried to be casual and acknowledge the general happiness in the room, yet he couldn't absorb it. The closer Phen got, the drier his throat became. He did more "how now brown cows" and added "the rabbit runs round the ragged rocks" to his repertoire. However, the moment he stood opposite her, his mind emptied and his mouth filled with sand.

"So, Mr Bogart, you like the stage? You a greasepaint and footlights man?"

Phen opened his mouth. Nothing came out.

"You like to strut your stuff on the boards?"

Phen couldn't even get his head to nod or shake.

"Enjoy a little stagecraft? Been to a pantomime?"

His mouth opened again, more in the way a fish gasps when pulled out the water.

"Movies? Drive-in? Books?"

He shrugged his shoulders imperceptibly.

"I like the theatre because you can be someone else. You can be free of yourself. Dream. Laugh. Give your head a little holiday. Don't you think who we're always told we have to be should occasionally get a vacation?"

His lips twitched. It was enough for Miss Delmont as acknowledgement of his confirmation.

"Therefore I would like to give you a critical part in the play." She raised one hand as if to push down the cold horror rising through Phen's body. He looked up to the cross. It was still empty. "*A Midsummer Night's Dream* is essentially an outdoor play. Nature abounds. Forests and glades – that sort of thing. And in the centre of all this I'd like you. I want you to be the tree that all the action happens around. Silent but gnarled. Full of wisdom, observing everything."

"B-b-b-books," he finally said. "I like books."

"Excellent! I'll take that as a yes then."

10

Patina

/pat'i-na/ noun

Phen walked home with a spring in his step. He even played a little hopscotch on the new paving outside the Ambassador Hotel. His first day back at school had not been as bad as he thought it would be. The Leb had spread a new mood. It was like sitting with a gangster in the class. De Sousa had shared his sandwich with him and Visser had let him sign his cast. Most importantly, the weight of his role in the school play had been lifted off his shoulders. Life was good. He had his haversack on one shoulder and his blazer on the other when he rounded the corner of O'Reilly and Catherine Avenue. There, sitting on the pavement, much like the black dog earlier in the day, was Heb Thirteen Two.

"How was school?"

"Okay."

"Okay is good."

"Not in the park?"

"Just bought some milk." He offered Phen the opened carton. "No germs, promise."

"No, thanks." Phen wiped his upper lip. Heb Thirteen Two took the hint and rubbed the white moustache off his face.

"You were right about the play. I'm a tree."

"Excellent."

"That's exactly what Miss Delmont s-s-said."

"And a fine piece of timber you shall be."

"I'm going to be gnarled and full of wisdom."

"Perfect casting."

Heb Thirteen Two stood up and offered the last inch of milk once more. "It's good for your bones."

Phen shook his head and watched him stroll off. "Where you going now?"

"Back to the park."

"Can I come?"

"Public space."

"I'll take that as a yes."

They lay in the shadow of the small willow tree, even though the park bench was in the shade too. Phen used his haversack as a pillow and Heb Thirteen Two used a rolled-up blanket he'd pulled from behind the Yesterday, Today and Tomorrow bush. Neither felt the need to talk. They spent most of their time just staring up at the clouds. These ones were more friendly than those that swept across the cover of his new history book. They weren't pitted with grey and didn't seem to be in a hurry. At times they'd pause to let the sun through and Heb Thirteen Two would be forced to close his eyes.

"You need sunglasses. My grandmother says staring at the sun can make you go blind … There's a new boy in our class, Adan Karim."

"Not Adam?"

"*Adan*. He's a Leb. He's not very big but everyone is scared of him. Even Mrs Smit."

"He *thinks* he's tough, so he is."

"Visser is much bigger … no one's really scared of him."

"Because he doesn't *think* he's a tough guy." Heb Thirteen Two pointed to the middle of his forehead. "It's who you *want* to be that counts. It's all in the mind."

Phen nodded. It felt like the mature thing to do.

"Watch out for people who want to manicure what's in your head. Trim your soul this way and that. Blessed are the curious for they shall have adventures. And hallelujah to those filled with imagination for they shall avoid the constipation of small minds."

Phen lifted his head off his haversack and watched Heb raise his hands. He then blessed Phen with a series of crosses, stars, exclamation marks and something that looked like the very curvaceous frame of a woman's figure. Both arms now tired, he fell back again and stared at the sky.

"The clouds are saying the same thing."

Phen returned to his previous position and tried to listen.

"Hear it?"

"No."

"You're not paying attention then. Is there any shape a cloud can't be?"

"No."

"I rest my case."

Phen wrestled himself up on one elbow again and tried to stare through Heb's shut eyes.

"Imagine if clouds were only allowed to be circles or squares. Maybe you'd make a good triangle or parallelogram. Maybe you wouldn't have any sharp lines or corners at all. Maybe you could be shaped like the inside of a seashell or a leaf."

"Vernon MacArthur says I'm shaped like a stick man. A s-s-stuttering s-s-stick man. He said my neck's so thin I can only eat s-s-spaghetti."

"That's just outside stuff. Don't let them leave their dirty footprints in your head. Let your mind develop its own patina. Protect the space between your ears; it belongs to you."

"My mother says I always have my head up in the clouds."

"There are many people with their heads up much worse places."

Heb Thirteen Two pulled his hat lower to protect his eyes and gently placed his arms across his chest. He stretched his long body and pointed his toes to the mine dumps that ringed southern Johannesburg. When the wind came up, the yellow sand whipped off the distant mountains like foam leaping from huge waves that threatened to advance, yet never did. Phen had looked up the meaning of "gnarled" in the dictionary before he'd left school and now realised it perfectly described the hands that lay across the paisley shirt. They seemed much older than the man's face, attached from another body. While Phen watched, the fingers began to strum gently on the intricate pattern. He wondered which tune was swirling in his head.

"The times they are a-changing," he warbled in reply.

"Bob Dylan."

"Not bad for a man who sings through his nose. Not the normal shape of a superstar. I'm sure a number of people, all who claimed to know better, would've told him his best contribution to singing would be to stop doing it." He continued:

> The line it is drawn
> The curse it is cast
> The slow one now
> Will later be fast
> As the present now
> Will later be past

The order is
Rapidly fadin'
And the first one now
Will later be last
For the times they are a-changin'!

Thankfully he mumbled-talked-sang and stayed flat on his back. Phen looked around but couldn't see anyone within earshot. The fingers did a final crescendo then fell silent.

"Can I ask you what you did, you know, before this?" Phen addressed the body as a whole. It seemed impolite to question a face with its eyes shut.

The chest heaved, indicating the answer carried a great amount of weight. Air escaped through his nose for an impossibly long time. "I'm not sure I can remember them all. I've been a farmer, a soldier, a sailor if serving slop down below makes you a man of the seas. It certainly didn't make me a cook. I remember running Ye Olde Tavern. I can see the Tudor beams. Forgettable office jobs came later. There's something about sitting in a cubicle that turns a man's spirit anaemic, bloodless. Geometric mummification. I've been a salesman. A dance instructor at Arthur Murray. I've hawked trinkets of all kinds, but never, I think, myself. I've sold vacuum cleaners. 'Madam, your carpet is begging you to let me inside and give you a demonstration.' And jukeboxes. 'One coin, sir, and Elvis Presley himself will ensure your customers can't help falling in love with you.' Most recently I've been an alcoholic. I'm still one, except I don't drink any more." The eyes stayed closed.

"So the dancing and singing comes from the dance studio and jukeboxes?"

"Maybe."

"My father was also a farmer a long time ago; it didn't work out. Now he's sick. He's not an alcoholic. He takes a lot of pills and injections, though. My gran says he likes the injections too much. She says sometimes the cure can be worse than the illness. He used to read all day, then his eyes got so bad that it became my job. Now that's stopped as well. I hate tape recorders."

"The march of technology."

Phen suddenly saw all the components of the Philips STÉRÉO CONTINENTAL "401" breaking into their individual parts. Led by the two reels, they formed a long column and began a victory parade towards his bedroom. He didn't really know what was in the machine, yet he imagined sprockets, screws, dials, switches, seals and flat metal frames all being trailed by yards of electrical wiring. Right at the back, the microphone still attached to its black cord tried to keep up.

Now it was Heb Thirteen Two's turn to lift himself up on his elbow and stare at Phen. They were like two bookends with nothing between them.

"Do you know what 'impaled' means?"

"Think so."

"It means to be speared, spiked, skewered, transfixed. Yet time moves around and through you whether you like it or not. You can't peg it down. Hammer it into the ground. So why try impale yourself on the here and now?"

Phen didn't even pretend he understood.

"Imagine you just stood here, in the park, for the rest of your life." Heb indicated Phen should stand up and move a few yards away. "Just wait there."

"I am."

"What's happening?"

"Nothing."

"Wrong! Everything is happening. You're happening. You're getting taller, bigger. Your nails are growing. So is your hair. Soon you'll get that stuff under your arms, on your chest and in a few other places. Your balls will drop and your voice will break."

Phen opened his stance slightly.

"And look around you. The grass, the flowers, this willow. Nothing is just staying the same. The clouds are different to how they were when you first stood up, the sun has moved across the sky. Even the children's pool over there will have a ripple in it that wasn't there before, because the wind's just changed direction. And that's only in the last few seconds. Imagine when day turns to night? Summer to winter?"

Phen watched an old lady shuffle to the bench behind them and slowly sit down. She took out half a loaf of bread from her shopping bag and dug her fist into it. Once she was finished punching it she pulled pieces out and threw them up in the air. Half of it landed back on top of her but she didn't seem to mind. Within seconds the doves and pigeons were all around her. One landed on her shoulder and was told to behave. She coaxed it down with a crust, cooed and tutted to them all, calling her favourites by name.

"Nothing stays the same. Nil, zero, zilch, nought, nix, nada is permanent. Everything waltzes around us. A one and a two … and a one and a two. I'll lead." Although Phen rebuffed the request to be his partner, Heb turned the park into a ballroom and spun around it by himself. With arms outstretched, he chose to dance in a wide circle. He disappeared behind the jacarandas and popped up on the other side of the acacias.

By the time he returned, the old lady was smothered

with pigeons. The largest one had landed on her lap. Phen couldn't work out if she thought this was acceptable behaviour or not. The bird was being scolded so gently it stayed there and pecked at a button on her jersey. She let out a ticklish giggle. Her legs widened as she laughed. Phen was embarrassed to see her stockings only went to just above her knee. Once there, they were folded back in a thick band like his school socks. Eventually the bird flew off. The old lady waved and watched it disappear into the blue. She stayed staring long after there was nothing to see. Sighing heavily she asked herself if there was any bread left and replied that it was all gone.

"Just remember the Three Times Truth and everything will start to make sense."

"Three Times Truth?"

Heb drew a large three in the air, paused and added a matching x. Phen wasn't keeping up. He stored the words in the hope that he might later make some sense of them.

"You like going to the movies?"

"Yes."

"What's your favourite?"

"*Lawrence of Arabia*."

"So, First Truth, the screen is full of Peter O'Toole's face as he says hello to Sherif Ali played by what's-his-name."

"Omar Sharif."

"Second Truth is the next shot, that shows both of them on screen but you can see Omar Sharif is pointing to something."

"Third Truth, a wide panoramic shot showing thousands of tribesmen on camels galloping towards them."

The old lady began to flick individual breadcrumbs off her skirt. She licked her fingertip and dabbed at those refusing to leave.

"You need all three to understand what's going on."

"Suppose so."

"We judge too quickly on the first truth."

It seemed they'd finally run out of things to say to one another. The old lady stood up, clutching her shopping bag, and waited. She looked at both of them, needing confirmation that it was all over and she could leave. Phen took his cue from her and fiddled unnecessarily with the latches on his haversack. Heb Thirteen Two was no help at all. He just stayed standing in exactly the same position and looked up at the sky. They were all equidistant from each other in a kind of triangle and no one wanted to break the symmetry.

Eventually the old lady patted her hair as if saying goodbye to it and began to shuffle away. Her slippers flattened the grass with each step. Phen watched from the corner of his eye as her dual trail inched towards the park gate. The bent grass reflected the sun, silver and strangely wet. He put his blazer on as slowly as he could and lifted his bag in stages to his shoulder. Heb Thirteen Two moved to the recently evacuated bench, sat down in the middle, and tapped his hat to make sure it was secure. He then spread each arm wide in an ambiguous style. The fluid movement, like the wings of an enormous bird, could be interpreted as either claiming ownership or inviting camaraderie. As Phen turned to go, he saw one finger on the top slat beckon him over. The invitation was both gentle and irresistible. The gold mines, more mustard than yellow now, miraged in the late afternoon.

"First Truth: at ten thirty this morning a black Humber Imperial with a silver roof roared to a stop outside number twenty O'Reilly Road."

"Doctor Weinner's car."

"The driver, at some haste, lifted his black doctor's bag from the passenger seat and charged into Duchess Court.

Second Truth: an hour later this same gentleman emerged with an attractive but tired-looking woman."

"My mother." Phen didn't want any more truths. He tried to remember if there actually was a scene in *Lawrence of Arabia* where Omar Sharif points to thousands of tribesmen galloping on camels.

"The doctor and your mother proceeded to have a long discussion outside on the stairs of Duchess Court. They did not see, or possibly chose not to notice, a man nearby in a felt hat. He waa sitting on the pavement trying to open a bottle of Mrs Ball's chutney which he'd found in a nearby dustbin. There were still a few inches left at the bottom, but the lid had set hard."

Phen stared in front of him. He remembered the tribesmen on camels attacking the port of Aqaba. The big Turkish gun was pointing the wrong way out to sea.

"Rheumatic fever, when not picked up as a child, can have long-lasting effects. You get damage to the heart valves and atrial fibrillation scar tissue. Your father might have had a heart attack. He's too sick so they can't take him to hospital to operate. His lungs are the main issue, can't take the anaesthetic. They've added to his medication and a specialist is coming tonight."

There were also lots of Arabs on camels when they slaughtered a column of the retreating Turkish army; however, he couldn't remember Omar Sharif being in that part. "No prisoners!" Lawrence had shouted because the Turks had recently killed all the people from the village of Tafas.

"Third Truth."

The mustard mine dumps were getting a purple topping.

Phen picked up his haversack, placed it on his lap, yet stayed seated. He'd never felt this tired before. His mind limped to a halt. He turned to the man in the hat, waiting for instructions.

"The Third Truth is now over to you. You must decide how far and wide you want to see."

"It's not just three times," he heard his voice say. "I'd like *Lawrence of Arabia* to end when he rides in his white-and-gold robes between the two mountains, and all the Bedouins stand on the ridge and call out his name. But everyone knows it ends when he dies in a motorcycle crash on a country road back in England."

Juxtaposition

/juks-te-pa-zishen/ noun

When Phen arrived home, his mother gave him a big hug and told him everything was fine before he could ask if anything was wrong. She offered him a cup of tea then laughed because she hadn't even given him the chance to take his backpack off. There had been a little incident this morning, just before she was about to go to work. It was pretty much sorted now and there was no need to worry. Mr Lansdown, her boss, had given her the whole week off! She made it sound as if it were a spontaneous holiday gesture and clapped her hands in delight. Plus, how about buying fish and chips from Manny's shop on the corner? There was absolutely no need to slave away in the kitchen on a Monday night, didn't he agree?

Phen agreed and enquired if the little incident had anything to do with his father. "Yes, it did." She paused to admire his detective work while hanging his school blazer over a dining-room chair. He was informed that another doctor would pop in tonight just to check on everything. "Better safe than sorry." He nodded as his mother brought him a cup of hot water. He could see the teabag resting on the breadboard, but said nothing. She sat down at the opposite side of the table and moved the empty fruit bowl sideways. Now that there was no obstruction between them, she smiled her widest smile and opened her eyes expectantly.

"Now tell me about *your* day. How was school?"

His mother was ecstatic to hear he was a tree and thought he'd be brilliant. She was sorry Mrs Tulip was gone. Although she'd never met her, she seemed like a nice person. She also hoped Kobus Visser's leg would soon mend. Adan Karim certainly sounded like an interesting young man. He should invite Jimmy the Greek around; he hadn't been to their flat in ages. Although there was no mention of Vernon MacArthur's rude words, she agreed with her son that he certainly had a high opinion of himself. His mother explained that those people got their own comeuppance and he shouldn't worry about it. "The wheel turns," she further elaborated. Finally all that was left was Wolraad Woltemade; however, he didn't feel like discussing a drowning horse.

"That's all," he said, and had a sip of warm water.

"Good!" His mother clapped her hands again in glee.

Phen nodded and began to stand. He knew sooner or later he had to get past the dining room and into the dark corridor. He also understood that at the end of that black tunnel his father's bedroom door would be closed. What he didn't know was what to expect on the other side. He had no idea what a heart attack looked like. It was a strange juxtaposition of words. It sounded so aggressive. Who had assaulted his father's heart? Was it a skirmish, a mugging or a full onslaught? And why was it that only hearts were attacked? Heads ached, stomachs cramped, ankles twisted, he'd heard that spleens, whatever they were, ruptured and necks whiplashed, but only hearts got attacked.

"Lots of vinegar," she said, "on my chips."

Phen had never seen his mother like this before. She was turning herself into another person. Determined to smile, even at the empty fruit bowl, she had found some mysterious source of energy. Her body seemed to have electricity running through it. Her hands jerked and her arms waved. She circled the dining-room table at high speed and laughed at jokes aimed at herself as she tied and untied her apron. Finally she decided to take it off and hang it behind the kitchen door. With a hand on each hip she stared at the unused teabag, shrugged and put it back in its box.

"You okay?"

"Perfect."

Phen saw the thick, almost caked powder strategically smoothed over the dark circles under her eyes. The lipstick was new and very red. She had wanted to put on a good face but was exposed by the bright dining-room light with its unshaded and relentless glare. Like a slightly crooked mask it accentuated rather than concealed. Quick to interpret the young boy's look, his mother turned to the mirror and dabbed her face with a tissue.

"Can I g-go … into his room?"

"Of course!" She immediately spun around and blocked his way. Then she hugged him again so suddenly he was caught off guard. His arms were trapped down by his sides with his body at an awkward angle. While he waited to be released he tried to stand tall and put on a man-size set of shoulders. When his arms were finally free he patted his mother on the back the way he'd seen Uncle Ed do. The gentle tapping, like Morse code, seemed to send a message they both understood. The electricity in his mother began to drain away. Her body slumped. She stepped back from her son but held on to his right hand. She squeezed it absent-mindedly before rubbing it vigorously.

Phen waited, arm outstretched. His mother's eyebrows arched as if she'd suddenly remembered something yet chose to remain silent. Finger by finger she let her son's hand go.

"Everything changes," Phen said.

"That it does."

"Nothing stands still."

"No, it doesn't."

"Even when we think nothing is happening, everything around us is moving. S-so we mustn't be impaled on the present."

"True. Well spoken." She nodded, impressed by the richness of his vocabulary. "We shall not allow ourselves to be harpooned by today."

Phen never saw his father that night or the next morning. Between leaving to get the fish and chips and his return, everything had changed. The illness of his father and what it meant could no longer be contained in a hug and the slow release of a hand. By the time he opened the front door, not one but two specialists were in the closed bedroom. His grandmother, wearing black stockings to match the rest of her outfit, was deliberately positioned with one foot in the dining room and one in the lounge. The human blockade held her nose.

"Did you order any fish and chips with your vinegar?"

Phen felt cheated; he'd been conned. He'd wanted to keep this small. He and his mother could cope if everyone just let them be a team. His gran, even the other doctors, weren't necessary. He could be the man of the house if he was left alone. When he heard Uncle Ed was also on his way, his annoyance reshaped itself into a brittle panic. There was obviously a direct relationship between the size and seriousness of the heart attack and the number of people getting involved. There were just too many. Like Wolraad Woltemade's horse, he was going to drown.

Uncle Ed arrived with a box of chocolates. "Not really appropriate," he said. "Couldn't think of anything else." Mairead thought it was a wonderful gesture, put them in the sideboard and locked the drawer. The lounge became the waiting room. The clicking of his gran's knitting needles, the ticking of the clock. After half an hour Uncle Ed asked if he may take his jacket off. His gran thought that that would be absolutely fine and patted her hair like the old lady in the park. In return, a second round of tea was offered as well as an apology for the stubborn smell of vinegar.

"It's the best I can do," she said, pointing disapprovingly to a side plate with Marie biscuits fanned out like a deck of cards.

"Quite alright, I've had dinner."

Without asking permission, Phen put the radio on and sat cross-legged six inches in front of the Grundig. He caught the beginning of Lux Radio Theatre presented this and every Monday night for your listening pleasure. The voice promised simply the finest in radio drama. A man had been found wandering on the windswept dunes of Swakopmund in South West Africa, yet he had no recollection of how he got there or who he was. The police feared he was up to no good. The diamond fields of the Skeleton Coast tended to attract an unsavoury bunch. Intriguingly, his well-tailored suit seemed to tell another story. Why was the only item found in his wallet a photograph of a beautiful woman? And who was she?

When Phen realised the gentle tapping at the door wasn't a sound effect he jumped up. As he invited Zelda Hillock in, Mairead moved to block her entry into the lounge. Uncle Ed beamed over her hunched shoulders that swayed like a cobra about to strike. As the man of the house, Phen chose to split her defence. He moved past his grandmother on the left while indicating to Zelda that she should move right. Uncle Ed shook her hand firmly and said he was delighted. Maintaining impeccable etiquette, Phen mentioned he was sure Mairead had met or seen Zelda before. Mairead nodded. Zelda gave her a little wave.

"I don't want to disturb. I just heard the news and wanted to know if I could help in any way."

"Won't you have a seat?" Uncle Ed ushered her to a chair. He then resumed his position opposite her and continued to smile. The thick cloth covering her swivel seat caught her white miniskirt and tugged it upwards. It took Zelda a few attempts to catch the material. Each time she lifted herself, the chair would spin left or right and emit a risqué squeak. Eventually she found the edge of her skirt and pulled it down. Now that she no longer had to wriggle, the chair fell silent. Zelda folded her hands across her lap and returned Uncle Edward's smile.

"Sorry," she said, "this knitted fabric gets caught on everything."

"Enchanted," said Ed.

"You say you think you're German yet your English is very good. And if I'm not mistaken, that's a Savile Row suit."

Phen wondered if he should turn the radio off.

The passage door opened and Phen's mother emerged with the two specialists. Her extreme exhaustion contrasted against their Laurel and Hardy-ness. They both wore dark suits, black ties and white shirts, but one was tall and thin, the other round with a thick black moustache. Phen immediately put bowler hats on both of them. They seemed somewhat surprised by the diversity of their audience. Each grabbed the back of a dining-room chair and held it like a lectern. Laurel spoke first, as befits the older, more serious-looking partner. He cleared his throat and touched his temple twice, the way a speaker taps a microphone to get your attention. Everyone stood and waited.

Maybe there comes a time when specialists feel an emotional connection gets in the way of science, when any attempt at a bedside manner becomes a distraction.

"We can," he said, "determine with some degree of certainty that the patient did have a heart attack this morning."

Hardy nodded.

"The severity of this incident is more difficult to ascertain. The heart muscle requires a perpetual supply of oxygen-rich blood to sustain its function. The coronary arteries feed this supply. If these become narrowed, this function is compromised."

"Compromised," said Hardy.

"This narrowing is caused by fatty deposits, something akin to plaque on your teeth. When this plaque gets hard, it breaks off and you have something called a plaque rupture. We believe this might have happened, leading to a blood clot forming around the plaque. This, in due course, blocked the artery, therefore starving the heart muscle of oxygen and thus precipitating a heart attack. This is all, of course, subjective hypothesis on our part, but our finding would be consistent with the symptoms displayed."

"Hypothesis," Hardy concurred.

Phen knew the individual words were English, yet the sentences were from another language. He'd never heard medical speak before. And they were clearly talking about a thing, not a human, and certainly not about his father. His father had a name and a face just like they did. He had to be more than a set of blocked parts.

"He needs rest," continued Laurel.

"Bed rest," added Hardy, perhaps worried that the eclectic crowd needed more specific instructions.

"And no excitement." Laurel's eyes briefly darted towards Zelda.

This furtive action brought about a stumbling silence that suddenly hardened. It was made more awkward because the gathered audience didn't know what to say or ask. Like students attending a lecture, they weren't even sure if they were allowed to speak. Laurel tapped his temple again yet declined to say any more. Hardy stared at the wedding photograph on the sideboard table, perhaps trying to place the bald man standing in front of him. Phen moved closer to his mother in an attempt to break the hush, although this seemed only to add to it. His mother put her finger to her lips, indicating that any sound was inappropriate. A strange staring contest developed. You could look anywhere provided it wasn't in the direction of another human being. It was left to Mairead to break the deadlock.

"Oh, my giddy aunt!" she said, holding a single knitting needle.

The two doctors looked confused, momentarily wondering if this was in reference to a medical condition. The tone, however, made it clear the exclamation was aimed at Dennis in the next room. The implication was that some silliness on his part had contributed to his present condition. Like a man who'd tripped over a spade in the garden, his negligence had knocked some plaque into one of his arteries. She looked back at the two in their suits and waited for confirmation of her assessment.

"Rest," was the best Laurel could do as he rubbed the slightly worn handle of his doctor's bag.

"And keep him comfortable," added Hardy. He had no doctor's bag. Instead, he stroked the back of the dining-room chair.

"I suppose," said Mairead, "whit's fur ye'll no go past ye." The doctors stared blankly ahead. "What will be will be."

"Right!" said Ed, suddenly emboldened and trying to take charge. However, his enthusiasm was short-lived as he immediately turned to the others for help.

It was at this point that Phen realised he'd been a fool to think it was all about what people said. It was all about what they *didn't* say. Words were used to talk *around* what really mattered. To surround and hide the truth. To keep it in some secret place. Grown-ups could claim they weren't lying because they were so good at camouflaging. It was the silence that leaked the truth through.

"*Ha, ha, ha, ha, haa! You must take me for a fool! Do you think because I'm stationed in Swakopmund I'm some country bumpkin? Now you claim the name Gustav rings a distant bell? We have a lot of fish on this coast, sir, and I smell a red herring.*"

Suddenly everyone was listening to the radio. The loud, bitter laughter had arced through the lounge and landed in the dining room. The two doctors didn't know what to do with the gleeful sniggering other than lean forward into the dialogue.

"*May I have some water, please?*" The upper-class accent turned the request into a demand.

"*Do you think that will help bring your memory back?*"

"*I've done nothing wrong, committed no crime.*"

"*That still waits to be determined. Sergeant! Keep this man in a cell overnight.*"

The firm slamming of the prison door snapped the room

out of its trance. By the time the metallic sound of keys turning in a lock was done, the room had found some movement. Zelda placed an arm around Phen's mother and whispered something in her ear. Mairead picked up the Marie-biscuit plate and dismissively offered tea. Sensing this was their moment, the doctors turned with military precision and headed towards their exit. Ed let out another "Right!", opened the door with a slight bow, then closed it behind them.

Again the silence that said everything.

"Don't worry."

Phen knew this was adult opposite-speak. He returned his mother's smile anyway.

"Everything will be fine," she said. "They are the best specialists. The top cardiologists – heart doctors – in the country."

"They look like Laurel and Hardy," Phen blurted. The words shot out his mouth with a velocity he'd never managed before. They flew off his tongue without any preparation.

The room was as stunned by the speed of the delivery as it was by the sentence itself. There were no stilted gaps between each word. No rehearsed pauses. The indignation, maybe even outrage, had melted the words into a perfect fusion. Phen watched Zelda's arm drop from his mother's shoulders as she spun towards him. Marie biscuits tumbled to the floor and rolled like mad wheels in the grooves of the parquet flooring. Ed, who was in the act of sitting down, hovered for a moment then relaunched himself into the vertical position.

Silence, but this time of a different kind.

It was Mairead, again, who released the group with a sound Phen could not recall ever having heard before. It was deep and rumbling and came from a place not often used. It grew in intensity and pitch as it tried to find a way out. Initially a cough trying to catch its breath, and then something else with a different rhythm. An erratic exhaling and inhaling – the sound was strange but not entirely unpleasant. And when the room realised this was how Mairead laughed, it became infectious.

Phen was amazed at the power of one sentence. Even as he tried to retrieve the runaway Marie-biscuit wheels from under the sideboard, the room still reverberated with the aftershock of his sentence. Uncle Ed snorted helplessly as if his laughter lived, tightly packed, up his nose. Zelda lay across the couch trying to get her breath back. She was stretched out with only one foot on the floor. Phen's mother giggled in continual bursts and moved sideways. She was leaning against the sliding door and her weight was slowly pushing it closed. Mairead unceremoniously fanned her face with the side plate and leaned hard on the Grundig, its bowed legs grimly determined to carry her weight.

The room had spontaneously erupted. Boom! Even Pal had charged out from under the telephone table, tennis ball in mouth, stubby tail wagging.

Slowly the noise died down as a kind of normalcy returned. Everyone apologised to everyone, although Phen didn't see the need. The odd chuckle or snigger still surfaced, especially when Zelda started hiccoughing. She sat up and arched her back. This tilted her breasts skywards. Uncle Edward followed their trajectory towards the ceiling. Mairead accepted the returned Marie biscuits onto the plate and noted only two were broken. "Nothing wrong with the rest. They can go back into the packet."

"Can I help you, Lil?" Ed extended a hand to Phen's tilting mother.

"Not much use at this angle, am I?"

After she'd straightened her skirt and centred her belt buckle, she nodded to her son, who was still holding a broken biscuit in each hand. "Thank you. We all needed that."

"I can still smell that vinegar." Mairead headed for the kitchen.

The first to leave was Zelda. This was seen as something of a moral victory by his grandmother. It was, however, diminished by her first spending twenty minutes talking quietly to his mother. Phen watched the two women cocoon themselves in discussion. He was envious of their easy chatter, the way their whispers bonded them.

As they talked, Mairead became more and more incensed. She emptied the dustbin, rattled the plates and washed the dishes in loud protest. She huffed and puffed to no avail. They were locked in a conversation and insulated from the outside world. The depth of this quarantine was made more obvious by Ed, who advanced three times, then peeled off as his presence went unnoticed. Mairead was somewhat mollified by Uncle Edward's offer to drive her home. Although this too was spoiled by him then referring to Zelda as a "perky little thing".

Once they'd left, the empty room confirmed that magic, by its very nature, had to disappear too. It only worked *because* it went away.

"Time for bed," his mother demanded and implored at the same time.

"Can I see him?"

"Tomorrow, maybe. Remember what Laurel and Hardy said? He needs rest."

Phen hated himself for feeling relieved. In an act of feigned dissatisfaction and defiance, he moved into the lounge instead of turning towards his bedroom. He'd make his own decisions. Now that everyone was gone he could be the man of the house again.

"*Your embassy has just been in contact with me.*"

"*Which one is that?*"

"*The British. Yet you are indeed Gustav. Gustav von Abendroth.*"

"*I am?*"

"*Your family fled Nazi Germany in the thirties. Your father would not yield to Hitler's fascist future. Having lost most of his industrial empire he escaped, with you as a young boy, to London.*"

"*But what am I doing in Swakopmund?*"

"*Part of that industrial empire included a diamond-mining concession on the Skeleton Coast. A concession your father thought was worthless. On his death last year, you became the executor of his estate and decided to check. Imagine your surprise when you found a working mine on what was meant to be a barren piece of desert.*"

"*It's coming back to me. I see the turning wheels of the headgear, large graders …*"

"*Probably the last thing you saw before being struck on the head, dumped in the back of a truck and driven twenty miles across the dunes to be left to die.*"

"*But who am I?*"

"*You are not just Gustav von Abendroth, you are Count Gustav von Abendroth!*"

"*I don't know what to say!*"

"*Maybe it is enough to note that life's mysteries unravel in an infinite kaleidoscope of possibilities. Who knows what drives the passions of man? Right now, though, let's celebrate that the greed of one was counterbalanced by the caring of another. If that wandering Bushman hadn't pondered why* tyre tracks crossed those of a gemsbok he was following, you would not be here today."

"Indeed."

"Now, I believe we should quench your thirst with something a little stronger than water!"

12

Anonymity

/e'non'im-iti/ noun

His mother had insisted on two full days before she'd allowed him in after the heart attack. Phen had made tiny baby steps towards his father and then found only a replica. His father was now made of wax. An effigy. He'd turned yellow and gummy as if his body was producing resin. Pasty yet peculiarly polished, a raised hand waved in recognition. He waved back.

The oxygen mask seemed bigger now. It kept creeping up and covering his father's eyes as if it had a mind of its own. Phen fiddled with the two bands of elastic behind his father's head, but the plastic cone still pushed upwards, tilting his glasses above his eyebrows. "Leave it. I can't see anyway." The voice was the only thing left that was still pretty much the same. A little softer and raspier, it was definitive enough to remind him that somewhere in that yellowed husk lay his father.

"Can I get you anything?"

"A new heart would be nice."

Phen straightened the already straight bedspread and puffed up the extra pillows lying on the chair. He wanted to push back the hair that had fallen across his father's forehead but was too scared to touch him. To feel the new stickiness of his skin. He looked ridiculous with a fringe yet Phen couldn't bring himself to do anything about it. It would have to wait for his mother.

"Failing that, you could refill my glass."

The jug was too heavy for Phen. Even using both hands, the water poured into the narrow glass too fast then gushed out, creating a small lake between the doily and the Mills Special box.

"Vic Falls."

For over a year the yellow tin had been three-quarters empty. Although his father no longer smoked, England's Luxury Cigarette had remained untouched at the base of the bedside lamp.

His father began to battle for breath. Phen was afraid if he did anything else the facsimile in front of him would feel obliged to talk, so he just stood still and stared. There was no embarrassment. Silence turned the man on the bed into a body. There was shape and form but no life unless it spoke. The hiss of oxygen, a lullaby or perhaps a requiem. By the time Phen turned to go, his father's hand had moved from his chest to his side and then, taking the arm with it, over the edge of the bed. He thought he heard snoring yet still lacked the courage to lift the hand and place it back on the white linen. The five fingers, white and limp, hung suspended as they called to the ground. Over dinner he and his mother didn't say a single word. It was the only way to have an honest conversation.

The next day, before first class, he stood next to Jimmy the Greek at the urinal. "Hey! Piss straight what, why splash all over my shoes." Phen apologised. "What's wrong? You more Sad Sack than usual." He tried to explain while they zipped up, washed hands and dried them on the back of their shorts. "Attack of the heart. Can't be good." He punched Phen on the chest. "My mother say not enough olive oil in this country. Everything get stuck." He dribbled his soccer ball out the door and down the corridor.

The war between Adan Karim and Mrs Smit continued unabated. It was a mix of spontaneous skirmishes and planned offensives. She now referred to him as Ad-dumb. He, in turn, added an H to her T. "It's Smit with a hard T," she'd yell. "I understand, Mrs Smith," he'd reply, and lisp the rest of his sentence. The speech impediment disappeared at break and returned like clockwork when he came back into class.

"Don't think I don't know what you're doing! And don't think I'm afraid to send you to the headmaster's office!"

"Yeth, Mrs Smith."

Mrs Smit was short and plump enough to ensure that wearing a belt would only accentuate the roll that undulated around her waist. This was not helped by her insistence on wearing dresses that were a little too tight and generally of a material that clung manfully to her body. The belt, usually a gleaming gold with an ostentatious buckle, set against a black knitted weave, started off too high anyway. The angrier she became, the more the shiny strap worked its way further north. It became a tidemark of her fury. The objective of the Leb was to get the belt as high as possible. On a good day it would be close to her armpits by first break, its inexhaustible rise stopped only by the conical ramparts of her bra.

Phen didn't understand it. The Leb had a pretend lisp and Jimmy the Greek scattered words across sentences at random, yet they were the two most popular boys in his class. They talked badly and didn't care. He shrivelled in silence, saying nothing. He'd give anything to be like them. To talk, not caring how it sounded. He desperately wanted to blurt again. He had proof his words could rocket straight out and at great speed. However, the more he thought about it, the less his tongue behaved. He practised blurting in front of the mirror by talking nonsense quickly. But what kind of nonsense? So you had to think, even a little. And the moment that happened, his tongue would cower in the bottom of his mouth, his cheeks would fill with air and his lips would tremble. He stared at the stupidness, the spazness, looking back at him.

"Mrs Smith?"

"Smit."

The Leb raised his arm proud and vertical. Mrs Smit tried to avoid him. She'd forced him into the front row and was now regretting that decision. His arm stayed thrust upwards like a beacon while the teacher pretended to search for something in her drawer. Phen sat directly behind him. The sharp hairs of his newly acquired brush cut needled the back of his collar. Having found a piece of chalk, Mrs Smit turned her back to the class and began to write on the board. The Leb waved his raised hand; the room snickered. Mrs Smit continued to write. The Leb folded a few fingers and gave her a peace sign. More snickering. The chalk continued to attack the blackboard. The hand turned one hundred and eighty degrees with the v of the fingers still in place.

The gasp from the class was immediate and audible. A giant sucking in of air seemed to pull at their teacher. She paused for a moment. Biology class had barely begun. She had spent most of her break drawing a locust and was now labelling it. Between the head and the abdomen lay the thorax. As she finished crossing the x she feigned moving up to the antennae but instead spun around. The Leb revealed his most sincere smile and a hand full of fingers.

"What?"

"I showed my brother, who's twenty-one, my history

book. He disagrees with page seventeen. He says whites made coloureds. He says if you go down to the local hardware store and mix white paint with black paint you get the Coon Carnival."

"Coloureds make up their own ethnic group."

"But who made them?"

"God," said Hettie Hattingh, placing her Bic pen in the wooden groove next to the hole where the inkwell used to go. "He made everything."

"How long do locust eggs take to hatch?" asked Mrs Smit, pointing to a hole at the rear end of her drawing.

Although Phen knew the answer was between six and eight weeks, he kept low. He was an expert at hiding and the Leb had allowed him to hone his craft. As Adan was the prime target he had all but disappeared by always being exactly behind him. The Leb was his shield and Phen was his shadow. By lowering his shoulders and stooping slightly, he copied his every move, ducking left and right as the blazer in front of him swayed to and fro. When the head in front dropped to read or write, so did his. They stretched in unison. Even the swivel into profile as he stared out the window was simultaneous. And the more incensed Mrs Smit became, the stronger his invisibility cloak grew.

This allowed his mind to roam while his teacher Gestapo-ed from her raised platform. A little moustache was all she needed. Every time she raised her hand he secretly Sieg-Heiled her back. He brought in an oompah band, turned the biology textbook into *Mein Kampf* and goose-stepped her to the window when she checked how the haricot-bean experiment was going. He painted a swastika on her tightly wrapped arse and made her fart at the end of the lesson as she bent over to pack her briefcase.

The Bavarians in their lederhosen all joined in, making matching rude noises with their trombones, clarinets and tubas.

"You're just outstretched arms and legs now, Sir Laurence," Miss Delmont said five minutes later. "However, I hear Arts and Crafts are creating a masterpiece. Soon you will be the finest tree in all the land. Remember, from tiny acorns do mighty oaks grow!"

Her Elizabethan bow, with one hand extended towards him, was so low all her hair fell forward in a red curtain. She paused in the position, almost tipping over and top-heavy. It was not far from a headstand. Just as Phen was about to panic, she whipped her neck back. He watched her hair open like a fan, then miraculously close perfectly behind her shoulders. Just like Zelda's, her hair wasn't something to tame, but rather to set free.

"You," she said, "will be the tree of life!"

The school play was proving relatively easy to endure. Phen suspected that Miss Delmont might even like him. She noticed him in the way Mrs Smit dismissed him. He even liked her gentle teasing. She spoke to him without ever demanding an answer. Most of all he loved her ability to celebrate words with flowing arms, angled hips and pulled faces. When Miss Delmont begged that the ensemble F-E-E-L the words, she puffed her chest out, grabbed her heart from under her poncho and offered it to the cast.

The perfect balance between anonymity and acknowledgement without a response being necessary could not last. It changed on the Monday of the third week of the new term. It came on the back of a strange weekend. The more Phen walked Pal, the more he felt Heb was there, the more he didn't see him. On Sunday evening he'd stopped and sat on the bench next to the willow. He was convinced Heb was in the park. He could feel him. Grey mantled the horizon and began to move up the hill. By the time it reached him and turned the grass to slate, there was no one left. Even the pigeons had gone to roost, settled in for the night and silent.

On his way out he found a single partially deflated water wing next to the pool. Phen wore it like a bracelet before hooking it on the corner of the sign stating that picking flowers was punishable by law. Convinced he was being watched, he spun around like Mrs Smit at the blackboard. No one was there. Instead, a dog broke through the bushes and trotted across a bed of marigolds. Their sturdy stems and firm orange centres bounced him on his way. With one ear up and one down, he recognised his old school escort. The dog stopped, lifted his chin and stared at him. Phen looked back slightly intimidated. The broken tail rose momentarily to emphasise their past familiarity. Pal acted as if he didn't exist at all. The two dogs stood facing each other, neither one acknowledging the other's presence. Eventually, the mongrel continued on his journey. He passed within inches of Pal, the kink at the end of his tail almost hooking the spaniel's ears. Uninterested, Pal stared forward.

"Snob," said Phen.

He bent down to put the lead on. By the time he looked up, the other dog had gone. The too-short legs attached to the too-long body had disappeared. Phen presumed he'd taken a short cut by burrowing through the privet hedge. On hands and knees, Phen stuck his head into the foliage and found nothing. Not willing to accept that a dog so clumsily put together could vanish so effortlessly, he began to whistle for him. The breathy, reedy notes barely made it out his mouth. Pal stayed motionless at his feet, scornful and detached.

The next morning Phen waited for the dog of many parts to walk him to school. The night before, he'd stretched out on his bed, stared at his macabre clown and decided that was what the animal had been trying to tell him. He dawdled outside Duchess Court and then pretended to hang around for Jimmy the Greek. There was no one there except a huge rock pigeon that cooed insistently from a jacaranda tree. The non-arrival of the dog made him uneasy. He could feel his confidence drain as every step brought him closer to school. The hole in his stomach was getting larger and heavier. He pulled his grey shorts up and his underpants down. He tightened his tie and straightened his cap.

Standing next to his desk, waiting for permission to sit down, Phen realised this was no false premonition. The morning school bell had barely stopped ringing when he knew he was in trouble. Mrs Smit gleefully read from a note delivered by the school secretary. Ad-dumb Karim would not be at school today as he was attending his grandfather's funeral. The gap between Phen and his teacher was now wide open and unprotected. He was in no-man's land, vulnerable and fully exposed. Ripped from his secret hiding spot, he was suddenly presented in full light, naked and on display. Mrs Smit looked at him as if for the first time, and smiled.

"Sit!" she said.

As one the class dropped to their seats, moved behind their desks and folded their arms. Buoyed by the precision of their obedience and the empty chair in the front row, Mrs Smit smiled again. It was the knowing grin of a woman who felt she was back in control. She sensed that without a ringleader, their courage was thin and easy to break. She spun the globe on her table absent-mindedly, playing for effect, enjoying the tension she was creating. She stabbed it with her finger and suddenly the world stopped.

"Alaska!" shouted Hettie Hattingh.

"Not geography yet."

Hettie bowed her head in apology. Kobus Visser let out the smallest of snickers. Mrs Smit turned her head serpent-like to the trapped boy with the broken leg. His cast was no longer white and was now covered in bad drawings of cowboys shooting each other with penis-shaped pistols. Anxiety filled the room as she slowly moved towards him. He tried to make himself smaller by sliding under his desk; the solid tunnel of plaster of Paris would not allow it.

"Al-as-ka."

She turned it into three lyrical, almost whispered words. Yet each one was a nail she intended driving into him. Her belt was still relatively low although her heavy breathing was already sending it slowly upwards. Mrs Smit was now so close to Kobus Visser he was forced to stare into her belly. She tapped his encased leg then allowed her fingers to play it like a piano.

"It is the largest and most sparsely populated state in America. What else can you tell me about it?"

"It's big."

Someone else cackled. Since the heartless laughter was caused by her manipulation, this was allowed, almost encouraged.

"I've already said that. What else?"

"It's got snow."

"It's got snow? That's all you know? For tomorrow a five-hundred-word essay on Al-as-ka. And don't use wide spacing. I'll count the words." She smiled again and withdrew her midriff.

The class let out a collective groan, half in sympathy and half in relief that it was not them. And that was the pattern of the day. Mrs Smit would maximise the absence of the Leb by keeping "her bunnies", as she suddenly started calling them, in purgatory. She would talk softly and be gentle as she put the knife in. She would try and keep her face one level above a smirk as she exacted her revenge. Only Hettie Hattingh and Margaret Wallace were not targeted. Hettie was rewarded for her ongoing ingratiating support and Margaret was skipped because everyone knew her parents were important and rich. She was dropped off each day in a large Pontiac. Even Vernon MacArthur, normally protected by his endless AS, felt the flick of her tongue as it slithered out of her smiling mouth.

"Vernon, what did you get for your arithmetic test?"

"Ninety-three per cent, Mrs Smit."

"It's funny how so many boys who do well at school just don't go on and achieve later in life."

Phen sat terrified and dead still. Like some small animal in the jungle, he knew his absolute lack of movement was his only protection. Even when the teacher moved past him to attack children in the back of the class he didn't turn around. He made it past second break yet could not shake off the feeling that he was being kept for last. Not substantial enough for the main course, he would make a perfect dessert. The final period of the day was Eng. Lit. Pot. He stared at the three words he'd had to amputate to fit into the last box of his timetable. The shadow that fell over his anthology book appeared patient, even serene. It just stood there. Phen therefore lifted his head slowly to find the cause.

"Glad you could join us."

Mrs Smit's domination of the class was now complete.

They begged for her approval. They howled to be part of her tribe. They were the most ardent supporters of her pogrom even as they were the subject of it. In return, she now let them participate. She would create the wound; they could then join in the frenzy and splash themselves in blood.

"Haven't seen much of you lately."

Phen disappeared down the inkwell. He imagined himself the size of an ant crawling upside down along the underside of the desk, dark with splinters the size of trees, but safe. He'd find a place where the uneven, rough wood had created a crevice and crawl in there. He would wedge himself deeper and deeper into the crack until he disappeared entirely. No one would find him there. Ever.

At the same time Mrs Smit was referring to a page number and suggesting he read from it. Because he was a little slow she opened his book for him and broke its spine. It lay disabled and spreadeagled on his desk. This mock politeness was cheered on by the class. Kobus Visser showed his delight by smacking his plastic ruler against his leg in superficial applause. Those at the back stood up for a better view.

"Turn around. Face your audience."

Mrs Smit pulled him up, spun him around and placed him at Adan's desk with his back to the blackboard. Like an unruly mob at the Colosseum, everyone leaned forward to watch the spectacle. Phen looked down at the page and saw the words dig themselves deeper into the paper. They weren't going anywhere without a fight. He cleared his throat and placed his finger under the first word. If he could just get started. The nursery-schoolness of his pointing brought a loud guffaw from Kobus, who offered his ruler instead. He passed it to Carlos de Sousa who brazenly walked across the classroom and offered it to Phen. Phen shook his head. Carlos threw it nonchalantly onto his desk with a shrug. Philip Denton drew circles next to his head with his finger. What can you do with a spaz?

"Frost, Robert," said Mrs Smit.

"Two," said Phen, mightily relieved. He heard laughter but tried to keep it outside his head.

"Yes?" she goaded.

"… roads … diverged … in … a … yellow … wood."

The victory was genuine enough. A whole line was out. He didn't know how long it had taken; still he knew it was done. For a moment his courage gathered. He briefly wondered if this could perhaps create a sprint of sorts. A crazy rattling off of words. This was not to be. Phen had concentrated so much on the first line, he hadn't seen the awaiting ambush.

"And?"

"And s-s-s-s-s-s-sorry …" The class went wild. Phen was the funniest thing they'd ever seen. Cheeks puffed like a chipmunk and lips quivering with sound on repeat. Philip Denton gave his best impersonation and even Mrs Smit had to put her hand to her mouth. However, not before everyone had heard her laugh.

"… I could … not … tr-tr-tr-travel … both / And … be … one … traveller, long … I … s-s-s-s-stood."

When Philip Denton said "You're not joking", the class became uncontrollable. In the midst of all the hysteria, Phen kept his chin on his chest. He continued to subdivide the sentence into individual words and those words into individual sounds. Sometimes he even broke the letters away from the words and wrestled with them individually before bringing them back together. He chopped up each word then moved his eyes right and hunted down the next one. By using this method, he finally arrived at the end of the first verse.

"And … looked … down … one … as … far … as … I … could / To … where … it … bent … in … the … undergrowth."

He said "undergrowth" twice to emphasise a completion of sorts. No one cared. Mrs Smit had moved back to her table on its raised platform. It was time to restore a semblance of order. A number of his classmates now looked like blowfish. They stared at each other to see who had the biggest cheeks and the poutiest trembling lips. Even Hettie Hattingh looked unbalanced. Somehow one of her two pigtails had become undone. She laughed and cried at the same time as she tried to rethread it. The *Chambers Twentieth Century Dictionary*, a newer version than his father's, was one thousand, six hundred and forty-nine pages thick. Phen knew this because Mrs Smit had often given them this information during her weekly threat to make them copy each and every page. He watched her lift it and bring it down three times on her desk. Aardvark to zythum smashed in her quest for silence.

"Thank you."

Phen moved to sit down.

"It's not a one-verse poem."

The class groaned. No longer sure if they were allowed to laugh, they felt comfortable in sharing their teacher's pain. Mrs Smit exhaled wearily, appreciative of the class's understanding.

"Alright, just the last verse."

"I … s-s-s-shall … be … telling … this … with … a … s-s-s-s-sigh / S-s-s-somewhere … ages … and … ages … h-h-h-hence."

"Alright! Alright! Enough! Class, open your books. We will *all* read to the end of the last verse."

Two roads diverged in the wood, and I –
I took the one less travelled by,
And that has made all the difference.

Phen sat down slowly. The consummate reader, the boy who had read more books than anyone else in the class, had needed their help to finish a poem. Their chorus of words had been sing-song and sarcastic. With a hot mist rising in his head, he moved towards the edge of the inkwell. Maybe it was Mrs Smit's barbed comment earlier that made Vernon MacArthur need to show he wasn't just academically bright, but street-smart too. As Phen dropped himself into the darkness, he heard Vernon address the class. He didn't turn around but imagined him standing with a thumb behind each lapel of his blazer.

"He doesn't get his school clothes from McCullagh & Bothwell, or John Orr's, or even Anstey's. He buys everything from Stuttafords."

13

Simpatico

/sim'patikeu/ adjective

The rest of the week came in dislocated pieces that refused to fit. Not that Phen tried too hard. He stopped battling to make sense of things and just watched. His life was zig-zagging of its own accord anyway. Everyone spoke their half-truths and he just nodded. He began to listen with his eyes. He now understood that when Mr Trentbridge "Boyo-ed" him with a firm slap on the back, he was also asking him not to mention that he'd found his flying duck tiepin in Zelda's flat. He'd uncovered it in the twisted strings of her shaggy white carpet next to the flattened bean bag. A wing had snapped off as the thick heel of his school shoe had squashed it flat.

"Well," said Zelda. "Stuck to a tie, I suppose, it wasn't flying anywhere anyway."

Straight after that on the way down from number forty-three, Mrs Kaplan caught him in the lift. She said she'd heard and offered him and his family a prayer. The words bounced around in the wooden box and ended perfectly with their arrival on the ground floor. The fact that he couldn't understand a word of her Yiddish seemed to make it all the more important and mystical. Like doctors, God had his own language. He pulled the metal grid back for her and she placed her hand on top of his head and squeezed. He wasn't sure if she wanted to force something in or out. As he peered down her sleeve he knew what was written underneath her forearm. Mr Trentbridge's eldest daughter, who was as precocious as Phen was shy, had asked her about it while she stood in the foyer waiting for her son. Mrs Kaplan had looked down at the tattooed markings and then into the eyes of the little girl. "That," she said, "is the telephone number of Hell."

Everyone was talking about the new tenant who had moved into Ziggy's old flat. It had been thought no one could be more exotic than the long-haired saxophone player, but Romolo Rossi, fresh from Florence, came close. He was immediately renamed Romeo in acknowledgement of his tight pants and sleek hair, jet black and shaped in the front like the bonnet of Margaret Wallace's parents' Pontiac. His T-shirt shamelessly revealed all, including the packet of cigarettes he kept tucked up his sleeve. The fact that he preened in public, often using the mirror in the crowded lift to admire himself, was considered outrageous by all.

"Catholic," said Mr Trentbridge.

Another layer of gossip was added when the caretaker, a man who normally kept to cleaning, plumbing and the spaghetti electricity board, declared that he'd have to watch him. As he scratched his one lamb chop of a sideburn, he said he'd heard that the new tenant liked a little bit of dark chocolate. Previously Phen's thoughts might have wandered to the potential evils of Cadbury but now he was beginning to understand the code. He saw the nudge of the elbow and the knowing smiles from all the men. They were in his tiny office, not just to collect their mail.

"Have to be careful," he said, handing out envelopes. "They sent a government inspector to check only last week. They call it the Immorality Act. I call it something else! Myself, I'm a milk-chocolate man."

Phen laughed along with the others.

Although the Leb returned to school and held his ground, it wasn't quite the same. The damage had been done. It would now be a more personal, one-on-one battle. The rest of the class were more muted in their support. His lisp hardly brought a reaction and even when he taped Mrs Smit's lunchbox to her ruler, the snickering was restrained. She stared at it like a fisherman with a surprise catch, yet fear flashed through the class more than hilarity. They'd lost their nerve. Vernon MacArthur, now deeply insecure about his future, offered his Swiss army knife to cut it free.

Phen continued to hide behind the Leb even though his cover was blown. His moves were less precise as he sensed he was of little or no importance to her. Mrs Smit had decimated him almost to the point of non-existence. His evaporation was confirmed by all the others. They didn't talk to him at break or include him in any of the teams. He tried to place himself equidistant between groups so he couldn't be accused of attempting to attach himself to anyone. He wasn't even important enough to make fun of any more. The last act of acknowledging his presence was the strawberry jam someone had scraped off their sandwich and into his history book. *Paul Kruger's Republic 1883–1900* would forever stay sealed by this red, sweet-smelling stickiness. He suspected Philip Denton. He'd overheard him saying he wanted to fuck up Stuttafords but wasn't sure he was worth the effort. "Like smacking candyfloss," he concluded.

"You are a somewhat withered oak today," said Miss Delmont. This time there was no poncho. Instead she wore a flowing tunic with a round cut at the neck. It was the sort of thing the Indians wore at the East African Pavilion when they served your curry. "Do your roots perhaps need water?"

He tried to smile. She stuck her arms out sideways and began to droop. The swirling mist, impossible to stop, moved into his head. Although he was far from his desk he went down the inkwell anyway. It was becoming a habit. Like with the black curtain behind the stage, he could just take a step to the side and disappear. A tear in his mind he could slip through. He would still be standing there but really be somewhere else.

"Chin up!" She patted him firmly on his trunk before spinning around to Margaret Wallace. "Sweetness, you're Titania, queen of the fairies, not a Barbie doll. Use those wings. Let's see them flap!"

Headmaster Kock made a brief entrance. He kept telling the children to sit, but only after they all stood up for him. Although his suit jacket was buttoned, his tie was a little long and tongued over his belt buckle. He walked in a slow circle around the entire hall, inspecting his troops. Occasionally he'd stop at a flower made of crinkle paper or a stuffed rabbit to give his approval – "Nice, very nice. Spot on!" – and then continue his tour. He was particularly impressed with the hollow head of a donkey made from cardboard and covered with the panels of brown carpet tiles. He poked his fingers through its sightless eyes. "Excellent, excellent." By the time he'd completed his circle he was standing in front of Miss Delmont and a tree with green baize up to its waist.

"I hope you asked the owner before you pulled that off his snooker table!"

"For never anything can be amiss, when simpleness and duty tender it," the director replied.

The headmaster didn't know what to do with the deep

bow that followed and stepped back to ensure he didn't stand on her hair. English was Mr Kock's second language. He preferred Afrikaans, which, to his mind, got straight to the point. English was finicky. And when people did this Ye Olde English thing it intimidated and irritated in equal measure. He had hoped for a more South African play – maybe a re-enactment of the Battle of Blood River and the slaughter of the Zulus. Instead, he had fairies and donkey heads and half-dressed trees. He tucked his tie tip behind his belt and stared at Phen one more time.

"Good luck. I hope the drought in your forest is soon broken."

Phen returned home to find Pal watching a corn cricket. It had lost two front legs on the right side and one on the left rear but otherwise seemed no worse for wear. Phen wasn't sure if his dog or the cat from number two was the cause. Either way, the armoured insect now jumped sideways. Although it could see the open door to the balcony, it could not stop ramming itself against the wall next to it. Phen felt simpatico with this strange ballet as he scooped up the cricket with a comic book and flicked it into the garden.

It wasn't much better in his father's bedroom. The patient no longer had the agility to sit upright and stretch for the Off button. Once the end of the reel was reached, it spun continuously until someone came into the room. Phen found that the brown tape had unravelled, first across the chair, then onto the floor and finally under the bed. It lay in vaguely concentric heaps as it tried to head for the wardrobe.

"I need the WC. The comfort station. The can. The head. The lavatory. Privy. Latrine, cloakroom, restroom, loo, bog. The throne."

Going to the bathroom had become a matter of pride.

Especially as his mother had had to go back to work and Mairead was forced to deputise. The slow shuffle took forever with every loose parquet strip being cursed along the way. His father had become so annoyed he'd kicked two out and refused to let them be placed back. The daunting indent lay just before the smooth tiles of the toilet. Clutching his pyjama pants in one hand and his walking stick in the other, he'd poke at the offending canyon.

"I fear not the Great Rift Valley."

As he leaped across he'd lift his foot a quarter of an inch higher and give an imperceptible hop. The only sign of additional movement was a slight ripple in his ruby-coloured dressing gown. The threadbare silk rolled up to his shoulders and splashed against his neck. The sound of flushing meant Phen had to open the door. His father could lift his pants up to his knees, but no further. It was a complicated task to help the folded body into an upright position while simultaneously lifting the bottom of his pants. The drawstring waistband often hooked on the toilet handle and occasionally the belt of his gown ended in the bowl.

By the time his father made it back to bed he was exhausted, and the waxy yellow of his skin full of per-spiration. He looked like a candle melting drop by drop. Immediately the damp flannel was placed on his forehead like a headband and the oxygen mask fixed over his face. The brass knob on top of the cylinder was turned to full, his sunken cheeks flattened and pushed downwards by the force of the air. The loud hiss made talking difficult but they tried anyway. His father gave a sarcastic thumbs up and tried to pull a tough-guy face.

"Mission accomplished," he said.

Mairead spent much of her time circling without actually entering the bedroom. A Scottish vulture, according to his father, who enjoyed riding the thermals of his discomfort. She stayed within earshot, hoping not to hear anything. She tidied, shopped, cooked then reverted to the chair in the corner of the lounge to read, knit and listen to the radio. Every hour, on the hour, she opened the door and called through the crack to see if Dennis wanted anything. Dennis normally didn't hear anyway; when he did he usually said uninterrupted sleep was at the top of his list.

Phen enjoyed having insider status. Afraid and purposeful, he'd come home and head straight for the darkened bedroom. Mairead would be standing over his lunch and a perfectly set table as he whisked past. He had to see his father first. If he was asleep, Phen did a reconnaissance patrol. Where was that second slipper? The reading glasses had to be unhooked from the lampshade, the saucer pushed back as it cantilevered over the edge. If he was awake, there were sentences to be traded, normally short and clipped, as Phen wiped his chin where the spittle, iced by the oxygen, had turned crusty like a frozen waterfall.

He still despised the tape recorder, but in that gloomy room, much of its power had been ceded back to him. Only he had the ability to make it work. *His* thumb pressed Play and his fingers set the volume. To remind the silver box who was boss, Phen continued to deliberately mangle and twist the tape as he threaded it. Although the tape recorder was still the voice of choice, more and more Phen determined when it spoke.

His grandmother reasserted her authority on his exit by insisting all homework was to be done after lunch and before the dog was taken for a walk. This assignment would be accompanied by absolute silence, a straight back, an elbow-free table and her knitting needles. Mairead would move from her corner chair to the dining-room table with the grim determination of a Depression-era farmer forced to go west. She'd begin her migration by sighing loudly and rocking herself off her chair. Heavily laden with handbag, knitting carryall, shawl, teacup and book, her body would lean forward and advance. Once at her destination, she'd meticulously unpack her balls of wool as if they were her only provisions for the long winter.

"Ah dinnae ken," she'd say every afternoon. "Ah dinnae ken. It's a jersey for your father, truth be told I have no idea of the size. He's shrinking every day."

His mother's return from work led to a military handover of responsibility. "Dennis fine. Homework done. Dustbin emptied. Bathroom latch still broken. Caretaker informed." Supper and the quantity thereof was confirmed. Although there were never any leftovers, Mairead always explained that eating yesterday's food never killed anyone. "A little starvation," she'd say, "made for a fine sauce." Feeling guilty, his mother would ask if she would like to stay for dinner and Mairead would stoically decline. "Not sure there's enough. Plus, I like to walk while there's a little light." Having suitably punished her daughter she'd gather her "bits and pieces" which were "strewn all the way to Timbuktu and back again".

"She means well."

Phen watched his mother crouch down to his height as the heels of Mairead's sensible shoes clipped away.

"How's school?"

"Fine."

"Look what Mr Lansdown gave me to give you."

It was a simple silver cross. She put it in the palm of his hand and let the fine links of the chain fall and curl around it in a tight circle.

"Why?"

"Well, you know, he's a lay preacher and a very nice man. I think he just thought it might help."

Phen was furious. Now even his mother's boss was interfering. Like Mr Trentbridge he also wore too much aftershave. Initially he'd thought that strong, stringent smell was the mark of successful and powerful men. Now he understood it was just another way to perfume the truth. At the company's Zoo-Day-Away, Mr Lansdown had sat on a tractor and pretended to be a farmer although his teeth were far too straight and white. He'd made Phen sit next to him and go for a drive in the engineless contraption. He'd bounced and swayed and sung "Old MacDonald Had a Farm", obviously thinking that because he didn't talk back Phen had the mental age of a four-year-old. He'd called him "partner" and insisted on helping him down, unaware he was fully capable of climbing off a stationary tractor himself.

"What am I meant to do with it?"

"Wear it, if you want to."

"Around my neck?"

"That's where they normally go … under your shirt. No one sees it."

Phen wasn't sure about religion. Like his grandmother's porridge it was a lumpy affair. And like that porridge, when he sought a little sugar, he found salt. He felt attracted to Jesus yet wasn't sure who to picture in his mind when he prayed. He particularly enjoyed the colour illustration in his Bible of Jesus preaching the Sermon on the Mount. With the wind tugging at his white, flowing robes and a camel in the background, he looked exactly like Lawrence of Arabia. And if you peered closer, you could see the yellow haze around his head was not caused by the setting sun, but rather by his own inner warmth. It was no wonder the woman was stretching out her baby towards him, begging for a blessing.

However, he could not bring himself to look at the same person hanging on a cross a few chapters later. Blood poured from his hands and feet and red dots stippled where his crown of thorns dug deep. How could this happen to a man who'd asked you to love your enemies? Mary was there, hugging the base of the cross, but where was everyone else from the Mount? He'd checked the page many times; the crowd was full of huge men with broad shoulders and massive beards. One minute they were waving palm fronds and hallelujahing him, the next they were looking the other way while a Roman soldier stuck a spear into his side.

Worst of all, the man on the cross with his ribcage forced forward and his empty stomach pushed back reminded him of his father. He, too, was now just protruding bone barely held together by a streched and yellowing skin. This Jesus also couldn't turn a tape recorder off. Or go to the bathroom by himself. You didn't want to burden this man with your prayers and pleas for help. He had enough on his plate already. He wanted the Lawrence of Arabia Jesus, but he couldn't get the sick and dying one out of his mind.

"So," said his mother, "here's a coincidence, you know, a fluke. Mr Lansdown will be preaching at our church on Sunday morning and I said we'd go and hear him."

Phen's anger continued to build. He was irritated that she thought he didn't know what coincidence meant and floored that she'd said "our church". She hardly ever went unless it was Christmas or Easter and now it was suddenly "our" church. She'd forced him into Sunday School on the basis that she would also become a regular churchgoer. He'd wanted to meet them on the tiny lawn next to the vestibule, like all the other children. After the service, tea was served and sandwiches without their crusts were offered. Here all the neatly dressed families huddled together. Everyone greeted you politely and wished you a good week when they said goodbye. This, he felt, was what normal was supposed to be.

"Uncle Ed will pop over to give us a break."

"I won't go to Sunday School. Just the service." He draped the cross around a large Outspan orange that sat in the fruit bowl. Not wanting to be too sacrilegious, he made sure it hung straight.

Phen felt a need to punish his mother for all the extraneous people she was bringing into their lives. Whatever was happening to them, whatever they were going through, he wanted to keep it private. She stood up slowly, rubbed her stiff thighs and said nothing. This was, in effect, confirmation of their deal. Phen was learning that silence in place of a negative equalled a positive. He lifted Pal's lead from the hat rack and stormed out the door, trying hard to show his displeasure. Zelda and Romeo were sitting outside on the low wall that offered a marginal protection to Duchess Court's slim garden. If you can smoke thoughtfully, that's what they were doing as they eyed each other in a professional way. Romeo's bright yellow Ducati was parked brazenly on the pavement, forcing pedestrians to walk around it. Zelda waved with her small finger and the Italian nodded; Phen headed to the park without pausing.

He decided to place his fury on Heb Thirteen Two. He'd

still not seen him. Yet whenever he went for a walk Phen thought he was being watched, maybe even followed. He tried everything to catch him out, even crawling behind the chrysanthemums outside Idlewide Mansions. He'd pulled Pal close and hidden behind the bushes. Someone had kept a steady fifty yards behind him no matter how fast or slow Phen had walked. However, the only person to stroll past was an off-duty bus driver whistling softly. He'd undone the two top buttons of his uniform and carried his shopping in a white plastic bag. Eyes at ground level, Phen watched a large tin of Lucky Star pilchards swing by. He waited patiently. Nothing. A fat rock pigeon mock-cooed him.

He arrived at church two days later in pretty much the same mood. He didn't know where to direct his ire, so he splashed it over everything. His mother was very grateful that Ed had suggested he drive them. Phen showed his thanks by slamming the door and eliciting a "Steady" from his normally compliant uncle. They sat in a pew second from the front – just the same as at school. He'd tried to peel off earlier, but his mother had insisted on dragging him down the royal-blue carpet. Now they both sat holding their prayer books, waiting for the minister to explain what to do with them.

Still, by the time Mr Lansdown climbed the wrought-iron steps to the raised lectern, Phen was well hidden. He had a tried-and-trusted strategy. The large lady in front of him made a perfect barrier. Not only was she three times the size of the Leb, but she also wore a yellow-and-brown hat that settled on her head like a cottage pie, its slightly burned crust flowing over her ears. Mr Lansdown bobbed and weaved to catch sight of Phen. Head down, he refused to show himself. It was even better when the congregation was asked to pray. Kneeling comfortably on the grey cushion, he disappeared entirely, his spindly knees making deep holes in the accommodating pillow. With his head against the pew in front, his nose filled with the smell of wood polish. And with everyone insisting he close his eyes, it wasn't too dissimilar from going down the inkwell.

"Phen! Phen!"

He must've drifted off. It was the combination of his mother's whispered exclamations and the pulling of his ear that brought him back to reality. Everyone was already sitting back upright in their seats and waiting. Someone in their row cleared his throat, confirming that piety needed to be punctual. Phen sprang up, exposing himself momentarily to Mr Lansdown, who smiled. The sweep of white reminded him of the ivory knuckleduster Carlos de Sousa had brought to class. Light broke through the stained-glass windows as Mr Lansdown gripped both sides of the lectern. He lifted his chin unto the Lord and let the shaft of dust beams mingle with his blond hair.

> *The Lord is my helper;*
> *I will not fear;*
> *What can man do to me?*

It occurred to Phen that man could do quite a lot, not that he was paying much attention. If you could swoon in church that's what the lady in front of him did. She didn't fall sideways with the back of her hand against her forehead; instead, she tilted as far back as she could go. Her cottage pie was inches from Phen's nose as she purred at the preacher. Her heavy breathing lifted at the end of each sentence, confirming her state of rapture. With chiselled torso, a wide square jaw and smouldering eyes, he was the

Charlton Heston of deacons. He drove the lectern like a chariot.

There were exhortations to faith and godliness. There were requests that we make our paths straight and narrow. The congregation was asked to endeavour to be perfect in every way. Everyone had to look diligently into themselves and root out bitterness; to endure chastening, and our conversations have to be without covetousness. Finally the gathered group was beseeched to trust in good conscience and to carry the light that is eternal within themselves. Phen was so hidden, he was almost under the back of the woman's hat when he heard the concluding sentence.

"Let brotherly love continue. And here I quote Hebrews 13:2: 'Be not forgetful to entertain strangers; for thereby some have entertained angels unawares.'"

As Phen lifted his head, the clouds once more parted and bathed the whole church in a rich, creamy light. Golden shafts poured through the windows just as they did in the biblical illustration of Daniel in the lion's den. He remembered their manes on fire, yet they did not pounce. They circled and circled but were made powerless by the holy luminescence. Mr Lansdown finally released the podium and let his hands float up higher and higher so they too could be illuminated. The woman in front of Phen gasped and straightened in a kind of ecstasy.

"Let us pray," Mr Lansdown said.

Over lunch afterwards Phen ate little and said even less. Could it be possible? Could the man in the park be an angel? Why else would he say his name was Heb Thirteen Two? Could it be a coincidence, a fluke? It all made sense and was complete nonsense. What angel needed underarm deodorant? What messenger from God would sing badly and show off dance steps he'd learned at Arthur Murray?

Why the felt hat and no socks? The detonated hair? What celestial being had a scar under his chin from a broken bottle? Where was he anyway? Was he gone? Had he just been passing through? What about the feeling Phen had of being followed or watched? The only solution was to stop thinking about it. His brain was too full. He hid his peas behind the mashed potato and obscured the view further with a half-eaten chop. Uncle Ed asked about the service and was a little taken aback by the emotional response of his mother. She checked that the corners of her mouth were clean with her starched Sunday serviette before gushing.

"Beautiful, just beautiful."

Unable to hide the jealousy in his voice Ed then directed the question specifically to Phen, who rolled his shoulders ambiguously and brought his knife and fork together, signifying both the meal and the conversation were over. A strange three-way silence followed. His mother seemed happier in a dreamy sort of way, yet that clearly made Uncle Ed sadder. Everyone stared at the gravy bowl, waiting for a sign of what to do next. In an attempt to re-establish his credentials, Ed decided to take the initiative. He folded his napkin into a half, then a quarter and then almost an eighth. Not quite flat, it opened its mouth towards the side plate.

"I have an idea," he said. He took a five-rand note out his pocket and slipped it into the gaping white cloth. "Why doesn't Phen take a friend for a milkshake this afternoon? What's the place he always talks about?"

"The Milky Lane." His mother was used to talking on his behalf.

"Or that ice-cream place?"

"Italian Gelato."

"That one. It's on me. Good for him to get out a little."

"That's an awful lot of money. He doesn't need five rand."

"In the circumstances, I don't think a little largesse would go amiss."

Phen should have been astonished, flabbergasted, even bewildered. This was treasure way beyond his reckoning. Instead that little hammer of anger began tapping again. He didn't like being spoken about as if he wasn't there and he knew he didn't have a friend to share his uncle's sudden generosity with. He didn't understand the word but if five rand was involved, he presumed it meant the same as large-ness. He'd never owned a five-rand note in his life. Just the maths of what he *could* buy with it jumbled his mind. What he really wanted to do with it was casually pull it out his pocket and hear all the whistles of amazement. He wanted Margaret Wallace to know that although his parents didn't own a Pontiac, or any car for that matter, he was still a man of substance. If his calculations were right, he was worth twenty milkshakes and twice that number of ice creams.

"Maybe Vakis?" his mother said, relenting and passing him the note as if it was somehow hers to give.

Phen took the note without looking at it and slipped it into his shorts, not sure if he was being bribed, if his absence was being bought. A few months ago he would've dashed straight to Jimmy the Greek. They would've double-scooped, always with the strawberry on the top. 'Never vanilla. It's sissy flavour.' After that it would probably have been the Florian Cafe for a sit-down toasted cheese. From outside on the first-floor balcony, Hillbrow breathed a little easier. The elevation helped release the congestion on the corner of Kotze and Twist. While pedestrians waited six deep for the lights to change, you rolled the stringy bits of melted cheese around your fork and above their heads. 'Crazy! It's sandwich. Why eat same way steak?'

Uncle Ed and his mother saw him to the door with great ceremony.

"Be careful," she said.

"He's going shopping, not trying to find the Northwest Passage." His uncle was trying to sound like his father.

Phen was surprised how awkward the folded note felt. He carried it gently in his hand in his pocket, careful not to wrinkle it. He held it like a small bird, occasionally pulling it out to give it some air. Jimmy the Greek would be the only person to share it with, but since Phen's reading of "The Road Not Taken", he'd kept his distance even more. A friend with two nicknames, Spaz and Stuttafords, was just too heavy a burden to bear. Phen thought Jimmy had waved at him once on the playground. He couldn't be sure, though. Margaret Wallace had been standing nearby and he knew Jimmy fancied her. Everyone did.

He stood outside the entrance to the Chelsea Hotel, tied his laces twice and pretended to be interested in the acorns at the base of the last remaining oak on the street. He dug his nail into their leathery shells and prised their cup-shaped hats off. Phen thought of Heb with one stuck on his forehead and wondered where he was. "Oooommmm," he soundlessly chanted to himself. Mrs Smit had told them the real name for the hat was a cupule. The curtains pulled back on the third floor where Jimmy lived. He waited twenty minutes; no one came down. Phen wondered if it would've made any difference to the Greek that a rich boy was waiting down below. If his absence from Duchess Court had been bought, he was ashamed to admit he was willing to buy a friend too. The noise of Hillbrow's traffic and the flick of its neon contrived an invitation. As he turned to go, a pigeon cooed him on his way.

It soon became obvious that the money would not be spent. Too many options paralysed him and an individual purchase that went into his mouth didn't warrant breaking the note. He loitered outside the Flying Saucer restaurant, indicating that he *could* sit at one of the outside tables if he so chose. Very continental, he reminded himself, noticing that the red-and-white check of the umbrellas matched the tablecloths. The five rand did, however, elevate his browsing at Estoril Books. He genuinely had the means to purchase a book or two and even lingered meaningfully in the hardcover section. Phen audaciously lifted up coffee-table books, went to the High Sierra with Ansel Adams, the Midwest with Norman Rockwell and joined Henri Cartier-Bresson on the streets of Paris. It was Gerhard Gronefeld's *Understanding Animals* that made him page the slowest, though. According to the inside flap of the cover, Gerhard, who was born in Berlin in 1911, could reveal many surprises in the behaviour of animals. He had conducted many field experiments himself. His research projects demonstrated that we should look at our fellow inhabitants with new, fresh eyes.

Phen closed the book and placed it back on the shelf. From the cover, a sacred grey langur from the Himalayas stared back at him. The black face was marooned in a thick mane of steely white hair. Its deep eyes would not let him go. They mirrored an honesty Phen could not ignore. It was time to admit he couldn't spend his five rand because he wasn't looking for a book, or magazine or comic. And the bare walls of his bedroom would stay that way because he wasn't looking for a poster either. He was searching for Heb Thirteen Two.

When he reached the park it was already dusk. Time in bookshops behaved differently to anywhere else. When he'd stepped outside and realised the whole afternoon was gone, he'd started to run to Nugget Hill. Down Banket and into Kapteijn, he began to sprint. By the time he'd crossed Catherine and reached Primrose, he was panting heavily. Everyone he passed looked behind to see what he was running from; no one presumed he was racing *to* something. Finally he arrived, gasping and wheezing. He bent over and stuck his fingers through the wire strands of the fence.

It was a silly barrier more for show than anything else; the fence was barely a yard high. Anyone could grab the metal posts and use the diamond-shaped mesh as footholds to climb over. Besides, on the south side, near the waterfall, there was nothing at all. You could scramble up from Hadfield Avenue and just step over a single row of logs. His mother had explained that decent people didn't go into parks at night. Once, he'd seen an excited sleeping bag worming itself across the lawn as it battled to get traction on the night-time dew. The moon had supplied just enough light for Phen to watch the bag rise and fall faster and faster as the two bodies inside slapped at each other.

He was tired of being told what to do and tired of not understanding why. Most of all he was weary of always being on the outside, of having to wait for permission to be invited in. He had five rand in his pocket and he was the man of the house. With one crisp leap, Phen was over the fence.

Away from the streetlights, his eyes had to adjust to the dark. The park was the last outpost of black left. Its unlit strip ran the whole length of Primrose Road, defiant even as tenants flicked switches and turned their apartments into boxes of light. They peered out to confirm the darkness then drew their curtains shut to keep it at bay. Phen moved to the edge of the park and looked down at Saratoga Avenue. Even the huge Catholic Cathedral of Christ the King looked small, the roadhouse dinky. The park felt much, much higher than it had ever been before. He was on the Hillbrow high sierra. He parted the branches of the young willow tree and stepped inside.

"Heb. Heb Thirteen Two?"

Inside it felt like a heavy blanket had been thrown over him. No light penetrated. He sat with his chin on his knees and held the five-rand note tightly in his palm. Where there should've been fear, a growing feeling of sanctuary emerged. His senses calmed and, at the same time, became more acute. Far away, a man demanded his dog return and a car radio arrived and departed within one chorus of "Strawberry Fields Forever". He was alone, yet in the right place. His job was to wait. Patience turned to serenity. It was the first time in his life he could honestly say he wasn't afraid of the dark.

Like its behaviour in the bookshop, time once again lost its normal calibration. Phen had no idea how long it took for the light to pierce his leafy shelter. It broke in from above and wrapped his head in a faint gold. Like Mr Lansdown, he held out his palms and let it do the same to his hands. The purple five-rand note turned transparent. Jan van Riebeeck's middle parting and the Voortrekker Monument glowed. The oxen pulling the wagon in the right-hand corner started to move, eager to complete their journey north. He looked up into the light but it was too bright. Blinded, he broke from the willowed womb and made his way through the drooping branches. Using the line of logs that marked the park's perimeter, he stumbled into the darkness.

Distance gave perspective. When he turned, there, high up in the acacia, he saw the molten glow. At first he thought the branch was on fire, but as his eyes adjusted he realised the source was contained, even as it breathed shafts of honeyed yellow. The light burst out and down, yet somehow was cocooned. Its form was human, although not totally so. As it stretched, a whiteness spread from both sides of its body to the edges of its unfurled arms. Two wings gleamed momentarily before folding inwardly again. On top of the head that stared straight into the night was a felt hat, tilted slightly to the left.

14

Enigmatic
/in-ig'mat-ik/ adjective

No one had to tell Phen that what he'd seen was to be kept a secret. He knew that instinctively. Who would he tell anyway? Besides, he could never trust himself to do the job. It wasn't the stuttering or stammering that worried him; he knew the words did not exist to explain what he saw. No one could describe the inexplicable or wrap a mystery in sentences stripped and borrowed from the world of the normal. What he'd seen was his alone to keep. The moment came with that deep vow. In the telling, the magic would seep out anyway. It was enough that he knew the truth.

This knowledge didn't necessarily make Phen more courageous; however, it did allow him to put his fear somewhere else. He now knew a parallel universe existed not just in his mind but in reality. It provided a place of safekeeping to store his deepest anxieties and his most exhilarating dreams. He'd often been chided for having too much of an imagination. Now he wondered if he had enough. Clearly there were other truths, other worlds that lay beyond his tiny, cramped existence. What he'd seen, what he'd witnessed, was big and powerful and full of light. The secret made him feel anchored, even if he didn't know to what. And that pushed much of the panic to one side. He now knew, even if you couldn't always glimpse it, that the world was more than the mundane detail it pushed in your face every day. Now, he felt if you changed your angle, perhaps you could see forever.

Phen needed a new, unimpeded perspective. He was standing in the middle of an intersection. School and the school play were driving full speed down one road. On the other, his father's ill health kept its foot on the accelerator. There were no stop streets as he waited for the inevitable collision. His mother spent more time at home than at work. Mairead continually circled, sometimes the flat, sometimes the entire block. Shopping for lunch could take her two hours. Uncle Edward popped in every night and sometimes even in the mornings just to check up. The man of the house spent one entire evening behind the large curtain listening to "Consider Your Verdict" and no one noticed.

To his utter shame, his thin frame, with tight fists, still lay awake at night and worried about the play. Phen knew he should be above this. He was a boy who'd seen an angel. He'd glimpsed the other side, pierced the veil, yet stayed chained to his potential humiliation. It was meant to be a comedy, although as Oberon and Titania danced around his trunk, it felt as if the purpose of the play was to mock him. He was hidden and on full display. As Puck and Peaseblossom swung from his sagging branches, how could they not be sniggering at his skinny arms? It didn't matter that Miss Delmont told them not to hang on for too long: Philip Denton was nearly thirteen and weighed a ton.

It also didn't help that Philip was jealous because Margaret Wallace, as Titania, spent a lot of time leaning against the tree. It was the closest Phen had ever been to her. The warmth of her body made his imagination boil. At one rehearsal she'd been forced to hug the trunk. His body had stiffened and his branches had shot up in surprised surrender. Two leaves unglued themselves and fluttered to the stage floor. In the changing rooms afterwards, Denton had thrown his fairy hat into the corner and asked if trees got woodies.

The only positive of the play was that Jimmy the Greek seemed prepared to talk to him if he was wearing his donkey head. He'd been a surprise choice for Bottom since the part involved a substantial amount of talking. Mrs Smit had been particularly mortified. Miss Delmont had, however, reminded her of the need for volume, especially with a head encased in cardboard. Besides, she had taken the role of narrator and would ensure the audience didn't lose track. Jimmy's eyes peered at Phen through the long tunnel of the donkey's mouth. A papier mâché knot in the tree allowed his left eye to look back.

"Crazy, crazy play!"

"I know."

"Old-time pixie story like hippie-drug party in garden. Love potion same as Durban Gold and crushed pills you get upstairs at Narnia Cafe behind counter. Also make you fly with the fairies … Be happy you don't have to say 'shivering shocks shall break the locks'. Delmont say I'm the donkey Bottom, the Leb call me the horse's arse. He's sour 'cause minstrel don't say much. Wear stripy pants too big. Look like he shat a brick in the back. Not even strings on his guitar."

Phen agreed. He peered through the wooden hole and hoped Jimmy could see him nodding. The donkey's head came closer and tilted upwards. From a distance it must've looked like he was trying to eat what little greenery remained.

"I heard," he whispered, "Mrs Smit make Leb's costume so he looks extra stupid. Hat like crashed flying saucer."

Phen was thankful for any conversation. Normally he just stood alone in the middle of the stage while people moved around him. Sometimes even Miss Delmont forgot he was in there. He'd stand for hours before she'd remember and suddenly shout, "Get that tree a chair." Now it was a little different. Wrapped in green felt, planks of wood and paper leaves, he thought about the acacia tree in the park and the light that had shone from it. Time didn't matter too much. Even as his legs became leaden and his arms chafed under the wooden struts, he didn't mind. He was somewhere else.

"You're a trouper, Olivier junior. Have your roots grown through the stage floor and found the water they were seeking?"

As he stood with outstretched arms and wrapped legs, Phen wondered what to do next with his revelation. It had been nearly a week; the golden light burned as fiercely in his mind as ever, yet he feared a revisit might extinguish it. What if Heb was no longer there? Would that make the memory stronger or weaker? What if Phen had witnessed some metamorphosis, a precursor to Heb disappearing entirely? Maybe that yellow light was now travelling through space, its glow registering for a moment in the lens of some vast telescope. He'd read somewhere about an observatory in Hawaii that could look all the way to the beginning of time.

Phen peered through the knot in the trunk to the clock on the far wall. The school day was nearly over. Besides his fear that Heb might no longer be there, he worried if this was a planned manifestation or was he culpable of the act of spying? He was sure of what he'd observed but this didn't stop his growing pangs of guilt. Confused and contrite, he pulled his eye from the hole.

"Right!" Miss Delmont once more clapped her hands high in the air. This time she dramatically brought them together above both shoulders with a Spanish spin of her body. "Let's finish off with the grand finale! Everyone on stage with your accoutrements. Mr Visser, esquire, bring your crutch too. We shall wrap it in purple crinkle paper. The strange beasts of the forest are allowed to hobble, provided they are colourful."

Margaret Wallace tucked in closely. Philip tugged the tree's branch down painfully. Jimmy the Greek played for laughs with his donkey head worn sideways, and the Leb strummed his banjo like an exaggerated Elvis. Hettie Hattingh rearranged the flowers on the front of her head while Vernon MacArthur undid them from behind.

"When you are all quite ready? … Thank you … Now where is my Portuguese Puck?"

Carlos de Sousa made his way to the centre of the stage. He had been another surprising piece of casting. His thick Lisbon accent would normally have banished him deep into the background. Two orange horns grew from his Brylcreemed wedge like the tips of carrots seeking air. He was not comfortable in a leotard and was very conscious of where it bulged. He held a flute which was really Leana van Wyk's recorder. Every time he put the instrument to his mouth she pulled a face. He centred himself in front of the tree and sighed.

"Now remember you are a mischievous sprite. Full of cheek and humour. You're shrewd, a merry wanderer of the night. This is your chance to wrap up the whole play. You talk directly to the audience and apologise for anything that might have offended them. And you suggest that they all pretend it was a dream."

Carlos wiped his mouth then blew a few mournful

notes on the recorder. He bowed, the tightness of his leotard stopping him from bending too low.

> *If we shadows have offended,*
> *Think but this, and all is mended,*
> *That you have but slumb'red here*
> *While these visions did appear.*
> *And this weak and idle theme,*
> *No more yielding than a dream,*
> *Gentles, do not reprehend.*
> *If you pardon, we will mend.*

Before Miss Delmont had even dismissed them, Phen knew what he had to do. He would not pretend it was a dream; he hadn't slumb'red there. It was no weak and idle theme. It was time to go back to Nugget Hill. He would confront this Arthur Murrayed angel who kept Life Savers in his hair. His oak had evolved from costume to carpentry so only Mr Swindon, the silent groundkeeper who was good with his hands, could de-tree him. He wedged apart the tongue–and-groove planks from around the base with a screwdriver, then quietly circled Phen as he unwrapped the felt. Finally, he gently pulled the brown-painted tubes off Phen's arms, careful not to lose any more leaves.

"In a rush."

Phen nodded. Not that it was a question. This three-word statement was the first time he'd ever heard the groundsman talk when not spoken to first. The pleasant smell of earth and grass surrounded him as he stacked the wood into two neat piles. Here was a man who moved at his own pace, who didn't let time bully him. Mr Swindon detached a piece of sticky tape from the schoolboy's sock and pointed to the cap folded in his blazer pocket.

"Once that's on your head and your tie is straight, you're ready to go."

Pal was, unusually, behind both the Grundig and the curtains. On hearing his master drop his school bag, it took some time to untangle himself. By the time he sniffed at the scuffed black school shoes, the front door was open again and his collar attached. To ensure his master couldn't change his mind, he tugged at his leash until they were well within the park gates. Once released, he immediately charged after a bulldog with a scarf around its neck, the coral-coloured linen a little feminine for its muscular body and squashed face. Suddenly it was important for Phen to feign casualness. He remembered Mr Swindon's steady, relaxed step and likewise tried to make time his own. His heart was pounding as he instructed his legs not to rush. He would amble with intent as he made his way towards the acacia. He'd read that rivers meandered and wondered if he could do the same.

"Greetings, Earthling."

Phen stopped in mid-stride and spun around. Heb was sitting on a park bench deep in the shade of the huge jacaranda. His legs were crossed, his arms spread wide. The sun reflected off the buildings that lined Primrose Terrace and backlit him slightly. The silhouette cocked its head, the hat tipped forward. Phen stalled. As excited and as relieved as he was to see Heb, he realised he'd been hoping for a more rapturous and euphoric reunion. A little levitation perhaps, or a glow that didn't come from the sun. All he could see that was different was Heb's placemat under his chin, which was now in a diamond shape.

The leather lead he'd been trailing behind him lay on the ground. It pointed towards Heb but had no source of energy at the end of it to draw him closer. He felt awkward with one end wrapped around his hand and the other lying in the freshly cut grass. He wasn't sure if there was some protocol he should follow. Should he slowly go down on his knees? Flatten himself entirely and spreadeagle himself on the ground? Did Heb know he knew? Did it even matter?

"Come here, boy!" Heb motioned to the invisible dog and slapped his lap.

Ridiculously Phen moved towards him, stood while Heb patted nothing, then sat down on the bench.

"How's the play going?"

"Fine."

"Fine terrible or fine fine?"

"Fine okay."

"When's the big night?"

"Friday."

"Anyone coming to watch?"

Phen looked sideways down his top, searching for a pulsating light.

"My father is too ill. My mother has to look after him. Uncle Edward has a business meeting and Mairead doesn't like theatre. She doesn't like the movies either, unless it's *The Sound of Music*, even if Julie Andrews looks like a boy."

"Everyone know their words?"

"I don't have any."

"I meant for those who have to speak."

"Miss Delmont says it'll be alright on the night. We have to trust the god of the theatre."

Heb began to sway from side to side as if in a trance. His eyes rolled so far back, the brilliant blue was replaced by a crisp white. He started to drool as he gnashed his teeth and whipped his head faster and faster from one side to the other. His face contorted horribly as a sneer cut across his mouth and stayed there. The locked jaw didn't stop the constant moaning of a man wanting to vomit. His hat fell onto the bench, then onto the ground. His hair became static and desperate to leave his head. His whole body jerked and jolted as his arms punched mindlessly in different directions. As instantly as he started, he stopped.

"Dionysus."

"What?"

"Dionysus. The Greek god of theatre. And of ritual madness. And of religious ecstasy. And of, by the way, wine."

"That was meant to be him?"

Heb shrugged his shoulders. "I thought you'd be good at charades."

Looking for some form of protection, Phen wrapped the lead around his arm.

"He's also the guardian of those who don't belong to conventional society. The outsiders. He symbolises the chaotic, the dangerous and the unexpected. The stuff that escapes human reason and can only be attributed to the unforeseeable action of the gods."

As Heb leaned forward to retrieve his hat, a still-stunned Phen checked the contours of his back. He was looking for something that might be folded tight against his skin. He wondered if Heb's spine didn't supply the rod from which two white feathered kites might hang.

Everything looked normal, though he couldn't be sure. The tie-dyed top was fairly tight. A psychedelic circle exploded out in a volcano of colour. Purples, reds and yellows radiated outwards and oozed down towards Heb's waist.

"New shirt?"

"Yes. Was a kaftan. Cheerfully hallucinogenic. I decided to cut it in half and make it a top. Offsets the pinstripe suit pants." He rolled the sleeves up to the tops of his shoulders. "And it can be worn in a number of different ways."

Trying hard to recover, Phen nodded politely and attempted to clear his head. He'd hoped for more than a believable act of madness and a diamond on a chin. Could that winged being be the same as this man in half a kaftan? He turned to face him again. And there, drawn with dark ink on the ball of his shoulder, like an ancient map, he saw it.

"Tattoo?"

The head half turned towards him.

"Haven't seen it before."

"It's from a time long, long ago."

"Spiral?"

The question was rewarded by Heb turning to face him directly. The face, for once clean-shaven and smooth, allowed the diamond even more prominence as it two-toned in black and grey. He pushed his hat so far back against the hedge of hair, the brim pointed to the sky.

"Is it spiralling up or down?"

"Don't know."

"Exactly."

"Exactly?"

"We're all orbiting. But in which direction?"

Heb closed his eyes and allowed the sun to hit his face. Phen noticed a hole in his left earlobe. Judging by the circumference, whatever had been in there before was large.

"I've worked it out."

It was Phen's second blurt. He'd spilled the beans. The cat didn't have his tongue; he'd let it out the bag. He was anxious and relieved at the same time. He needed this man-angel to understand that he, Phen, was different now. That he was part of a deeper knowledge.

"I said, I've worked it out." He slowly repeated the sentence, trying to give it a pointed direction.

Heb didn't react one way or the other.

"Heb Thirteen Two. Hebrews chapter thirteen, verse two. Be not forgetful to entertain strangers; for thereby some have entertained angels unawares."

"I said you'd work it out. You're smart. Well done. Gold star."

Phen had been expecting more, much more. The man he'd just accused of being an angel didn't even open his eyes. The polished, tanned face and heaving chest stayed oblivious. Catherine wheels of colour expanded and contracted at an even pace. To relax his eyes from the kaleidoscope, he moved back to the dark blue of the tattoo. It was stationary yet whirled at the same time. It reminded him of the snake's eyes in *The Jungle Book*. If he looked at it for long enough, would he be hypnotised like Mowgli? The even sweep of the continuous curve pulled him closer and closer. The entire universe sat on his shoulder.

"Cut away a nautilus shell and it's there," said Heb, still with closed eyes. "You see it in the whorls of a sunflower head. Stare up at the galaxy and that spiral stares back at you … Dab-a-dab-a-doo, yes sir, right back at you." Heb was starting to sing, "No need to be blue, yabba, yabba, yabba, do! 'Cause you're in that spiral too!" He stopped clicking his fingers and opened his eyes.

"Right!" Heb pulled his sleeves down and suddenly stood up. He then tried to touch his toes and missed by six inches. This was followed by a few half-hearted star jumps. Every time his arms windmilled up, a flash of only moderately firm midriff showed. The push-ups were even less impressive. After the first two his knees stayed on the ground as he battled to lift his shoulders off the grass. He then rolled onto his back and attempted to cycle in the air. His dirty tennis shoes pawed at the blue sky, battling to find traction.

Pal returned to check on his master. It was a brief visit. One pat on his head and he was gone again. Heb used the interruption to bring his gymnastics display to a close. He lay like a starfish on the ground before slowly getting to his knees and finally standing up. He bowed, acknowledging this physical crescendo, did two laps of honour around the bench, then used the kaftan top to dab at his non-existent perspiration.

"Nervous about the play?" he asked.

"A little. I don't want people to make fun of me. Everyone knows I'm a tree because I don't speak properly."

"Lots of other people don't have speaking parts?"

"Not because they can't talk normally."

"Everyone dances around you? The actors all act around you? You stand in the middle of the stage?"

"Yes."

"Even their dreams dream around you?"

"Yes."

"So, you are either a poor little mute tree, or the centre of the spiral. Everything spins out from you. Your choice."

Phen felt a growing frustration. He didn't know exactly what he'd expected. He had hoped it would involve some mystical angel–boy camaraderie. At least a manly arm around the shoulder, like a captain acknowledging you've just scored the winning run. Instead he felt blocked, boxed in. Outmanoeuvred. He was being asked the questions and he thought it should be the other way around. Angels weren't meant to be cornered into revealing the universe. He was looking for sacred light and heavenly music and secret doors into other worlds. Dab-a-dab-a-do wasn't cutting it.

"You appear confused."

Phen didn't know how to reply. He looked down at the Catholic cathedral, more distant yet still huge, and then at the roller-skating waitresses of the roadhouse. He'd accept assistance from anywhere.

"You must know things that normal people don't. Special stuff. Wisdom … understanding … only you …" He ran out of words.

Heb placed a profound look across his face and slowly ran both hands through his hair. There seemed to be some ceremony involved, the momentary untangling of the mass of curls also serving to straighten his thinking. "Ankles and elbows," he said. "Very few people appreciate them. Little bony pieces no one pays any attention to." Heb demonstrated by first pulling up his trousers and then his kaftan sleeves. "But wait until they stop working. Suddenly they're not just jagged bits of joinery. Can't cruise like a cushioned Homo sapien any more. Can't get food or drink into your mouth. And you can forget tennis entirely. Holy commandment number eleven: honour thy ankles and thy elbows."

15

Epiphany

/e-pif'a-ni/ noun

Mairead said the rain was very unseasonal. Which is what she said whenever it rained. Scotland had four proper seasons; you knew where you stood. In Johannesburg the weather was all over the place. Ill-disciplined and unexpected, the rain hit the lounge windows and furrowed down to the red-polished sill. From there it channelled between the grooves of the tilting stone and poured into the garden. Already the palm was surrounded in a circle of water. She parted the net curtains and tugged at the handle of the closed window, trying to seal some invisible gap.

"Look at it! It's coming in sideways now!"

This was clearly no way for rain to behave. She checked the other closed windows and moved the potpourri from the Grundig although it was in no danger of getting wet. Next she prodded the towel that was lying snake-like at the bottom of the balcony door. She hid her annoyance that it was still dry by complaining that it would soon be sopping. Mairead then questioned the state of the world which allowed a half-inch gap between door and floor to be acceptable. Craftsmanship was dying, pride in your work was seen as an old-fashioned concept. No one wanted to be an apprentice any more, it took too much time. Everyone was in a rush. It didn't matter where you were going to as long as you got there quickly.

"You don't have a spring," she said to no one in particular.

"Winter stops and summer barges in. Same with autumn; blink and it's gone. Not that it's a proper winter, anyway. No snow. Well, once in a blue moon. Then everyone runs outside like crazed banshees."

Phen sat at the dining-room table, pretending to do his homework. He'd noticed his grandmother talking more and more, even when there was no one there to chat to. This dialogue with herself seemed to be when she was at her happiest. Phen never interrupted; he knew about other worlds and how you could be in two places at the same time. It was a rare connection he had with her. A bond he could never acknowledge, but one of the few things he understood. It made him feel strangely reassured as he watched his own life mend a little then fall apart once more. He spiralled into the centre only to be pulled out again. He had no idea whether he was spinning up or down and no control of its direction anyway.

Even his school lunch wasn't under his jurisdiction any more. He'd been very happy with the thick slices of Bovril and cheese he'd begun to make himself. Now Mairead insisted on skinny egg-and-lettuce sandwiches. "More protein, the lettuce is just for show." He hated eggs. He hated lettuce.

He was also no longer allowed free access to his father's bedroom. "Maybe later, not now," was all his mother would say as the door closed behind her. Forced grins split sad faces horribly from side to side.

The only time he was free to make his own plans was when he was out with Pal. This meant walking as fast as he could, without actually running, straight to the park. He no longer pretended he was doing something else while he looked for Heb. The man in the fedora was mostly found at the far end of the green strip on a bench between the young willow tree and the almost completed waterfall. He was usually asleep, sunbathing or reading whatever newspaper or magazine he could find. On his "intellectual days" he'd play chess against himself. He kept the pieces and fold-up board in a toffee tin. "Damn, I'm good," he'd say. "Never lost a game yet." Occasionally his head would be perfectly still as his eyes scanned way beyond the horizon line. At these times Phen would slow his approach, sensing something private and personal was in progress. He'd sit quietly next to him and follow his gaze. Sitting without speaking was becoming his favourite form of communication.

However, for all this comfort and easy camaraderie, Heb's puzzle was far from completed. The more Phen saw of him, the more he felt he knew only his outer edges. He knew *what* he was, yet that had proved, surprisingly, not to be the full answer. He hadn't thought there would be more to know about a man who glowed at night and had wings. He had presumed this knowledge would unlock all the necessary questions. Finding an angel in your local park seemed like the end of the story. This was not proving to be the case. Surely he knew he'd been seen? Didn't divine messengers know everything? Was God's envoy keeping quiet because he didn't like being spied on?

Paul had seen a burning bush on his way to Damascus and everything had changed. A light had flashed around him and he'd fallen to the ground. A voice had spoken to him. Most importantly, afterwards he'd known exactly what to do. He was a changed man. Phen had a picture of him in his Bible. His eyes were suddenly filled with a steely blue. His wavy hair turned white with a wide middle parting like the Red Sea, going left and right. His skin pushed back as he felt the G-forces of the Lord. His legs transformed to a polished marble by the furnace of the sacred fire. Nothing like this had happened to Phen. His balls hadn't even dropped.

The problem was that a question to Heb, no matter how directly it was asked, always just produced another question. The school play was a case in point. Heb told him to stop worrying, that he would have an "okay evening". When Phen asked how he knew it would be okay, Heb asked if he was a well-rehearsed tree or not.

Phen almost hoped for some catastrophe just to prove him wrong. Wrapped in his green baize and planks, he'd tried to watch the audience with one eye through the hole in his trunk. The only truly unexpected moment was the arrival of a huge rock pigeon. It flew in through the top window of the hall, cooed twice as if to announce its arrival, then made itself comfortable on the rafters. Mrs Smit stood on a chair and shook a broom at it. The younger children in the hall, thinking she was part of the play, clapped politely and waved at her. The pigeon was unperturbed. It spread its wings and began to preen. The lights dimmed, and Miss Delmont strode to the centre of the stage. She was dressed as some form of mythical forest creature and it was clear her costume had not passed through the school's sewing class.

Phen noticed the headmaster, who was sitting in the front row, suddenly sit bolt upright and scrunch his programme into a tight ball. From behind, the tasselled brown moccasins launched a pair of green tights that sucked at her body. These, in turn, gave way to a smooth-fitting white blouse which highlighted the thick curls of her red hair. At its apex this fiery auburn was crowned by a pair of antlers that waved to the audience as she turned her head. What Phen wasn't aware of at the time, and what he heard again and again afterwards, was that as she pranced in the spotlight, her nipples stood out "like cherries on a cupcake".

This moment of potential scandal was quickly subdued when it became evident that, as the narrator, much of her time would be spent in the darkness of the wings. Margaret Wallace stole the show, leading other female cast members to spread the rumour she'd had her hair *professionally* done. Besides Mustardseed flying into an unsighted Bottom, forcing his left donkey ear to point south, all went pretty much to plan. The Leb couldn't resist doing his Elvis swivel whenever he was on stage. This led to good-natured laughter and therefore escaped sanction. Kobus Visser received an extra round of applause for enchanting the forest with a goblin's-hat-rugby-scrum-cap *and* a crutch. His broken leg made him the only other cast member who could not take a bow. Phen shook his branches, not that anyone noticed. He was standing right at the back with the entire ensemble in front of him.

He'd tried to imagine himself at the centre of some magical spiral rather than just a tree in the background. Sometimes it worked. He was inside himself and inside the play. And everything did spin around him. If the performance had an epicentre, he was surely it. Did it matter that no one could actually see him? Somewhere near the middle, while Puck was placing the flower's juice on Lysander's eyes, he went back to his father's bedroom. He saw him lying at peace, fast asleep. This time, though, he pushed the hair away from his father's forehead and gently brushed it back.

By the time Mr Swindon announced "the tree feller is here" and the planks lay on the stage in neat piles, the hall was almost empty. The pigeon sat plump and fast asleep up in the roof while down below Hettie Hattingh's family took pictures of her. The flash exploded off the wooden board behind her, turning the gold lettering of past headmasters silver. Her father asked her not to pose so much and she asked what the point was then. She'd taken some of the flowers from her hair and placed them sideways in her mouth. When Phen walked past, he nodded at her mother's greeting. "He was the tree," was all Hettie said.

The children were invited for tea afterwards although this really meant Lecol orange squash in a paper cup at their own table. They were allowed to mix with their parents only once the teachers had made sure the adults were sufficiently refreshed. The scones and koeksusters were not for juvenile mouths until Mr Kock said so. Once this happened, Phen was not fast enough. Carlos de Sousa, however, pulled a plaited piece of dough from his pocket and offered him a piece. A Wicks bubblegum wrapper and a piece of fingernail had to be removed before he placed it in his mouth.

"Now the hungry lion roars, and the wolf behowls the moon." The Portuguese Puck punched him on the shoulder and headed for the exit. For the rest of the term Carlos would say that line over and over. Whether he passed biology, scored a goal, or saw a pretty girl, lions and wolves would be involved.

From what Phen could gather it had been a fairly successful night. Miss Delmont was much in demand although she now wore a small waist-high riding jacket over her blouse. Her horns were gone, yet she still looked like some bewitched and beautiful creature of the woodlands. She seemed ready to join in the hunt for the fox or, if needed, become the prey itself. With her cup sliding dangerously across her saucer she explained that a story didn't have to be linear. The atmospherics of the telling was often as important as the tale itself. We had to be authentic to the author's ambience as much as to his play. The men were enraptured; the women drifted off.

Mr Kock thanked Miss Delmont and simultaneously suggested something more South African for next time. Once more he mentioned his preference for the Battle of Blood River. "Four hundred and seventy Voortrekkers held twenty thousand Zulu at bay," he reminded her. "We could build a laager right across the stage. The girls could make themselves kappies. You know, bonnets." He used his hands as blinkers down the side of his head in case she didn't quite get it. "And inter alia the boys, they love a little action, guns, spears and boot polish." His fingers circled his cheeks as he pretended to blacken them.

In the car park Phen heard Philip Denton's older brother say Miss Delmont looked like Bambi with tits. It sounded more like a compliment than an insult. Phen waited at the gate hoping to walk home with Jimmy. Once the last car had gone he realised he must've missed him and turned to go. He was halfway across the road when a rusted Anglia drove through the side entrance from the fields and hooted at him. It was only when the window was wound down that Mr Swindon's face became recognisable beneath his gnawed-at straw hat.

"Want a lift?"

"Are you going to Hillbrow?"

"What a coincidence."

With the play out of the way Phen had hoped his existence would weave together a little more evenly. His gran was now knitting obsessively "against the clock". All the while she complained that the object of her work continued to get smaller and smaller. She'd finished his father's jersey and that had led to an awkward fitting. Firstly he wasn't a fan of the colour. "Teal," he said, "is a confused green, looking for an identity. The offspring of over-optimistic parents." Once his head had been pushed through the v-neck and his arms helped through the sleeves, he sat there like a liquid. The jersey was so large his upper body seemed to flow off the bed. "Perfect," he'd observed, "for those nights I wish to disguise myself as a river." Mairead was now working on a pair of slippers. "Call them booties if you like. Feet don't shrink and they'll be practical in winter."

Although there was little Phen could do to alter events that swerved and crashed around him, he'd expected more from an angel. Discussions about spirals, ankles and elbows were fine, but he was in the mood for miracles. "Talk," his grandmother never tired of telling him, "wasn't worth the paper it was written on." He felt that Heb was under-delivering, playing it too casual. A seed of resentment was beginning to grow. Perhaps he hadn't been direct enough.

He rehearsed his lines, using Pal as his prop, for some reason checked his hair was neatly combed and then went in search of the kaftaned messenger of God. He found him next to the willow tree, trying to fly in slow motion.

"White crane spreads its wings." He then stepped back and pushed at nothing. "Repulse the monkey." He bent over awkwardly: "Snake creeps down." Finally, he tried to stand on one leg: "Golden cockerel on right leg." He wobbled dangerously, waiting for Phen to comment.

"I'm guessing you haven't been introduced to t'ai chi before? Clever, those ancient Chinese. A defensive martial art that's also full of health benefits." He brought his other foot down onto the ground. "Let me 'Pat the wild horse's mane', then we can sit down."

Phen parked himself on the bench while Heb took one step forward very slowly and raised his hand to shoulder height. After a long pause he began to smooth the air left and right. Finally he turned to face Phen, sat on the ground like a venerable sage and crossed his legs in the lotus position. "You have questions to ask."

Heb's knees pointed more up than out. Before Phen could even reply, they had to be untangled. The sage tried to use both hands to undo his feet and rolled onto his side as they stayed stuck.

"You alright?"

"Fine."

Having unknotted himself, Heb straightened his legs and blew symbolically on his knees to cool them.

"Continue."

As his rehearsed lines dispersed, Phen decided to slow himself down. He thought if he talked like Mr Swindon walked, he'd be fine. It also helped that he was higher than Heb. He looked down on his face as it tried to radiate serenity. Phen had a rare sense of authority and control.

"I want to make it clear that I saw everything. Everything. I didn't tell you before in case you thought I was spying. I was in the willow," he pointed to it, "when the light suddenly burst through. Then I went out over there," he pointed again, "and saw the cocoon of fire and" – he paused for a long time – "your wings. I wasn't even ten yards away."

"Interesting," said Heb, straightening his back.

"What?"

"You never stutter when you're with me any more. Even spying wasn't s-s-s-spying."

Phen knew not to be distracted. He waited for him to

deny everything but Heb didn't. He did mention that he slept in a massive white T-shirt he'd found at the Student Nurses' Jumble Sale. He called it his Victorian nightgown. When he lifted his arms the sail between his body and his wrists made him think he could fly. Or at least launch himself and glide all the way down Nugget Hill. He also disclosed that his bed was a threadbare sleeping bag. Phen watched him as he pretended to roll it out. Evidently there were two parallel branches, like the slats of the bench, which allowed him to dream in relative comfort. Heb also said he liked to read in bed and the powerful torch he used might even punch holes through the tattered bottom of his bag.

That's what he said.

Phen, however, knew the games words could play. He was learning they were never spoken in isolation. The actions surrounding them were equally important. Context was everything. Why had Heb suddenly stood up as he started to talk? Why had he put his hat back on and pulled it so low? What was the sudden attraction of the distant mine dumps? Besides the words and the context, it was also the *way* he spoke. If Phen's tone had been challenging, Heb's on the other hand offered no defences. His words floated out his mouth almost in a whisper before disappearing entirely. It was as if he was speaking from memory. The sentences came from long ago. Frail and delicate, they vanished when exposed to the air.

Phen wanted to push home this advantage. Although the afternoon seemed in no hurry to reach evening he felt their conversation needed a speedy conclusion. He stood up and, in a pose borrowed from Mrs Smit, placed his hands on his hips. A little power to the suddenly self-righteous is a dangerous mixture. As Heb sat down on the bench, Phen felt the right to advance, up close. He tilted his head under the brim and stared straight into Heb's eyes. He was pierced and pulled upright in one moment. The blue had turned to steel. These were exactly the same eyes as Paul's on his way to Damascus.

"Tell me," he said, battling to finish his sentence, "tell me you're not an angel."

Heb used his index finger to push up his fedora. Then he made it travel in a semicircle across his forehead to ensure it was level. "The mind," he said, "is powerful beyond, and yet always in need of, understanding and belief. It's all we have to feel the full width of the universe." He was talking to the mine dumps, this time with more volume and clear diction. "Do you believe I am an angel?"

Phen didn't even have to think. "Of course!"

"Then you have your answer."

He had it. Confirmation from the source. The original epiphany had been validated. In return he apologised for watching him unawares and promised never to do it again. Heb, nonplussed, noted it probably wasn't a good idea to secretly watch people as they went to bed. The elation lingered, although not as long as Phen had anticipated. He wondered how long the burning bush stayed ablaze and when Paul's legs of marble returned to flesh and bone. It didn't matter that the world resumed a veneer of normality, the truth was out. As Heb went back to the grass and experimented with different yoga positions, Phen felt a deep calmness slowly move through his body. While he worked his way through an endless cycle of breakfast, lunch and dinner, whole universes hovered and orbited around him. That's what he'd seen in the changing blue of those eyes. That was the spiral Heb had tried to explain.

"May I ask you a last question?"

Heb gave a tranquil sign of consent by fluttering his left hand like the wing of a small bird.

Over time Phen had begun to speculate whether Heb existed only for him. He'd stared at the crack in his bedroom ceiling and watched the balls of his clown spin and levitate and wondered if he had created Heb out of some desperate need. "Your mind's overactive," his grandmother had said, "like Aunt Aida's thyroid." He realised he'd never touched Heb before. What if he was the only one who could see him? He certainly could smell him. But what if that slightly rancid odour was for his nose alone? Maybe he was just made of light, projected like a movie only his eyes could see. Perhaps the back of Phen's mind was the screen.

"Do angels shake hands?"

"It's a request not often asked."

"Can I shake your hand?"

"You want to be formally introduced?"

"Yes."

Heb stood up, walked around the bench, then rang an invisible doorbell. It took Phen a few seconds to understand he was meant to open an invisible door.

"Greetings."

"Hi."

"I'm Heb … Heb Thirteen Two."

"Phen … Stephen … Stephen Baxter."

"Pleased to meet you."

"Likewise."

They shook hands. Flesh met flesh. The palm was warm and rough. The firm grip contrasted with the ancient fingers and knuckles.

"Gnarled." Heb read his mind. "Manual labour."

Phen wasn't sure how long he should hang on for. He

enjoyed the heat being transferred to him, although this also made him slightly embarrassed. By the time their hands slipped apart, his whole body felt as if it had slowly been set on fire. He was confused. His palm was hotter than it had ever been before; he was also blushing. The crimson in his cheeks moved up and scorched his temples. He'd turned himself into something awkward and clumsy and wasn't certain what had been confirmed or achieved.

"It's just an ever-changing shell."

"What is?"

"Your body. It's just an outer wrapping. Teeth and hair and skin and bone aren't the important bits."

Phen returned home with a palpable sense of satisfaction and a tangible angel. Yet while endless galaxies spun for those who could see, and seraphs glowed like lanterns in trees for those who believed, the old reality continued to squat over his life once he opened the door at number four Duchess Court. Everyone tried to live a life as if constructed from his Meccano set. They battled endlessly to get everything to sit flush. The more their days were bent out of shape, the more they tried to correct them with a fantasy of braces and buttresses. They attempted to create some edifice, some structure that would allow them to cantilever over the truth. Although now there wasn't sufficient material to work with. Seemingly strong struts collapsed, metal plates buckled and pieces went missing. There weren't enough corner brackets to hold sections that went in opposite directions. The interconnecting bolts were too short for diverging lives.

Try as they may, no one could reassemble what was happening in the square box that was his father's bedroom. It was here that Phen hoped his self-confessed angel would produce the miracle. He'd asked for Heb's help as he was leaving. Deep in meditation, he thought he saw a nod. Now Phen was annoyed he hadn't been specific enough. He'd presumed celestial beings knew these things in advance. Yet, as he lay on his bed, he was having doubts. Was this a lack of faith? The very evil that Mr Lansdown and Reverend Clayburn had warned him against? To play it safe he thought he'd better cut another deal. Over prayers he made a pact – with whom he didn't know exactly, but he looked like Christ of Arabia – that he would accept stuttering for all his life if his father recovered. He even added that if that wasn't enough, he could be struck dumb in return for his father's good health. Shamelessly he imagined himself arriving at school to the collective sympathy of the class as he was forced to communicate in sign language. Margaret Wallace would squeeze his hand affectionately and be aghast to see his eyes had changed to a steely blue. They'd give him a new nickname: Saint Phen.

He stayed on his knees for a long time. The more he prayed, the more Margaret Wallace wandered around clad in the tight costume she'd worn in *A Midsummer Night's Dream*. By the time he stood up, his mother was standing at the door. She thought it was time she found out how school was going. He opened his geography book and let her look. She loved his drawing of a volcano and was particularly impressed by his magma chamber. Sedimentary was spelled incorrectly but, besides that, it was a beautiful Mount Vesuvius. He pointed to his underlined heading, which very clearly said Krakatoa. Phen knew that although his mother's body was sitting next to him at the dining-room table, most of her wasn't actually there.

Phen wanted to stay spiritual but found himself getting angry with her instead. It was his only choice. He was too scared of his grandmother and his father was always asleep or drugged. As she paged through his projects he grew furious with the way she mollycoddled Drs Klevansky and Baldwin. He hated the way they arrived with their white coats, self-importantly flinging them on the backs of chairs, as if they owned the place. His mother immediately made them tea, like a servant, and they often didn't drink it. She tiptoed around them even when fatty Baldwin consoled her too often and for too long. A handshake wasn't meant to last forever and there was no need for an extra squeeze after it was done. His belly always rotated to point towards her. It was obscene.

Most of all, Phen was incensed that they continued to speak about his father as if he didn't exist or even have a name. The more they worked with the body that lay shrinking in the bed, the colder and more distant the doctors became. They never chuckled at his one-liners, or talked about any of the books he was listening to. The *patient's heart* was still under enormous strain. *Valves* were not responding as they should. *Arteries* were a problem and *pulmonary veins* were a concern. The *left ventricle* was not performing and *septum tissue* was an issue. Never a word about Dennis, father of Phen, husband of Lily.

Edward and Mairead were also too respectful during the doctors' visits. "Medical VIPs," was all Ed would say as he happily played butler and doorman. In diffidence to their high rank, his gran would occasionally serve a few slabs of shortbread with their tea. "Scotland," she reassured them, "still has a fine knack for producing many of the world's most famous physicians."

By the time his mother reached the end of Phen's geography book, she was absent-mindedly impressed.

"Wonderful," she said.

"I hate the doctors."

"We've run out of money, we can't pay them; they don't have to come here."

"Krakatoa," was all he could reply, "not Vesuvius."

16

Gesticulate

/jes-tik'y-lät/ verb

The one advantage to number four playing host to so many guests was that it also contributed to twisting time out of shape. The days were incredibly long, the weeks fairly quick and the months flashed past like greased lightning. When Phen woke to the last day of term he could hardly believe it. He checked his homework diary and there it was. The final square of the semester had detonated a mushroom-shaped cloud he'd drawn with his ballpoint pen. Vernon MacArthur had said the communists also had the atomic bomb, so if we made it to the holiday break we should all remember it might be our last. Kobus Visser made the mistake of challenging this point of view. He said South Africa had a huge army, navy and air force too. We had to because there were so many blacks. MacArthur did not like his intellectual prowess being challenged, especially by Visser, who came near the bottom of the class and now had one leg that was much skinnier than the other. "That's what the Japs said," he sneered. Visser had no idea why the people who made Toyotas were suddenly being brought into the picture. He looked blank.

"Hiroshima!"

"Hiroshima yourself!" he said, and lifted a middle finger.

Although presents were normally reserved for the end of the year, Hettie Hattingh brought Mrs Smit a bunch of flowers. Her curtsy was interrupted halfway down when

Margaret Wallace produced a brooch beautifully wrapped in a velvet jewellery box. It was clear the second present was more to Mrs Smit's liking. By first break the strelitzias still hadn't been put in water. All through maths, Afrikaans and religious studies, the spiky orange petals pointed accusingly at the teacher. By the time Mrs Smit explained that Joseph was more loved than all the other children and *that's* why he'd received the coat of many colours, Hettie was beside herself. It had never occurred to her that *she* might not be the chosen one.

At second break she took matters into her own hands. When the class reconvened, all the glass jam jars they had collected for the avocado-pip experiment were now filled with individual strelitzias. The stems stood tall in their see-through shoes as the light shone through the two inches of water like defiant bursts of sunshine. That the teacher's pet could perform an act of such wild rebellion left her fellow students happily dazed. Even Mrs Smit wasn't sure what to do. When Hettie received a wink from the Leb she got such a fright she dropped her pencil case. Crayons rolled everywhere, sending colourful ripples across the polished floor. In a display of last-day camaraderie, Mr Karim apologised in advance and dropped his too. He spent ages crawling on all fours while his teacher fiddled with the new shiny butterfly on her lapel and tried to regain her composure.

English was the last lesson of the day. She had been tempted to cancel "Oh my word" but a collective groan from the class persuaded her to proceed. They promised to behave and in return anyone who used the word correctly would receive double points. "Wait, wait, wait," she warned them. This meant it would have to be a particularly difficult word. She opened her dictionary at random and slowly ran her finger down the page. As the tension mounted, Vernon MacArthur leaned forward and allowed his elbow to lift from his desk. He was ready to shoot his arm up like a rocket blasting off from Cape Kennedy. He was always first and he always got it right unless Mrs Smit chose not to see him. The bar graph next to the map of South Africa's national parks showed how far ahead he was. One more right answer and his skyscraper had nowhere else to go. The last day of term was the perfect time to cross the white-stringed finish line held taut on either side by thumbtacks.

Mrs Smit smirked as she made her decision. She closed the thick book slowly in conspiratorial glee while keeping her finger in place as a bookmark. She moved back onto her raised platform; it appeared the word might need a little extra height. Like athletes in their starting blocks, everyone strained for the beginning of a sound.

"It starts with a P."

She then opened the dictionary again, pretending to check once more. Her eyes looked up from the page and scanned the classroom. It was a moment to relish: a group of young, highly focused minds waiting to be triggered. Aside from the Leb, who fiddled noisily as he tried to slide the wooden roof of his pencil box closed, there was dead silence. She pulled her belt down and waited with one hand on the buckle. Her lips moved, first teasing, then finally loud and clear.

"The word is 'pro-ver-bi-al'. I repeat, the word is 'proverbial'."

The class all turned to Vernon MacArthur. His hand launched skyward, lost altitude and hovered around his ear. He knotted his eyebrows as he sought the answer and repeated the word soundlessly. It was all an act. He didn't know the answer and everyone knew it. The more time Mrs Smit gave him, the more obvious it became. Vernon soldiered on, determined to portray it as a lack of memory and not of knowledge. His hand stayed half up as his head began to droop. Mrs Smit now allowed another kind of tension to develop. She would not put him out of his misery until his humiliation was complete. His pride needed to be slow-roasted. It was the last day of school; it would end on her terms. She was so caught up in Vernon's degradation that her eyes failed to see another hand slowly rise and crest the back of the Leb's head.

Phen had never spontaneously answered a question at school. Not once. Possibly the courage came from Hettie's act of defiance. Perhaps it was because it was the last day of term and his final chance to remind his classmates that he existed. No one spoke to him at school any more. He wasn't sure if the class had planned this or if it had happened naturally. Jimmy would let him walk home with him but only after they were a few blocks from the school. Maybe he thought it was time to be at the centre of his spiral. Or at least nudge it upwards. His world continued to spin with no brakes. Could this be a sign his life was about to change? Coincidence?

He couldn't believe his luck when Mrs Smit had said the word. Phen didn't know the meaning of proverbial but it didn't matter. As fortune would have it, he had heard the word being used the night before in his kitchen. So he had it attached to a sentence as well. The sink had blocked and the caretaker had called the plumber. They had both battled with the corroded flange that joined the large s-pipe before it disappeared into the wall. They'd wrestled with wrenches and spanners and all types of tools before they'd managed to get it to budge.

The Leb flattened himself across his desk to ensure Mrs Smit had a clear line of sight. She saw yet she didn't believe. Her eyes registered both annoyance and surprise. Attention was now being diverted from a broken Vernon to Phen, who stubbornly kept his hand in the air. The entire class shifted in their seats to address this new phenomenon. Centre row, two from the front housed the boy who was always at a loss for words. He didn't talk; he certainly didn't participate. Now he was suddenly the hushed centre of attraction. Mrs Smit pulled her finger out of the dictionary, put it down on the table, and crossed her arms. She flicked a single eyebrow up, combining permission and ridicule in one movement.

Phen stood up, faced her squarely and tried to calmly slice the sentence into individual sounds, then words and finally a full sentence.

"I-i-i-it's tighter than a nun's proverbial."

"I beg your pardon?"

Phen repeated the sentence. "I-i-i-it's tighter than a nun's proverbial."

After a difficult start, he thought he'd done very well. The sentence was a little staccato. It certainly wasn't a blurt. He'd had to cut proverbial into four. All in all, though, he was happy with his articulation. Phen initially thought Mrs Smit's stunned expression was due to the relative smoothness of his delivery. It was only when he began to feel a strange, almost bewildered reaction from the class that a sense of unease developed. Since none of the students knew what proverbial meant in the first place, it took some time for a full understanding of the sentence to filter through. Although the classroom was picking up ricocheting signals from everywhere, they were battling to interpret them. The sustained look of shock on their teacher's face was the biggest clue. Her mouth stayed open as everyone began to whisper and gesticulate towards its real meaning.

Philip Denton got it first.

Being a year older and having a brother in high school contributed greatly to a brain that might determine the various tightnesses of a nun. Vernon MacArthur didn't believe him. "It wasn't the proverbial I remembered." The Leb wasn't far behind Philip. He spun around in his desk and stared at Phen with a mixture of pure delight and astonishment. Carlos crossed himself and Jimmy the Greek was left floundering. He would later have Philip Denton break it down for him in anatomical terms. This would lead him to ask, "Why she give him such filthy word then?"

The girls, when they finally understood, took it personally and fell into a sanctimonious silence. They were appalled beyond words. Sisters in shock. As the boys warmed to the topic, the girls froze. Struck dumb by the horror of the sentence, Hettie Hattingh began to cry. It had been a horrible day anyway and now it was even worse. Phen could sense all this but couldn't understand any of it. He stayed standing as the realisation slowly dawned that he was not going to get double points. Mrs Smit emerged from her trauma, staggered to her desk and began to write. Phen took this as his cue to sit down.

Being sent to the headmaster's office with a note and having to wait in the secretary's office for an hour meant he missed the rest of school. By the time he'd been ushered into the only room with wall-to-wall carpets, everyone else had gone home. Mr Kock was signing report cards and didn't look up. Phen stared at the top of his head for so long he thought he was becoming disrespectful and turned sideways. There he found another Mr Kock in shorts and a floppy hat. He was smiling as he held a fish with teeth that pointed in sharp, different directions like the petals of Hettie Hattingh's strelitzias. The speedboat he was standing in was called *Lekker-Dekker* and, although it was a black-and-white photograph, Phen was sure it was painted in some bright colour.

"Tiger fish. Zambezi."

Phen spun back into position.

"Africa's piranha. Not really."

Although the headmaster wanted to be in holiday mode, a sea of paperwork blocked his exit. He carried the air of a man in a good mood against all odds. Phen handed over his note and he added it to the pile with a playful grimace. When the boy didn't leave, he corrected himself and grabbed the envelope back.

"I thought it was for just now, not now."

Whatever had been written, Mr Kock had to read a few times. At one stage he even turned the letter sideways hoping some better understanding would laterally reveal itself. He then opened the pocket-sized dictionary he kept next to his glass ashtray. The type was small so he had to put his glasses on as he licked the tip of his finger and turned the pages. Having found what he was looking for, he seemed to lose himself in the text. Phen drifted off to *Lekker-Dekker* again and thought of *The Old Man and the Sea*. He wondered if his headmaster knew who DiMaggio was and if he'd ever fished in the Gulf Stream. Had he ever used a harpoon and caught a fish so big he had to tie it to the side of a boat?

"Youngster!"

Phen left the glowing lights of Havana and returned to Roseneath School. He watched the mouth as teeth bit into a lower lip and a finger stroked the hairs of a brown moustache into place. It was thicker and more toothbrush-like under the nose before flattening out towards the sides.

"Inter alia the correspondence, were you fully aware of the usage of said word in said context?"

Phen didn't understand the question although he immediately knew the answer. Just to be sure, Mr Kock hinted by shaking his head. He tried to answer instantly. Sounds, not words, jerked out. The harder he tried the more he stammered. He wanted to pause, to get his breath, but was scared the silence would be seen as insolence. All he had to say was "no". Two letters, one sound. His mouth could machine-gun the N, yet proved useless in reaching the o.

"Whoa safari!" The headmaster rubbed his moustache again. This time using his thumb and forefinger to smooth it left and right. "Inhale. Let the air in."

Phen refilled his lungs and fell silent. To be beaten by a word of two letters left his humiliation with nowhere to hide. It didn't even have an s in it. It was taking all his control not to cry. By the time he looked up, Mr Kock had put his glasses back on even though he wasn't reading. The thick, black rims, similar to his father's, made him look important, like a judge waiting to pass sentence. It took Phen a few moments to realise his eyes were closed. Was he praying? Or already dreaming of his holiday? When he opened them, a kindness settled over his face. He took off his glasses, rubbed his eyes and allowed the faintest of smiles. Then he playfully flicked at the glass ashtray. It tinged like a bell signifying time was up.

"Go and enjoy your holiday … and watch out for those English words. Some have got more teeth on them than a tiger fish."

When Phen told Heb about his last day of school it made him suddenly stand up and do stretch exercises with his back to him. When he finally sat down he said if the intent was pure, no man could be held to account for a well-meaning action that had gone awry. He then explained what awry meant. They were seeing each other every day now. Sometimes even mornings and afternoons if Phen could slip out the flat or combine a chore to the shops with a walk for the dog.

He had to escape. The growing presence of the patient was felt everywhere. Even his smells slipped from under the closed door and permeated the other rooms. Mairead sprayed toilet deodoriser everywhere. Phen's egg-and-lettuce sandwiches tasted of lavender. His father demanded attention then piteously rejected it. He scorned help on the way to the bathroom and insisted on it on his way back. He didn't need oxygen then scolded everyone for not knowing that he did. The tape recorder spun forward then back as whole chapters were missed or told again and again. Reels snapped and were sticky-taped together to produce a reading that jumped, fell silent or jittered like Phen on a bad day.

It wasn't difficult keeping Heb a secret. The bigger Hillbrow grew, the more invisible its inhabitants became. Everyone was on the move. He and Heb seemed to be the only ones standing still. Hillbrow was the junction on the way to somewhere else. Only the sick, disillusioned and directionless stayed. Like a refugee camp, it was filling up every day with more and more people who had excitedly arrived knowing this wasn't their final destination. Cranes and concrete mixers rested only on the Sabbath as they tried to accommodate the influx. As each new apartment building was finished, it was immediately crammed with a smorgasbord of humanity. They spoke in different tongues, and those from the Mediterranean were suspiciously dark for a white South Africa. Mairead often referenced the Tower of Babel.

In this frenzied to-ing and fro-ing, who would notice two figures sitting on a park bench? It might seem strange to some that a young boy would be spending time with a hobo. With a lead in his hand, though, those strolling past presumed it was a moment of proximity while the skinny boy walked his dog. The only other person who might have asked questions was Jimmy the Greek. He sometimes came to the park to kick his soccer ball and frighten the pigeons. But he had gone to his uncle's caravan somewhere in the Transkei. He was "swimming the sea with body board, trust me, not horse". Everyone blurred past while Phen and Heb sat and stared at the horizon.

It was almost a week into the holidays when Phen presented Heb with his mother's old sunglasses. It didn't feel like stealing; she hadn't worn them for years. He'd found them when looking for a pack of cards. They'd been hidden under a theatre programme for *Fiddler on the Roof*. On the cover, a man in a cloth cap leaned against a chimney holding a violin while a black cat stared at him.

"I noticed you're always squinting into the sun."

"Very nice."

"You don't have to use your hands to cover your eyes any more."

Heb put them on enthusiastically and marvelled at the quality of the lenses. He said he'd always loved pink. He particularly liked the diamond bits that swept up the corner of the frame. They reminded him of the twinkling of stars at night.

"Cat-eye sunglasses, I believe they're called. Thank you,"

he said. He pushed them further up the steep bridge of his nose.

"I thought you could also wear them when you practised t'ai chi or yoga."

"Add to the serenity of my being. Ooooom. Mani padme. Hummmmmmm," he chanted.

Although the sunglasses were a gift and not a bribe, Phen hoped they would add to his serenity too. He still waiting for his miracle. He'd mentioned to Heb, in a very direct manner, that his father was not getting any better. He'd shared his dislike for the doctors, especially fatty Baldwin, yet this had led to only a muted response. He enjoyed the time they spent together in the park. They could sit for hours discussing the different shapes of the clouds and how the mine dumps always moved yet never went anywhere. But back at Duchess Court he wanted action. Things needed to change, and fast.

"I have to go now. My father's so sick we need to take turns at his bedside to give my mom a break."

Heb nodded, keeping his sunglasses on.

"The doctors come nearly every day. I overheard them saying there wasn't much they could do."

Heb continued to nod. The sun ricocheted off the corners of his frames. Tiny starbursts exploded in front of his temples.

Back in his father's bedroom he continued the truce with the tape recorder. It could talk provided he couldn't hear it. While his father slept, he turned the volume down to a barely audible mumble. Kurt Vonnegut's *Cat's Cradle* muttered and grumbled to itself as he watched the tiny chest rise, hold, then deflate. The oxygen played its usual song, background music that was now never turned off.

Phen stared at all the books lined up above his father's

head. Spines pushed out; closed and erect, they looked like soldiers on parade. Eager and ready, they waited for a call to action. Phen sat uncomfortably on the arm of the leather chair while the two reels turned. Occasionally they'd catch the edge of his shorts, stutter momentarily, then continue. His father was alternately too hot or too cold. Right now, the thick duvet made the bottom of his body disappear entirely. Phen looked for his knees and feet but even they were made flat and invisible.

He bent down onto his knees to pick up the glasses case that had fallen on the floor and decided to stay there. Phen created his own Trinity by placing Jesus between Peter O'Toole and Omar Sharif. The bowed head reiterated that he would be happy to stutter all his life or be struck dumb, if only his father would recover. He bit his lip until he felt blood in his mouth and dug his nail deeply into the fleshy part of his palm. In a mixture of frustration, anger and pleading, he made Heb join the Holy Three. He begged for help, couldn't hear the answer and couldn't stop them all from putting on cat-eye sunglasses and doing t'ai chi.

"Bugle," his father said.

"What?" Phen stood up.

"If you want to call the US Cavalry, try blowing a bugle."

He showed him the glass case in a weak attempt at an alibi. His father squeezed his hand in thanks. There was so little power in it, Phen wasn't sure if he should squeeze back.

"Perhaps you could ask your mother to bring me a cup of tea, a ginger snap to dip in it and a soupçon of morphine to wash it all down?"

17

Parody

/par'e-di/ noun

Phen continued not to know what to do with his angel. He'd had a glimpse of another world, been teased by its possibilities, yet found no way to take advantage of it. What use was this awareness of a parallel universe if you couldn't bring it in to help your own? It wasn't knowledge, if that was the right word, that he could just park outside and stare at like Mr Trentbridge did with his Ford Cortina. Not that his immediate environment was conducive to vacant gazing. Within the walls of number four he could sense the exhausted gears that turned their lives were slipping more and more. Everyone was yanking at their levers harder and harder, with less and less effect.

Mairead had launched into a tirade about a store in the new Highpoint complex that claimed it would sell roasted chickens twenty-four hours a day. Fontana would be open every day and night of the week. The huge construction had barely been completed and the thought of poultry being consumed at three in the morning drove her into "quite a lather", as Ed put it. Mairead was also incensed that they would be selling hot rolls and French loaves at the same time. She found the French unclean, full of garlic and their torpedo bread hopeless for making intelligent sandwiches. The point was, she questioned anyone who crossed her path, was it a bakery or a butchery? And why on God's green earth would you choose to mix the two?

Uncle Edward, for his part, wandered in the background, telling everyone he didn't want to be a nuisance. Mairead smiled demurely and perpetually told him he wasn't. Phen wasn't so sure. His mother seemed to want him out of the way on the leatherette lounge chair where his grandmother could feed him tea and shortbread. Every time Lil went from the bedroom to the kitchen to fetch boiling water or throw away the used ampoules, he'd stand, embarrassed that his only contribution was his good manners. Once she was gone he'd hover like some ever-hopeful bystander until Mairead patted the cushions and suggested he sit down again.

The cause of all this skittish behaviour was the sudden deterioration of the patient's health. Ed had told Phen not to worry because his father was not himself. Yet he could cast no light on who he had become. His father's mind seemed to be trapped in a shifting fog. Usually the morphine made him sleepy and unintelligible yet when the clouds cleared he seemed to see further than anyone else. He recalled the minutiae of the past and spoke of the future without being burdened by it.

He'd watched his father open his eyes, move further up his wall of pillows and scan the room as if for the first time. He needed a few minutes to come to terms with what the box that was his bedroom contained. Could a man's life be so compacted? How could vast dreams end up with boundary lines measured by the reach to an oxygen mask or a stretch to a bedpan? He'd try to wave away the twilight, not sure if it was in his mind or in the room, then slowly turn and put the bedside lamp on. The triangle of light caught Phen's knee as he sat sharing the chair with the tape recorder. His father traced it back over his body and up to his face.

"Laurel and Hardy," he said. "Well, that's another fine mess you've got me into." He tried to put an exclamation at the end of the sentence but didn't have the strength.

His father enjoyed the quick smile and easy silence that followed. It caused him to look at his son differently, as if seeing something he'd not noticed before. To align their height, he moved higher up his pillows. Father to son, eye to eye. Phen enjoyed seeing the top half of the patient vertical for a change. Although he continued to shrivel, his pyjamas gave him broad shoulders and a firm chest as the thick flannel armoured his body. It was only the thin neck that could not be disguised. Even with the top button fastened, a huge moat circled the sagging skin.

"You look uncomfortable."

"Don't want to damage the tape recorder."

"Put it on the floor."

"Then you won't be able to reach it."

His father shrugged. Phen imagined the gaunt collar-bones tensing as they tried to lift the scrawny shoulders. It was only after the Philips had been tucked under the bed that he fully understood the implication of his actions. His father thrust a bony finger towards him and simply said, "You." He was back. Reader-in-chief. Storyteller to the man on the pillowed throne. Phen looked up at the bookcase waiting to do the king's bidding. Instead, the emaciated neck swivelled left and right within its flannel collar. The Adam's apple looked dangerously too big and in need of scaffolding to hold it in place.

"There's not enough time for long stories and elaborate plots. Tick tock. Tick tock. Side table by the window. Bottom drawer."

Phen stood up and moved around to the other side of the bedroom. He pulled at the little plastic handle and eventually managed to work it open.

"Under the Milk of Magnesia."

He lifted out the dark-blue glass bottle and saw a large book as thick and as wide as an encyclopaedia. Besides being a little frayed at the top and bottom of its spine, it was otherwise in good condition. The pages looked stuck together the way only time could seal them. The cover lay flat, heavy and silent like an unused door. Phen ran his hand across the five characters of the title and was surprised to find it deeply embossed. His fingers disappeared into what was once silver lettering but now shone with an oxidised green.

"*Chums* annual. Nineteen twenty-seven. My Christmas present when I was your age."

Phen stared at the cover and tried to imagine his father as a young boy holding the book. The cowboy had crested the hill and was now galloping on his trusted steed straight towards the reader. A line of pines guided his way while the horse's hooves created clouds of dust. Lasso at the ready, it formed a loose circle behind his Stetson and ensnared the bottom of the H and the U. His father could've used the scarf that was neatly tied around the buckaroo's neck. His belt appeared too big for him, the pistol in its leather holster bouncing far from his hip.

"Open it."

The book was so heavy he had to put it on the bed. He watched his father exhaust himself by lifting his hips and moving sideways to make room. Once he'd got his breath back and had a sip of water, he gave the order again.

"Open it."

The first page was a black-and-white lithograph of another cowboy riding up a hill pursued by four Indians. Phen wondered if this had any relationship to the action on the front cover. It was a brave man who took on four rampant Sioux with a few yards of circular rope. On the left side was a fold-out that released itself into three panels, each lined with deep crevices. "Wonders Beneath the Street" was a set of diagrams, all precisely labelled, showing the engineering feats of London's underground railway system. Tunnels, like tin cans stuck together, wormed their way from Camden Town to Kennington New Street. They burrowed under Tottenham Court, Oxford Circus and Charing Cross, coming up for air at Bank, Liverpool Street and Canonbury.

It was a Jules Verne world, although there was nothing to fear. The Dead Man's Handle was explained. Should the Motor Man be suddenly taken ill whilst driving, his hand would be removed from the driving handle. A button immediately sprang up and the brakes were instantly applied. Likewise, a cross-section drawing of the lift shaft, not dissimilar to Phen's Krakatoa, described how a rotating ball governor ensured that the cage ascended and descended at a regular pace. In addition, a safety catch was fitted so the lift could not be started until the gate was shut. Phen pondered what the cowboy and four Indians would think if they ever made it across to the other page.

He stood beside the bed with a flat hand on each page. The Reverend Clayburn did this at his church just before he began to preach or give a reading. Perhaps he thought the good book could be absorbed quicker through his fingers. Phen pretended he was at the lectern, straightened his back and waited for his congregation of one to tell him what to do. Even in this room, reeking of illness, the honest smell of stored paper lifted off the book's pages. His father seemed to catch the musty scent too. He lifted his nose and closed his eyes.

"Just the colour plates," he said. "Read the captions under

the colour plates. I know the stories. I've read them each a thousand times."

The first one he found was a group of fierce-looking nomads who blocked the way of two men dressed in khaki. They hovered around their desert vehicle not sure whether to reach for their guns or not. Both looked more stoic than terrified. Their upright posture and steady gaze from under their pith helmets showed they would not be cowed.

"A Crisis in the Desert," Phen read. "'No ordinary Arabs these, but fearless and daring, with eyes that flashed and glinted as s-s-s-savagely as the eyes of their mounts. The arm that held the s-s-spear was bent backwards, it had only to move forward and the s-s-spearhead would dart towards the white man's chest like a s-s-s-serpent's tongue!'" Then it s-s-says in brackets ..."

"See Sparrow-Hawk's exciting yarn 'The Spear-Arabs'," his father completed the sentence. "Go to the pirate one."

Phen found the "Marooned" colour plate opposite "Stamp Corner" by Stanley Phillips. "Cutlass took off his hat and made a s-s-sweeping bow. 'Farewell, Picaroon! Farewell, Martain Lacy!' he cried. 'Here on Doom Island, you'll be fellow captives until one of you dies.'"

"From S. Walkey's thrilling story 'Marooned'." His father smiled at the memory of it.

Phen stared at the picture of the downcast teenager manacled to a tough-looking pirate with an anchor tattoo on his wrist. They were chained ankle to ankle, yet he seemed more thoughtful than worried. Even with the rest of the crew setting off on a rowing boat back to the ship, he remained nothing more than pensive.

"The Fourth Throw," his father asked.

A young boy about Phen's age was tied to the massive trunk of a tree. His shirt was tucked into the top of his jodhpurs, which in turn were neatly pushed into knee-high leather boots. His arms were stretched sideways; one spear pierced the cotton cuff although it had missed his wrist. The pupils of his eyes were wide, yet the squareness of his jaw and clenched mouth showed a grim determination. A highly muscled warrior with a skin tied around his waist and a red-feathered headdress was about to hurl another spear straight at him. A group of his tribesmen, clutching their shields, looked on with mild interest.

"Derek realised that Zumtewayo was balancing for the throw, and as the great black arm rose to the level of the plumed head, his knees s-s-shook with terror."

"The Witchdoctor's Victim."

His father fell silent. Not sure if he was drifting back to sleep, Phen turned to the next colour plate. High up in the Alps, a powerful motorbike seemed to be racing a train. As they both roared around the bend, Phen saw the motorcyclist was on the ledge of a wall that curved around the railway track. Wheels blurred with speed as he flattened himself behind the handlebars and desperately tried to avoid falling down the yawning precipice. Behind him, black smoke poured from the oncoming locomotive in relentless pursuit. "'Unhesitatingly, Terry opened the throttle to the limit, felt the bike leap beneath him and saw the bay under the front wheel' ... Allen's thrilling story, 'Dynamite Devine.'"

He turned to his father to await instructions. The halo of the bedside lamp illuminated a pair of moist cheeks. The tears ran down his face without being absorbed. There was no sound to the crying. The eyes stayed closed even as they leaked. There was no attempt to brush the weeping away. The water raced to the edge of his jaw, gathered in drops, then leaped onto his pyjama top.

"Adventure. I was scared of living a little life." His eyes remained closed. "Terrified if you drew a map of what I'd done you'd find no contours. Just flat … frightened I'd wake up at the end and not be able to remember any of it."

His face was streaked with rivulets. They ran faster now over his thin, shiny skin. Some formed tributaries as they coursed downwards, zigzagging between the stubble. Phen wanted to reach for the tissues on the bedside table but he stood still. He'd never seen his father cry before. Ever. The face looked rained-on under the light.

"Weights or wings. Get dragged through or try fly above." Again the shoulders shrugged like some skinny puppet manipulated from above. He looked around the room again. "Unhesitatingly, Dynamite Dad leaves the bedpan on the sideboard and all-powerfully, inch by inch, strides magnificently across the unknown frontier towards the toilet. All he has at his side is his trusty scout Phen. Will they make it? Or is their incredible adventure doomed to failure?"

Phen helped his father twist sideways and placed his slippers directly beneath his waiting soles. His toes hung down pink and baby-like. The fur lining of the slippers smothered his ankles and grew up towards his shins. To stand, the knees, then back, then neck had to unfold themselves in three separate stages like the foldout in the *Chums* annual. He moved forward, sliding his feet slowly, then stopped as if waiting for acknowledgement that he'd made it halfway across the parquet badlands.

"I once peed into the Limpopo from the bank. It was only June but it was already long dry. Didn't make any difference, although I felt I'd contributed. Does it matter being insignificant, if we are uniquely so? Either way, in the end, we become a parody of ourselves."

Phen waited at the closed door for his father to finish. Pal passed with the tennis ball in his mouth and could not be persuaded to stay. It mattered less now that he was no longer scared of this part of the apartment. The narrow passageway didn't squeeze at his stomach the way it used to. The absurd dado rail running horizontally and into itself like a snake eating its own tail didn't unnerve him any more. Still, he wanted to be somewhere else. He wanted to be older and wiser and sure of himself. He leaned against the wall and decided he was in an important hall in a renowned university. Perhaps Oxford or Cambridge. Church-like windows allowed the light to fall on him, as it did on Mr Lansdown. Long, golden shafts illuminated him and the eager crowd he waited to address. With a pipe still smouldering in the pocket of his tweed jacket, he peered over the thick frames of his glasses and began his lecture. Margaret Wallace, now a university student in a white miniskirt shamelessly borrowed from Zelda, swooned at his every sentence, mesmerised by the depth of his erudition.

"Apologies for the delay," his father called out, trying to be jolly and taking deep breaths after every second word. "It appears I'm full of sound and fury. So far it has signified nothing."

The body that made it to the bathroom needed four stops on its journey back to the bedroom. His skeleton offered no ledge to stop his pants from falling down. "Every time a coconut." Phen would retrieve them from the slippers and slide them up to his chest. Clutching the waistband at heart height they edged forward. Phen could hold him on the elbow but was not allowed to put his arm around his father's body. "We're walking, not dancing." They inched past "Lily's folly", the folded, never-used wheelchair, flat and sandwiched between the wall and the wardrobe. "If I was meant to have wheels, I'd have been assembled in Detroit."

It took his father a full ten minutes to recover. The bravado in the bathroom and the walk back left him panting and white. He breathed so heavily into the oxygen mask it filled with condensation and made the middle of his face disappear. While Phen waited he kept the *Chums* annual closed and on his lap. It had assumed a sacredness. "How to Build your own Valve Radio", "Sportsmanship in the Ring" and "How Eskimos Count" were all part of the holy text. He would not open it without permission. Being reinstated as reader-in-chief didn't mean you could just randomly flick through your father's paged and printed past.

"Keep it," he said.

The oxygen mask was pushed up off his face. The elastic at the back of his neck kept it tightly wedged at the top of his forehead. The air continued to blast through, making his hair dance in the plastic cone. It hissed differently, angry and annoyed at its abuse.

"It's yours. Keep it."

Phen held up the book to confirm the meaning of his words. He didn't like the wave of his father's hand. It was too urgent, too impatient. As if he was chasing something away. He had to take the book *now*. The book must leave. Phen understood that by getting the colour plates, the diagrams, the stories, he was losing his father. He looked down at the cover. The cowboy kept his lasso in a lazy loop and his horse kept galloping down the mountain. The pines stayed rooted and in their straight lines, the story would remain the same forever, but not the reader.

Phen stood up, holding the annual to his chest. He waited to be dismissed, not sure if the wave of the hand included him as well as the book. His father turned sideways, allowing himself to be profiled in the pillow, and watched him with one eye. His hair still swayed and twirled in its plastic dome. Although the curtains were drawn he knew the afternoon sun was low. It was time to take Pal for his walk. His self-control was beginning to crumble. He was desperate to get out and determined to stay. He saw the tape recorder at his feet and wished he could push Pause. Everything was happening too fast.

"Can I ask you a favour?"

"Yes."

"I would ask your mother, but she won't. And my eyes are too bad. I'm due for a shot any minute. The morphine takes the pain away. Unfortunately my mind goes with it, so we'd have to do it now."

"What?"

"Under the Milk of Magnesia bottle, once more."

Phen walked to the other side of the bedroom again and opened the drawer. The light was poor, and at first he didn't see it.

"In the back, far corner."

The book was small, pocket-sized. Unlike the *Chums* annual, the cover was broken and deeply scarred. A crack up the centre caused the leather to erupt and peel. The brown skin clung on, bent and fraying yet refusing to let go. If the cover had a title it had been rubbed off a long time ago. It had disappeared against the rough fabric of a hundred different pockets. The corners had been forced inwards to accommodate the tighter pouches. A thin strand of cotton lay hooked in the blistered surface. It was clear the cover was not meant to serve as an announcement of its contents; rather it was a shield, a protective layer of what lay within. Phen opened it as carefully as possible. The spine seemed to groan, like someone forced to stretch. The pages stayed in an upright v, refusing to go any wider.

"Page sixty-seven."

As he delicately leafed through the book he noticed the square verses displayed with military precision under their slightly bolder headings. "That Sanity be Kept". "The Seed-at-Zero", "This Side of the Truth". He liked the short sentences and large gaps between stanzas. Words proud in their sturdy and brief building blocks. There seemed less room for camouflage here. And yet, he turned the pages slower and slower, scared of what he might find.

"I don't want to be mawkish or even worse, obvious …" His father ran out of words. Phen kept the book in its tight v, scared of the damage opening it any wider might cause. This made getting any illumination very difficult. He had to bow under the bedside lamp and tilt the words towards the light.

> *Do not go gentle into that good night,*
> *Old age s-s-s-should burn and rave at close of*
> *day;*
> *Rage, rage against the dying of the light.*
>
> *Though wise men at their end know dark is*
> *right,*
> *Because their words had forked no lightning*
> *they*
> *Do not go gentle into that good night.*
>
> *Good men, the last wave by, crying how bright*
> *Their frail deeds might have danced in a green*
> *bay,*
> *Rage, rage against the dying of the light.*

As he read, his father began to breathe more evenly. Phen placed his voice above the swirl of the oxygen. Forced to face the lamp, he wanted to be sure his father could hear. Halfway through, he turned to face him and found him no longer staring into the wardrobe mirror, but up towards the ceiling. His head swayed imperceptibly as his eyes followed what his son couldn't see.

> *Wild men who caught and s-s-sang the s-s-sun*
>   *in flight,*
> *And learn, too late, they grieved it on its way*
> *Do not go gentle into that good night.*
>
> *Grave men, near death, who s-s-see with*
>   *blinding s-sight*
> *Blind eyes could blaze like meteors and be gay,*
> *Rage, rage against the dying of the light.*
>
> *And you, my father, there on the sad height,*
> *Curse, bless, me now with your fierce tears, I*
>   *pray.*
> *Do not go gentle into that good night.*
> *Rage, rage against the dying of the light.*

"Well read. Again."

18

Succumb

/se-kum/ verb

The question was, did the white lily staring straight at him also have a secret spiral to it like the nautilus shell? If you cut it down the middle would it reveal a curve on a plane that winds around a fixed centre at a continuously increasing or decreasing distance from a point? It seemed highly likely. It had a conical shape, wide at one end then tapering towards its long, green stem. If that stem was hollow you could blow through it like a musical instrument. They were called calla lilies but "trumpet" or "spiral" would've been a better name. There was a large pile of them on the gleaming lid. One, however, had broken away from the arrangement and continued to peer at Phen.

He was thankful for the attention. The throat of the lily carried the gentlest hint of yellow, like an early sunrise. Or sunset? If it did contain a spiral he had no idea which way it was going. He was helped to his feet and pushed to his knees. He had his own prayer book yet his mother insisted he share with her. He couldn't see over her hand but pretended to read anyway. They sang hymn four hundred and fifty. Evidently everyone was going to meet at the fountain when they reached glory-land. It was bright and fair there. The only fountain he could conjure up was the drinking one at Nugget Hill Park. They'd have to be careful. If you turned the tap on too much the water shot out straight up your nose.

Mr Lansdown was there with his aftershave. He'd tried but couldn't get any closer to his mother. Uncle Edward had spread his legs wide, taking up two seats of the narrow pew. Phen wasn't sure if being his mother's boss qualified Mr Lansdown for the long bench reserved for family and close friends. They were a little short of relatives so he'd obviously thought he could fill the gap. He'd attempted to push past Ed's splayed knees but the barriers had stayed firm. Instead, Phen's uncle had shuffled his body to the right, allowing Mr Lansdown to sit next to Mairead rather than the widow. Mr Lansdown gave a strange cough at this thoughtfulness and studied the simple cross above the altar without blinking.

Phen didn't like being in the front row, nor did he understand why a straight back was necessary. There was no Leb or fat lady to hide behind. He could feel a thousand pairs of eyes staring at the back of his head. In front, the Reverend Clayburn kept solemnly looking at him over his white collar. He was trapped on both sides and furious because he'd had to wear his school blazer. Uncle Ed had volunteered to buy him a "proper jacket" but they'd run out of time. It didn't match his longs but was still better than his mother's suggestion to wear short pants. Mairead turned to the back of the church and said she was amazed at such a good turnout. She was her usual mountain of black. The white tissue on her lap dazzled in unseemly brightness and was quickly tucked into her sleeve. She apologised twice to Mr Lansdown for having to wedge her handbag against his thigh. He said it was no trouble at all.

The reverend knelt and dipped his chin onto his chest in a private prayer. It looked like he was sticking his head out of a ship's porthole. Having established an open line to his god, he thoughtfully made his way up to the lectern. If he was waiting for some holy light to burst through the window, it never arrived. Eventually he explained that the Lord was his shepherd. As he read Psalm 23, Phen tried to lie down in its green pastures but found himself stretched out at the park next to Heb. The sun was gone, the clouds were black and the wind whipped the felt hat off the tangled mass of hair and across the lawn. It cartwheeled into the children's pool and slowly sank. He couldn't see why goodness and mercy would surely follow him all the days of his life. The lily still lay open and fluted. It invited him in and he didn't have the strength to resist.

It was pleasant to have sounds so far away. Words blurred like distant figures you chose to keep out of focus. The light was different too, more diffused and soft. Gentle curves protected you from the brittle edges of good intentions. Handshakes too firm, smiles too sincere, squeezes on the shoulder that hurt or were too light. And always the rubbish that time would heal all. What if time just gave you more space to remember? Why didn't they just say the body that had been Dennis Baxter wasn't working any more? The stuttering and spluttering through blocked arteries and faulty valves had finally ceased. His father would not be coming back. The wound might close, the scar would remain. He'd already been told hair and teeth and bone and skin didn't last forever – he just wanted to know what did. Was a memory enough or should he expect more?

His mother tugged at his blazer and pulled him down. He and Mairead's handbag were the only two still sitting on the bench. He was out of sync again. Everyone else had slid forward onto their knees and politely closed their eyes. The reverend grinned at him, waiting to say the closing prayers. It worried Phen that sickness and death caused so many smiles. The blast of the organ rattled him back to reality as did the "amen" sung three times with mounting gusto. The last one was clearly designed to float upwards and deliver a sense of finality. Like hosts who'd already waved goodbye at the front door and at the car and now really wanted the guests to know it was time to go.

For a while thereafter absolutely nothing happened. This was because neither he nor his mother realised they had to leave first so everyone could follow behind them. The deadlock was only broken when Ed stood up like an usher and showed them the way. Phen wasn't sure how to lead the procession. He started off too fast and had to wait for his mother to catch up. She gently placed an arm around his shoulder as they looked forward, and slowly walked towards the light of the open door. He expected bells and maybe white doves, but there were neither. One slightly dishevelled pigeon sat on the outside notice board, staring at them. Phen noted that Tuesday evening's choir practice would now take place on Thursday. Those involved were asked to please be punctual. It was his first funeral and he'd presumed something more dramatic would happen to say it was all over. Amen, however often it was repeated, didn't seem enough.

He couldn't believe you just walked into the little garden and stopped. Even worse, the people that were behind now surrounded you and said the same thing they'd said before. Phen was astounded by the stupidity of it all. Plus the grass was full of confetti; how could they allow the remains of someone's happiness to carpet their sorrow? Mrs Kaplan was the only one who seemed to understand. She didn't smile, chat or pat. She just looked at him and threw her hands in the air. Although death was final, its ceremony sauntered on. He shrugged back at her. His mother interpreted it as him not wanting her arm on his shoulder. She lifted her hand and asked Ed to fetch the car.

Earlier that morning Phen had promised himself he would not cry and it appeared as if he had achieved that goal. Any rope that had tied him to some sense of calm and control had long been cut. He just didn't want to embarrass himself or his mother. If he wasn't the man of the house he didn't have to be the wailing little child either. This was put to the test with the unexpected appearance of the coffin coming out of the side door. As the men from the funeral parlour battled down the uneven stairs, he thought he heard something roll inside. It was the first time he fully understood his father was crated within the box. He was being transported the same way a removal company would take away an awkward piece of furniture. The casket was clearly too big. Did they not know how much he'd shrunk? Were there blankets in there, or shredded paper, Styrofoam chips and bubble wrap to ensure he was kept steady and secure? As he moved towards them, Mrs Kaplan appeared from behind the rose bush and cut him off.

"He is not there," was all she said.

They danced a little as she followed him first to the left and then to the right. By the time Phen could look past her, the coffin was being pushed into the back of a black station wagon by a man too round for his waistcoat. The last button could not be fastened, and split his stomach in two. He tried to close the tailgate gently but couldn't get the latch to lock. He ended up having to slam it shut and hold it in place with his knee. His assistant came to see if everything was okay and offered him a cigarette. He undid another two buttons and let his stomach free. They both lit up. White smoke drifted above the hedge and towards the steeple, following the last amen.

Mairead advanced with confetti on the soles of her shoes to say Ed had brought the car around. She acted as a battering ram to ensure their escape was unhindered. At the car, Mr Lansdown had finally found Phen's mother and was comforting her. They leaned against the passenger door and spoke in low tones. Trapped behind the steering wheel, Uncle Ed fumed. By the time everyone was ready to go, the car was a heady mix of emotions. Mairead worried about the cake she'd left in the oven, Ed was silent, the effect of the tranquilliser his mother had taken was beginning to wane, and Phen couldn't stop thinking about his father. He was concerned about the corners and the roundabouts. He kept seeing his father's body tilt onto its side, his face squashing against the hard wood, before flopping onto his back again. Would they check at the crematorium if his tie was still straight and lapels unruffled?

The Church of England in South Africa in Hillbrow was forced into a gentle triangle by Clarendon and Twist streets. Caroline Street creates the base of the triangle yet, for reasons that only town planners understand, was made a one-way. While Mr Lansdown was offering every condolence, a more watchful Ed would have noticed the hearse trying to do a four-point turn in his rear-view mirror. The length of their vehicle, the cars parked on both sides of the road and the impossibly tight corner up Edith Cavell made an exit via Twist Street the only way out.

It was difficult to tell who was the more surprised when the hearse drew level with Ed's car. The parlour man gave a sheepish smile and a very quick wave. In a show of diffidence he rolled the window down and flicked his cigarette out. The light had just turned red; there was nowhere for anyone to go. In an attempt to release the tension he moved forward. This brought the coffin directly opposite the Wolseley. The two cars were barely an inch apart. Phen had never been this close to the elongated box before. Without the lilies resting on the lid, it looked merely functional. The ornate silver handles appeared silly, like something added on later as a joke. The curtains on the hearse's windows and the grey wall-to-wall carpeting turned the back of the station wagon into a home. It was impossible not to peer in on your neighbour.

Uncle Edward was the first to go. He apologised in advance, placed his chin on the steering wheel and began to sob. Lil patted him reassuringly on the knee, called him Eddie and then likewise broke down. Mairead found the tissue up her sleeve, studied the cream interior of the Wolseley's roof and started to shudder. Phen tried to hold on. He tried to distract himself with detail. The carpet was badly worn where the coffins would first land, scrape then roll into the back. The left curtain in the second window was not tied back like the rest. It had slipped its gold clasp and swayed cheekily even though the car wasn't moving. Its fringed edge trailed a single thread similar in colour and length to the one he'd found on the cover of Dylan Thomas's *Selected Poems*. Huge scratch marks above the rear mudguard bore testimony to a miscalculated corner. Inside, the world howled; outside it was as it always had been.

He could've coped. By putting big events into small compartments he might've managed. With enough individual storage facilities you can give the appearance of taming the unmanageable and the incomprehensible. You take what you cannot understand, put it in a number of tiny spaces, lock the door and feign control. By worrying about the roadworthiness of the hearse Phen didn't have to think of his father about to be set on fire and turned to ash. The same thing had happened to the Leb's grandfather. "A braaivleis," he'd said, trying to prove how tough he was.

He could've got through if the two vehicles hadn't started moving. Suddenly there was nothing to cling to, to focus on. With everything else in transition it was cruelly unfair to make the two cars do likewise. He just needed something to be static, stationary and tangible. Speed was the enemy; he couldn't keep up. Whatever the game was, the rules kept on being broken. No one waited for your feelings to catch up. And it didn't matter where you left them, no one was going back with you to find them.

When the hearse turned right up Twist Street and Ed turned left to go down, the metaphor was complete. Phen buried his face in the crook of his arm and disappeared. He had been leaning against the door and now collapsed into his own lap. Later on he saw how wet his sleeve was, so he must've cried, yet that was not what he remembered. It was as if his earlier request to press the Pause button had finally come through. Everything stopped. Everything returned to its place. It wasn't a dream. *He* hadn't placed himself there. He was filled with a great stillness. Whatever had been had fallen in on itself. He was part of this and also on the other side of it. He'd been folded into a safe place.

It wasn't quite over yet, though. Mourning, he learned to his surprise, had an appetite. It had to continue back at Duchess Court over snacks and tea. He was put in charge of sausage rolls and wandered from group to group with two outstretched arms. He was still in a dazed state and didn't mind the job too much. His mother said she'd had to shake him three times to wake him up in the car, although he kept telling her he was never asleep. Zelda was the most popular mourner. She had to break out of a circle to accept his sausage-roll offering. Phen hadn't noticed her at the church; however, her demure black dress, tasteful but tight, had ensured everyone else had. Mr Trentbridge pulled him to one side and made him put the plates down. "That's life, Boyo," he said. "That's life." Then he explained how *his* father had died when he was only eight. Phen offered his condolences. It was quite a relief to hear the words going the other way.

Even with all the cakes and shortbread being homemade there's only so much stuffing a funeral can take. From her high command in the kitchen, Mairead noted that even her raspberry oatmeal meringue could not induce thirds. Someone had the temerity to ask if there was anything stronger than tea. She curtly explained it was not a wake, nor were they Irish. As Phen sausage-rolled the crowd he heard again and again that "Dennis had left a little early". Like a bus or train that had surprised everyone by its unscheduled departure. He wanted to say that in his last days his father was the oldest man he'd ever met. That pain and a clogged-up heart and arms full of purple bruises and punctured veins ran the clock forward at a demented speed.

With a dishcloth wrapped around her left fist, Mairead told Aunt Aida that Dennis had succumbed in his sleep. She made this sound slightly cowardly, as if he'd taken the easy way out. A number of people said his father was "in a better place" but could add no detail, verification or geography. He also heard Dennis had "popped his clogs" from someone in Zelda's group, although he couldn't trace the exact source.

Uncle Ed was the head waiter. He took orders from Mairead and passed them on. He was also the carrier of trays filled with rows of cups that wobbled as the parquet flooring bobbled. He demanded to be seen and be invisible at the same time. The delivery would be made with some ceremony, only for him to immediately melt away. Phen noticed that death was a very earnest business. It wore black and offered lots of advice. This only changed a little when the caretaker arrived and explained he couldn't make the funeral because of a burst pipe on the second floor. Still wearing his grey overalls, he offered a jar of pickled beetroot to express his sorrow. This shift in atmosphere was compounded by the surprise late appearance of Romeo Rossi. In exchange for a sausage roll he said, "Rest in pizz," and went to join the entourage around Zelda.

Phen looked across the room at his mother. Both widow and hostess, she accepted their sympathy and simultaneously offered more Swiss roll. She beckoned that he come join her. He held up his two plates to indicate there was still work to be done. She pulled an exaggerated sad face. Like Zelda, she also had her admirers. Phen wasn't jealous, although, right now, he didn't want to be just one of them. He was happy to orbit the room. He knew it was a mindless spiral but, for once, he could deliver on the obligations it placed on him.

"Ahem."

Phen turned around to find Mrs Kaplan right at his back.

"Death doesn't need a waiter forever."

Phen looked blank. She pretended to burp. Death had clearly eaten too much.

"I'm old. I walk with a stick." She bent over double to illustrate the point. "My hips don't move and my joints are stickier than my farfel kugel, which your grandmother still refuses to serve." She pointed to the kitchen.

He offered her a sausage roll. She waved the plate away.

"Don't you think it would be good manners for a young man like you to escort an old woman like me back up to my flat? And while you're doing that you can bring your dog along. And after you've got me to the fourth floor, isn't it time you took him for a walk to the park? I'll tell your mother while you fetch the lead."

Mr Otis behaved relatively well. As they were yanked upwards, Mrs Kaplan readied herself by leaning forward on her stick and bracing herself for the stop. Unlike his father's wooden walking stick, hers multiplied as it reached the bottom. Three fat metal fingers suddenly sprouted and clawed the ground with their rubber stoppers. Although he opened the grill gate for her, she needed no help with the six-inch step-up and seemed puzzled that Phen had walked her to her apartment. She placed the key in the door but would not open it until he left. She lifted her stick, aimed three muzzles at him and waited for him to go.

"Tough day?" Heb only half turned towards him as he approached.

Phen nodded.

"The Great Inevitable always presented as the Great Surprise."

"Wasn't sure you'd still be here."

"Why?"

"Just 'cause."

He'd found Heb in his normal place on the bench next to the willow tree. Heb had put the cat-eye sunglasses on as Phen and Pal arrived, although there was no sun to speak of. He was still wearing the psychedelic shirt with his suit pants and had added a bedspread, which he wore across his shoulders like a shawl. It was light and cottony. It bunched up behind his neck and pushed his hat forward. Phen hesitated before sitting down. He searched his memory for a picture of a tired angel and couldn't find one. The sun-burned face was a little pale; the normally outstretched arms hugged a slightly stooped frame. Heb seemed spent, like a man who'd run a marathon and needed time to recover.

"Sometimes you get a little burned in the fullness of the light."

"Actually you look a little whiter than normal." Inexplicably Phen began to look on the ground for confetti.

"Don't close the blinds entirely. You're man enough to take the brightness. Sometimes it's got to hurt to illuminate."

Phen didn't know what he was talking about yet instantly felt offended.

"It's just a space that wasn't there before," said Heb.

"What is?"

"Death. You get to choose how you fill it. Deliberately not remembering isn't a good start."

"I'm not deliberately not remembering."

"Good. Don't be one of those people who never buys lilies because they remind you of your father's death. Buy lilies all the time because they remind you of your father's death."

"Why?"

"Because that's how you keep the empty space filled. And that's how you remind yourself the space *you* take up isn't forever."

On today of all days Phen didn't feel like being lectured to.

"My mother said before my father died he saw people in his room. They were floating. His eyes followed them around. I heard him talking to them through the door. Was that you?"

Heb shook his head slowly. "Those are fetchers. Usually family. They come to explain what happens next."

"Afterwards he asked for the 'Moonlight Sonata' and had a bowl of soup. We had to turn the volume to full so he could hear it in the bedroom."

"Beethoven." Heb flicked the tails of his jacket over his chair and straightened his bow tie before beginning to play the piano. As his hands floated across the keyboard, the bedspread gently rocked from side to side on his shoulders. Phen waited for the sound effects, but none came. The finger movements seemed meticulous, the head bowed in concentration. Behind the sunglasses there was no way of telling if the eyes were open or closed. The silent music seemed to reinvigorate Heb. He played on and on, finally allowing his thrashing torso to bring the piece to its full and complete climax.

"First movement."

"So?"

"You, sort of, heard it the way Beethoven would've. He was going deaf when he wrote it."

Phen had kept his school blazer on as a respectful reminder of the day and had presumed, at the very least, Heb would've been more sensitive to the moment. Was it too much to ask for angels to understand the need for sympathy and compassion? He wanted a deep, even mystical sharing of sorrow. Something that would lift him above his pain and grief. Something that would explain how his father could bounce around in an ill-fitting box, get burned to no more than the leftovers in an ashtray, while everyone else politely nibbled sausage rolls and sipped tea. Instead he'd received a silent sonata. The grey mist that had begun to fill his head turned to red.

"The heck with you," he said.

"The heck? I don't know what that means."

"The hell with you."

"Oh."

Phen took off his blazer as he stormed away. Not satisfied that he had expressed his anger to its full extent, he searched for the worst word he could find. He thought of "swine", "bastard" and "rogue". Ridiculously "cad" and "scoundrel" also flicked through his mind. Eventually he found the word. It was so horrible and vile he couldn't bring himself to say it out loud or even pronounce it correctly. Despite that, by the time he reached Duchess Court, he was still calling Heb a sunt.

19

Incandescent

/in-kan-des'ent/ adjective

Being on holiday without a father was hard. Phen now wore Mr Lansdown's cross retrospectively. Maybe it was a little late but he still had a mother and he didn't want to take any chances. The more he tried to fill the empty space the more it drained away. He tried music and replaced Beethoven's "Moonlight Sonata" with the Animals' "House of the Rising Sun". He finally broke his five-rand note, went to the OK Bazaars record bar and bought the single. The melancholy introduction and the devastation caused by that abode in New Orleans spoke to his soul. It had been the ruin of many a poor boy, and Phen loved singing at the top of his voice that God knew that he was one. Sitting on the carpet in front of the Grundig, he played it again and again as he shouted his hurt to the world.

The flat was now an empty space too. His mother was back at work and his gran had retreated to Ivanhoe Mansions "to get her breath back". The main bedroom still had hospital smells and a circular mark on the parquet where the oxygen cylinder had stood. Now that the curtains were always open you could see the thinnest crust of dirt running along the top of the skirting board. The Salvation Army had come to collect his father's clothes. Phen had let them in and shown them to the wardrobe. His mother had insisted on keeping one smart dark suit. It hung spaciously from its lonely hanger and spun in a slow circle when you opened the door. By mistake, his slippers had been left behind. Tufts of the fur lining still stood upright even though there were no legs for them to climb.

All the pills were thrown into the toilet. The capsules tended to float and needed a second flushing. They happily bobbed up and down, reflecting their many colours before yielding to the swirl. No one knew what to do with the hypodermic syringe. Made of glass and metal, it seemed to have some inherent value. In the end it replaced the sunglasses underneath the *Fiddler on the Roof* programme. The steel needles were placed in an empty Eno bottle. The stumpy flask was then wrapped in black masking tape before it was dropped into the dustbin. This was to ensure it would be of no use to scavenging hippie drug addicts.

"Now that the deed is done," Mairead had explained, "it's pointless hanging about." She'd spring-cleaned a number of times and washed all the bed linen twice just to be sure. It was only after all the activities had died down that Phen realised there were some things you couldn't scrub away. No one sat in his father's chair in the lounge. No one lay on his side of the bed. His shaving brush stayed upright and defiant in the bathroom cabinet. Although their fingers moved around it every morning and night as they reached for the toothpaste, no hand had the courage to lift it and put it in the bin. Likewise the *Chums* annual now lay in the bottom of his cupboard, impossible to open.

Phen tried to go to his other worlds. He pulled *Seven Pillars of Wisdom* out of his father's bookcase and stared at the charcoal sketch of Lawrence of Arabia on the cover. The desert stayed still. His mighty warriors sat silent and unmoving on their camels. Le Carré's spy did not come in from the cold. Even his war comics remained on the page. He reread *The Dark Terror*, one of his favourites. The paratroopers dropped behind enemy lines were brave yet distant. When Jim Robson burst into the room to save the captured Professor Rennard, the startled look on the German's face was genuine, just not gripping. The speech bubble told Jerry to freeze or he'd be dead. "Himmel! Englanders!" was the reply, but Phen could take it no further. He stood in front of the bookcase and stared at the vacant bed. Did death take all other forms of escape with it? Was it so final and powerful it buried everything else? Would the rows of books against the wall be not just his father's, but also his, epitaph? Here lie father and son. Rest in pizz.

The tape recorder was lying in exactly the same position, half hidden under the bed. Mairead's spring cleaning had given "the machinery" a wide berth. She'd declared it futuristic mumbo-jumbo. He thought about plugging in the microphone. The two reels were still threaded, stopped midway in whatever tale they'd been telling. He just had to press Record and his voice would take over the story. *He* could interrupt mid-sentence and tell it his way. He could even wipe everything out and start from the beginning. He just didn't know what to say.

There was only one way to resolve this once and for all. The pen was in his Oxford stationery tin and a full prescription pad had been left behind by Dr Klevansky. He took his time, slowly making notes of thoughts that had been in his head for too long. He wrote calmly and clearly. The long list of degrees behind Dr Klevansky's name forced him to reread his sentences and check his spelling. Pal sensed they were heading for the park and waited patiently at the door. If Heb was still there, it was time for a showdown. "Enough of this bullshit," Phen heard himself say. He liked the adult sound of the sentence and repeated it to Pal.

They found him engrossed in a *Drum* magazine. It stretched across his face with only his forehead showing. Phen
had to clear his throat twice before the eyes and nose
appeared. A stalemate ensued when the magazine didn't
drop any lower. They looked at each other, waiting for the
next move.

"You still talking to me?"

"Business," said Phen, holding up his paper and pen.

"I'm just reading about a town without a soul. How
Fordsburg was bulldozed to a new place called Lenasia."

Phen would not allow himself to be detoured. He sat
down on the bench and flipped open the pad. "I have a
school project I have to hand in on the first day of next
term. An essay."

"What's the topic?"

"What I learned during the school holidays."

Heb folded the magazine in half then took off his
sunglasses. He stuck them deep into his hair. While his
blue eyes stared down at Phen, his glasses scanned the
horizon. Phen would not be distracted and kept his finger
on the first line.

"What does heaven look like?"

"You want it to be a place?"

"Isn't it?"

"Do you want it to be?"

"I asked first."

"If you want white fluffy clouds and beautiful blonde
women playing golden harps, you can have that. If you'd
prefer a giant Scalextric track – it can be a thousand times
bigger than the one in the window at Hutson's Toys – you
can have that too. Personally, I prefer a magnificent shallow
bowl that stretches across the universe. It's perfectly woven
with every colour ever made and each colour is an individual

note in the most beautiful piece of music ever heard. And as you move to the middle, it gets better and better."

"Why?"

"Because when you're at the centre, equidistant from all sides, there is nothing except absolute silence."

Phen wasn't sure what to write down. His pen remained poised.

"Heaven is exactly what you need it to be. That's why it's heaven."

Phen moved on to his next question. "Do you get different kinds of angels?"

"Yes and no."

Phen sighed and tapped his pen against his pad.

"Angels are angels. However, they are assigned different tasks."

"Like?"

"I've already mentioned fetchers. Another example would be guardians or witnesses."

"What do they do?"

"They watch and offer assistance, if possible."

"If possible! Can't angels do anything and everything?"

"Not if you want to stay human."

Heb fell silent. A struggling Phen doodled on his pad, pretending it was helping him think. He drew a ladder up the side of the page.

"You have free will, so angels can only point and suggest. They can't force you to do anything. Angels can't do frontal lobotomies. It's not part of the code."

"Code?"

"Like traffic circles, it pays to follow the signs."

"I've seen your wings at night. Why don't I ever see them during the day?"

"It's also not in the angels' code to give pigeons heart attacks."

Heb pointed to the flock that queued impatiently to drill holes in leftover French loaf. It protruded from a brown-paper Fontana Bakery bag. There were tiny eruptions as flakes of crust burst into the air.

"Of course angels also want to avoid cardiac arrest among the general population. The whole thing works best incognito. Wings are fine for paintings, mausoleums and monuments, but a little impractical in the field."

"You're undercover?"

"You could say so."

Phen checked his list. He'd put an exclamation mark behind question four.

"How do you qualify to become an angel? Do you have to have lived a perfect life?"

"Not quite. Look at it this way: if all angels had perfect lives, how could they help someone who was having a not-so-perfect one?"

"I don't understand."

"I once watched a school swimming gala. The boys were about your age. The winner was a terrific swimmer. Broad shoulders, athletic body. He came first by five lengths. Stood on top of the podium and held the cup up high. The boy who came last suffered from muscular dystrophy. All he could do was paddle away like a dog. Halfway through, everyone thought he was going to drown. He paused, exhausted, then kept on going until he reached the end. Now, which of those two boys is best qualified to help someone who's terrified about getting into the pool?"

The pen stayed motionless. Like the French loaf, Phen's mind was having holes picked in it. He drew more steps in his ladder.

"Could you explain that again?"

"Let's look at this a different way. We are all everything and its opposite at the same time. We are scared *and* courageous. Good *and* bad. Sad *and* happy. Deep *and* shallow. It's just that angels have learned which side to turn to the light. They've worked out which to illuminate and from that choice everything else is decided. I'm an alcoholic who doesn't drink alcohol, so I can help people who do. It's that simple."

Phen wasn't so sure. He looked down at his notes again.

"Number five." He hoped by saying the number he'd show some semblance of control. "Are all angels white?"

"We come in all colours."

"Even black?"

"Of course."

"Isn't black evil? The serpent in the garden of Eden is always black."

"And the mushroom cloud of an atomic bomb is always white. Colour is on, not in. It doesn't matter. First you are a human. Then a man or a woman. Only after that are you a colour, a religion or a nationality. Be honest, be kind. Kindness always has purpose. The rest will sort itself out."

"Then why does the bench we're sitting on say it's only for whites?"

"Because those people have turned the wrong side to the light."

Heb grabbed a microphone and began to tap his foot as he searched for the rhythm. He turned the empty park into a nightclub and began to acknowledge patrons at different tables. He pointed at them individually as he tried to sound like Dean Martin.

Before you're black, white, yellow or of
   cappuccino hue,
When you're brand new,
You are, you are, you are just you.

Before Christian, Buddhist, Muslim or Jew,
Better believe it,
You are, you are, you are just you.

Before agnostic, atheist, animist, nihilist too,
That's right, folks,
You are, you are, you are just you.

While Heb searched for a fourth verse, Phen stood up and walked away. He was tired of this singing angel. The pigeons were in such a feeding frenzy they let him get up close. It wasn't just the bread they were attacking. A large round of salami was being thrown in the air as different beaks pecked at it. It spun and turned like the pizzas at Bella Napoli before they were put into the oven. A robin took advantage of the chaos. It swooped in, stuck its head into the bulbous end of the loaf, feasted, and flew off. Phen watched it disappear into the mauve haze above the mine dumps; it was already late afternoon. By the time he'd returned, the lower angle of the sun had forced the sunglasses back on and the singing had stopped.

Phen consulted his pad again.

"If you're an angel and you can be a human, can you be anything else?"

"Form, like colour, is just an outer layer. It is irrelevant."

"But can you change … into other things?"

"What difference would it make if I said I could be a dog, or, say, a pigeon?"

268

"If it's the dog that walked me to school or that rock pigeon that's always around, that came to my concert and then came to the church, it *would* make a difference."

"Why? In *form* it's still just a mongrel or a clump of feathers. You decide whether it's an angel or not. It's up to you to see past the exterior and decide. My saying so doesn't make it real. You believing it does."

The sun was beginning to set. The shadows lay far behind them. The black trunk of the jacaranda stretched across the park, up and over the parked cars and across Primrose Terrace. The wind blew up his too-wide shorts and puffed them up around his hips. He flattened them by putting his hands in his pockets. As a second thought, he also pulled his white tennis socks up from his ankles to his mid-shins. They wouldn't stay there long, but momentarily made him feel more businesslike.

Question number seven was the only one he'd written in capitals. It was the last question yet it had always been the first, and perhaps the only. He took a deep breath and turned to face Heb more squarely.

"Why didn't you help my father? All I could do at the end was read to him – badly! No help whatsoever."

"Massive help. Forever. Your father didn't want you to read to him. He wanted you to hear the words. His death is a gift. It's opened a space you can now fill. *How* you fill it is up to you. He was giving you clues."

"Adventure," Phen heard himself say. "No ordinary Arabs these," he continued in his mind, "but fearless and daring …" He saw the tears run down his father's cheeks again and watched as they leaped from his chin onto the flannel top.

"You could've done *something*."

"Angels aren't in the business of forcing themselves between the little hand and the big hand."

Phen stood up; he had to go.

"Like me smashing your watch to stop time."

There wasn't a single answer written on his pad. The wide gaps he'd carefully left between each question were blank. He clipped the lead to Pal's collar and put the pen in the pocket of his shorts. He wasn't sure what to do with the pad, so he held it to his chest the way he imagined doctors did on their rounds. The birds were all gone and the first crickets greeted the night. Far away in the kiddies' pool a frog burped. Phen imagined it sitting on the ceramic nose of the smiling dolphin. A woman with a peace sign on her bag pushed a pram towards the early glow of the street lamp. They were the only ones left in the park.

"You could've helped, but you didn't. You're pathetic. The only mystical thing you've done is produce a packet of Life Savers from the back of your head. You turned nothing to the light. Made no difference. An angel that deliberately clips its own wings." He wasn't sure if he'd made a metaphor or not. "You're like all the others. You just talk. Or sing. Or dance. You dress differently, you have too much hair and you change the shape of your beard under your chin. Square, diamond, now it's a circle, but the only difference it makes is to yourself. You're not a guardian, you're a waste of time. Show me—"

"Adventure," Heb interrupted.

"What?"

"Adventure! See you back here after dinner."

Phen was so stunned by the invitation he couldn't speak.

"About nine o'clock should be fine." He looked up to the sky, cleaned his teeth with his tongue and traced the circle under his chin with his finger.

The dining-room table was proof that two was an even

number and three was not. Although his mother sat directly opposite him, this accentuated the empty seat at the head of the table. The space in front of it was vacant yet still taken. The bowl of peas or the gravy boat could not trespass there. Although that specific space had been unoccupied for over a year, it had always been reserved for the pending return of his father. The fact that this was no longer possible didn't seem to change anything. A funeral and a container of grey dust was less final than the relinquishing of a dining position.

Most meals started noisily and ended in silence. His mother tried hard, adding bits of office gossip as the silences between the sentences grew longer and longer. The lengths of skirts and the width of ties were discussed. Believe it or not, Beverley in the typing pool was through to the ballroom-dancing Transvaal Champs. Mr Henderson, of all people, had got an Afro. They say to cover his bald spot. Phen nodded constantly in an attempt to look interested. He knew his mother was desperately searching for a dialogue; there just wasn't much for him to say. Jimmy the Greek still hadn't come around, although Phen knew he was back from holiday. All his conversations had been with a dog and an undercover angel.

After dinner they both read *The Star*. Phen started from the back, his mother from the front. They tried to go at equal speeds to ensure no one was left waiting when they reached the middle. This was a much more relaxed time. The dining-room table served a less melancholy purpose as they spread the newspaper sheets wide and pinned them down with their elbows. She didn't like this prime minister B.J. Vorster. "Looks cruel. Balthazar," she said, "reminds me of Beelzebub." Phen wondered why Cassius Clay had changed his name to Muhammad Ali. The powerful boxer was pointing angrily to the camera as if getting ready to punch it. The article said he'd refused to go into the US army so that was the end of him.

After they'd finished the main body of the paper his mother always had a more than cursory glance at the classifieds. She never wanted to buy anything but was interested in what people were prepared to sell. From here they drifted towards the radiogram. He wasn't a great fan of "The Epic Casebook", and immediately demonstrated his boredom by stretching and yawning. As Inspector Carr started to investigate, he excused himself and went in search of the torch. He finally found the Ray-o-Vac next to the old hamster cage. The heavily ribbed silver metal felt comfortable in his hand although the batteries were old and the light the torch projected pretty dull. It would have to do. He hated lying to his mother when asked what the flashlight was for. All he could think of was the frog, its throat exploding downwards as it croaked.

"Krrrrug," he said, making a joke of his deceit. "Looking f-for f-f-f-frogs on the walk. Heard them this afternoon."

His mother's eyebrows arched, returned and asked no more questions. Phen waved and let Pal out. Once he'd turned right down O'Reilly he pulled the pad from the back of his shorts and checked his pen was still in his pocket. He'd presumed the adventure was linked to the answers he had not received earlier in the afternoon. If his questions were about to receive replies he wanted to be ready. The overweight moon sat on the telephone wire and turned the spaniel a coppery ginger. It was much brighter than he'd anticipated. The torch might not even be necessary.

Heb was standing outside the park on the other side of the fence. "Adventure," he confirmed, looking quizzically at the notepad. "We're not going far, just high."

They crossed Primrose and turned down Fife. He'd never seen Heb walk so fast or far before. His sunglasses, facing backwards and clinging to his fedora, bobbed with each step. He was wearing a holey cardigan to keep out the night's chill. Red Christmas reindeer pranced with stiff legs, pointed hooves and straight necks across his back. The thick wool could not accommodate buttons. Instead, wooden toggles an inch long bounced off their leather straps as they cornered into Prospect Road. They were getting very close to Duchess Court again. Phen tried to hide his panic by watching a red nose crease into Heb's neck, then fold back with the knitted collar.

"Don't worry."

"I'm not."

They stopped at two huge gates made from three layers of corrugated iron. Each gate had a square cut out of it through which a massive chain was threaded. This chain was then secured by the biggest padlock Phen had ever seen. The moon, now slightly above the telephone wires, cast their shadows twenty feet high against the door. The moment couldn't have been any more exaggerated. As Pal lifted his head he turned into a wolf. Heb added a soft howl as Phen looked to see if anyone was watching. The silver torch in his hand clearly marked him as an accomplice. He began rehearsing his story to the police. His only alibi was his mother. She'd confirm he was really just looking for frogs. Would the lie-detector tests show this, too, was an untruth? Fear began to outpace his initial enthusiasm. When Heb had said they were going high he'd hoped for more of a religious experience, perhaps a quick visit to his shallow bowl that stretched across the universe.

"Ever been to a building site at night?"

"No. And there's no chance we'll ever open that." Phen pointed to the lock and turned to go.

"Never judge a book …"

Heb pulled at the lock. The thick steel arch gave way immediately. Within seconds the chain was being yanked through the square. As soon as the doors could open they slipped through. Once inside they leaned against the crossbeams and closed the gates as gently as they could. Metal screeched against metal and then a walled silence. There was no going back now. Not only were they trespassing, they'd also chosen to imprison themselves.

"The foreman lost the key. Been like this for weeks. Deceive the eye and the mind follows."

They sat on packets of cement and tried to focus. The moon was of less help here. The darkness had thickened, the moon's light having been blocked by the high fence. Strange shapes teased their eyes. Phen probed rather pathetically with his torch. It was much tidier than he had imagined. Even the spades were gathered in neat bundles. In groups of twelve their handles leaned against each other, forming a long row of tents. Wooden brooms with wire bristles lined the wall in front of them like sentries quietly on guard. Feeling intimidated, Phen moved away and immediately fell over and into a wheelbarrow. Nothing stirred. Adding to the pantomime, his torch's light went out.

"Careful. It's twenty storeys high." Heb pointed skywards. "The stairway is finished but it goes around an open lift shaft. There are no handrails. Hug the wall and you'll be fine."

Phen stood up and tried to digest what he'd just heard. If he'd understood it correctly, the purpose of the exercise was to climb the inside of a pitch-black building.

"You hold on to your dog and I'll hold on to you."

Suddenly Phen saw them like blind rats clinging to each other as they clawed their way around the inside of some vast chasm. Deprived of light and rope, only a potential fall of alpine proportions kept them bonded together. Instinctively, he made Pal's lead shorter and pulled him towards his legs. This was not how he'd thought this evening would go. He'd left the flat with a sense of mission and a vague feeling of being in charge. Now his knees were starting to tremble, touching against each other involuntarily. He wanted to go home, back to his newspaper. There epic events had headlines and neat columns. Horror and inspiration, joy and sadness, arrived and left with the wide arc of a turn of the page. You could participate without leaving the comfort of your dining-room chair.

"You don't have to come." Heb sat back down on the packets of cement.

Phen needed to think. Who goes climbing with a dog, a torch, a pad and a pen? He wanted to suggest that tomorrow might be a better day. If he'd known what the night would entail he would've arrived early. More light. No dog. Certainly tennis shoes instead of slip-slops. He'd also have gone to the bathroom. He was under-prepared on all counts. His legs felt weak and the flu his mother had said was doing the rounds had definitely appeared. There was a slight buzzing in his ears. He felt his cheeks. It was also clear his sinus had returned. He sniffed uncomfortably to remove the blockage.

"I'm ready," he said.

The first two flights were as dark as coal but hardly terrifying. He'd climbed trees this high before. A fall from here could end up in a broken leg or maybe a collarbone. Kobus Visser had survived similar injuries; he could too. He even felt embarrassed about holding Heb's rough hand. Initially he was more concerned that he might come across as a sissy. Even on the ground floor he'd felt awkward and uncoordinated. He had too much stuff. The pad had to return to the back of his shorts and, to ensure a free hand, his torch had been forced into his right pocket. He tried to push it in as deep as possible, but the silver stalk still hung out by two inches. The point of his pen poked his thigh from the other side. Everything felt wrong.

By the third floor he was no longer worried about his torch or pen. Or the coarse hand he gripped more and more tightly. Academic fear had blossomed into physical terror. They were mindlessly moving up in a series of square circles. Mrs Smit had shown them an Escher drawing in art class and now he knew what it was like to be in one. To ensure they kept their backs to the wall, each step was climbed crab-like, their spines never leaving the rough, unplastered surface behind them. Terrified of the darkness in front, he rubbed himself hard against the blackness behind. The more he shuffled upwards, the more the sightless horror in front of him grew. Hell had come to visit.

He was no longer holding Heb's hand. The grip had moved up his wrist to just under his elbow. Pal's leash was six inches long. Half strangled, the dog had learned the art of moving sideways and one step at a time. By halfway Phen could no longer tell if he was climbing around the lift shaft or around some deep hole in his mind. Vertigo set in; he could feel a spinning height yet could see neither up nor down. His back was rubbed raw but the pain was the only thing that scraped a sense of dimension and direction out of him. Tied on either side by a leather strap and a muscular forearm, he inched his way around the unseen dread. His head had been turned inside out; he was stumbling on that outer edge too.

Full of the madness of a man who'd gouged his own

eyes out, Phen began to shake uncontrollably. No matter what he did he could not find the next step. He put his right leg out again and again, it was just not there. He was lifting his knee higher and higher into nothing. Even worse, the arm that had been so firm was slipping away. He tried to hold on to the hand and then the fingers. After a brief struggle, it was all gone. Now he understood: this is what falling felt like. It wasn't so much the rush of air against your body, it was the disappearance of all other contact. He leaned back for confirmation and found the wall had gone too. He felt the pull of the lead. Pal must be falling with him.

"You can open your eyes now."

Although Phen heard the voice it came to him as a distant echo. He could not immediately obey.

"And you can put your leg down."

The absurd nature of the instruction, repeated twice, finally penetrated his brain. As his foot found the concrete floor his lids flicked up.

"Welcome to the presidential penthouse."

It was the most beautiful thing Phen had ever seen. They had the entire twentieth floor to themselves. The concrete, smooth and uninterrupted, swept like a vast runway in front of him. The deck lay firm beneath his feet with no walls or ceiling to impede his view. He was suspended on a floating platform, walking in space. There were no edges, no boundaries, just a horizontal he could travel on. The stars wrapped around them tightly and added infinite distance at the same time. As far as his eyes could see, lights below answered the glow from above. Totally insignificant and central to everything, he looked over the park, above the neon cross of the Catholic cathedral and beyond the mine dumps.

"I wouldn't go any further." The rough hand had him by the shoulder.

He'd wanted to join the view. One slip-slop rocked backwards and forwards, testing the edge of the concrete. Heb wheeled him around and walked him in the opposite direction. As they moved across the dark plain, Phen wondered if he was hallucinating. He'd never been so aware of his mind and body being in two separate parts. One was buoyant and floating, the other more visible and fixed. They housed each other but were not the same. When they reached the other side of the building he waited for them to rejoin. They chose to stay apart.

"Counterpoint."

Across and below, Crown Towers spread itself out. Two storeys shorter, it took up an entire block. Each apartment was framed by an identical blue aluminium square. This blue lived within a larger silver grid that sliced the building from top to bottom and from side to side. There were no balconies, and two windows per square opened at varying degrees. Although most of the curtains were drawn, higher up a number of them still stayed open. Phen watched four men play cards at a kitchen table. As the dealer flicked left to right a bored woman sat on the couch and stared at her shoes. Her feet rested on a pile of magazines which grew out of a black-and-white-chequered carpet. Everyone had a cigarette in their mouth. Smoke blurred their faces before lifting and circling in the light.

"That's a big box of humanity. A cube on top of a cube next to a cube beneath a cube. Human honeycomb."

Heb started singing. Although it wasn't particularly loud, it wasn't a whisper either. He stepped forward, bowed to Crown Towers and cleared his throat. He nodded to the invisible band behind him, clicked his fingers to give the beat and began.

Little boxes on the hillside
Little boxes made of ticky-tacky
Little boxes on the hillside
Little boxes all the same
There's a pink one and a green one
And a blue one and a yellow one
And they're all made out of ticky-tacky
And they all look just the same

And the people in the houses
All went to the university
Where they were put in boxes
And they came out all the same.

Heb bowed deeply three times as he swivelled to acknowledge the full one hundred and eighty degrees of his audience. Then he turned to face Phen.

"Lose the fear, lose the fear, loooooooose the fear!" He sang at the top of his voice as if it were the last line in a dramatic opera. Still with puffed-out chest, he turned himself into a signboard, arms outstretched pointing north and south. One finger directed at Crown Towers, the other to the horizon studded with stars. "Which side are you going to turn to?"

Phen took a deep breath and followed Heb as they walked back towards the endless sky. Far below a whistle blew, a car wouldn't start and a woman laughed more in derision than merriment. As if in reply to Heb's song, someone turned their radio up. He'd forgotten entirely about Pal, who lay where he'd left him, a brick on the handle of his lead pretending to anchor him. He wished everyone could stay and allow themselves to be so politely pinned down.

"You're leaving, aren't you? Like my father, you have to go. Part of the code."

"Sometimes the thing you feel you have to cling to is the very thing that's holding you back."

Phen sat down next to his dog and let him put his chin on his thigh. Heb remained standing.

"Any more of those questions?"

"Doesn't matter." He pulled the pad from out the back of his shorts. He had a torch that didn't work, a pen that hadn't written and a pad he couldn't see. "I was also going to ask if you could stop me from stuttering."

"You never stutter any more when you talk to me."

"But with other people."

"When I was growing up my head was full of sharp edges and loud noises. I began to imagine some crazy bird lived in there, all beak and claw. It kept scratching my skull from the inside, screeching, making me do bad things. Realised I had to tame him. So I built a perch for him from ear to ear. Over time I trained him to sit on it and relax … sometimes even sing. These days he does a lot of that."

Phen looked up at Heb's head, surprisingly silhouetted against a curve of the brightest white.

"Why don't you go one better than me? Why don't you put a bird in there you *already* like. Keep it calm from the very beginning. It'll settle your mind from day one."

"It'll have to be a swan."

"That's a lot of bird."

"I love swans."

"I was imagining more of a sparrow. Still, swans are very peaceful and beautiful. And you have a huge mind. Less of a perch, maybe a small lake. Keep him paddling round serenely and you might be pleasantly surprised."

"I'll try."

The curve of white climbed up the side of the building and presented itself as a giant polished and pockmarked ball. Spotlighted, everyone stood up and huddled together. Pal, excited and nervous, barked into the glow. The sound echoed then echoed again before spilling off the side and falling all twenty floors. The moon didn't pause for long. Having made its point, it continued on its upward journey. The higher it moved, the more it flattened the concrete floor, giving what was already smooth a thin film of fluorescence. By the time they turned to go, the stairwell was a container of the purest light and each spiral incandescent and golden.

20

What I learned in my holidays

by Stephen Baxter

The first thing I learned in my holidays was that skin and bone and hair and teeth aren't the things that last forever. I also learned that if you only believe the things you can see and touch, you are going to have a very small life. Funerals don't have a proper ending but maybe that's right – who knows if life on earth has one either? You can say amen as many times as you like, that doesn't prove the dead person is actually gone. Maybe he's just slipped backstage like Miss Delmont did in *A Midsummer Night's Dream*. She was there, you could hear her, you just couldn't see through the curtain.

I also learned heaven is what you need it to be. So my father is in the world's biggest library and all the books have huge print. I hope they don't allow tape recorders up there.

Everyone should read Hebrews chapter thirteen, verse two. I won't say more than that.

Kindness always has a purpose.

Dogs love you all the time, no matter what. Mothers hug when they don't know what to say and grandmothers bake.

We all have everything and its opposite inside us. Love and hate. Anger and calmness. Meanness and friendliness. Which one you choose to show the world is the proverbial sixty-four-thousand-dollar question.

Appreciate your ankles and elbows more.

Some people always come first, which is fine. But they don't learn as much as those who are always knocked down. Provided those who are always knocked down always stand up again.

You don't just die when you die. Many people are dead because they've stopped living. Their hearts have grown hard and cold. Like a chicken from the deep freeze that won't thaw.

One of the most difficult things I learned this holiday was that my father's death was a gift. He gave me a big space I can fill any way I want. The trick is to fill it, not fall into it. Beethoven filled his deaf space with beautiful music so that's a good example to keep in mind.

If you want adventures, stay curious. Or you'll end up with a constipated mind. Then, at the end of your life, you won't be able to remember any of it.

People often don't say what they mean. A man who likes chocolate isn't always talking about Cadbury's. Tongues don't slip and cats don't get them. I could go on and on.

I learned we should all study spirals more. You find them in everything from flowers and shells to staircases. The galaxy is a spiral and so is your life. See your birth as the centre and Monday to Sunday is what spins around it. Are you moving up or down? Well, that's for you to decide. All I can say is even when it's pitch dark it pays to keep climbing.

Also, as confusing as it sounds, tomorrow is just today in one day's time. This means we should celebrate but not get impaled on the present. Time moves around and through you whether you like it or not. And that's why we should not be superficial with the truth, because it's always moving from somewhere on its way to someplace else.

I know everyone calls me Spaz or Stuttafords and I know why. But the other thing I learned at the end of the holidays is that those names are just part of the outer layer. Porky the Pig stutters, so everyone thinks it's funny when real people do. It's not. A friend suggested I put a bird in my head to see if it helps. I chose a swan. That's something else people might laugh at. It's a big bird but I'm managing to keep him calm, so maybe it'll work.

Right now he's swimming on a very still lake. The water is blue and the sun is shining off it. He has an orangey-red beak and black markings that look like make-up going towards his eyes. He looks like he's just floating but you can't see his feet working hard paddling underneath. His neck is like a question mark. That's because he's always asking me, "Have you lost the fear yet?"

Acknowledgements

The excerpts quoted on pp. 24 and 25 are from Ernest Hemingway's *The Old Man and the Sea* (Charles Scribner's Sons, 1952).

The lines reproduced on p. 33 are from *In Cold Blood* by Truman Capote (Penguin Books, 2017). Text copyright © Truman Capote, 1966.

On pp. 41–2 the poem quoted is Rudyard Kipling's "The White Man's Burden", first published in *The New York Sun* on 10 February 1899.

The excerpt on p. 58 is from *Siddhartha* by Hermann Hesse, copyright © 2006 by Random House, Inc. Used by permission of Modern Library, an imprint of Random House, a division of Penguin Random House LLC. All rights reserved.

The excerpt that appears on pp. 73–4 is from John Le Carré's *The Spy Who Came in from the Cold* (Victor Gollancz & Pan, 1963).

The excerpt on p. 86 is taken from *The Tulip Tree* by Kathryn Blair. Text copyright © 1976 Kathryn Blair. Permission to reproduce text granted by Harlequin Books S.A.

The lines from "Beasts of England" reproduced on p. 88 are from *Animal Farm* by George Orwell (Copyright © George Orwell, 1945). Reprinted by permission of Bill Hamilton as the Literary Executor of the Estate of the Late Sonia Brownell Orwell.